MENACING SHADOWS

HORROR STORIES AND NIGHTMARES

DARKENBROOK

Order this book online at www.trafford.com
or email orders@trafford.com

Most Trafford titles are also available at major online book retailers.

Print information available on the last page.

ISBN: 978-1-4907-8363-5 (sc)
ISBN: 978-1-4907-8364-2 (hc)
ISBN: 978-1-4907-8365-9 (e)

Library of Congress Control Number: 2017911357

Trafford rev. 07/27/2017

 www.trafford.com

North America & international
toll-free: 1 888 232 4444 (USA & Canada)
fax: 812 355 4082

CONTENTS

PREFACE

I HAD A TERRIBLE SECRET, AND the secret pounded away beneath the floorboards of my brain. I felt just like Edgar Allan Poe's mad narrator in "The Tell-Tale Heart." In my ninth-grade English class with Ms. Klaussen, I learned to perfect the "five paragraph essay" format, discovered *Huckleberry Finn* and *Romeo and Juliet* for the first time, diagrammed subordinate clauses and prepositional phrases, and encountered Poe's short story that would change my life.

I was the son of a preacher, and every Sunday my mother, older brother and I went to church out of duty to see my dad preach. My brother was the high school football star, and every Sunday the men of the church congratulated him on his latest headline in the sports section of our hometown newspaper. I remember the church sanctuary had fuzzy orange pews and a kaleidoscope of stained glass all around the sanctuary windows. My father preached passionate sermons, his hands wrestling with the powerful words that came from his mouth and spread across the audience, but I sat there daydreaming and playing with the rubber rings that lined the communion cup holders on the back of the pew.

Despite being the preacher's son, I didn't study the Bible very much at all. I stayed away from it, in fact, except when I had to study it in Sunday school. One day during Sunday school, I asked the teacher if my dad was being literal in his sermon when he had said, "Satan always tries to throw chains over our hearts," a line that woke me up from my daydreaming. The Sunday school teacher, a man with tall curly hair, paused for a moment, and I could see I put him a tough spot. Here I was, the preacher's son, asking him to question what my dad said in the sermon. He mumbled something about Jesus freeing us from the chains, and then he moved on to the next subject, but he didn't answer the question about whether or not Satan was literally trying get us. Obviously, the part about "throwing chains over our hearts" was a metaphor, but was Satan a metaphor too?

In the Junior High cafeteria, the subject of demonic possession and Ouija boards was a popular topic of conversation. My friend Ethan told me the entire story of *The Exorcist* from beginning to end, a movie that my dad would never let me watch. And despite all of the Catholic parts of the story—we were Dutch Christian Reformed—I really questioned whether all of that could happen, and I really wanted to know if Satan could come and possess me. In addition to *The Exorcist*, I heard a variety of stories from my friends about strange experiences with the Ouija Board: disturbing messages, demonic encounters, and attempts to destroy the Ouija Board; it was indestructible, not even fire could destroy it.

Around the same time I asked my Sunday School teacher about Satan, in my English class we finished the unit on *Huckleberry Finn*, and we read a disturbing story by Shirley Jackson called "The Lottery." I had never read anything like it before; the ending was so unexpected, so shocking, and our minds reeled at what it all meant. That story paved the way for what we would read next, Poe's "The Tell-Tale Heart." Just like "The Lottery," this story had a surprising ending: after the narrator chops up and buries his murder victim beneath the floorboards, and he has seemingly gotten away with the crime, he suddenly confesses because he hears the pounding of his victim's heart, which drives him to confess. The police detectives, who are also in the room and suspect nothing, can't hear the heart at all, so is the pounding heart just in the narrator's imagination? Is he insane, or is some supernatural force driving him insane? It was the first time I encountered an "unreliable narrator." Poe's narrator reveals himself to be insane by all of the outlandish, paranoid things that he says, all the while trying to convince the reader that he is not insane, which undermines his credibility even more.

Poe's story impacted me on a much deeper and personal level too; the more I worried about Satan, the more I became convinced that horror stories were how Satan found people to possess. I knew that thinking about horror stories would be like a flashing beacon for Satan to notice me and come collect me. I didn't dare share this with anyone, but one day after class I gathered up enough courage to ask Ms. Klaussen a question.

When everyone else had left the classroom, while Ms. Klaussen erased the chalkboard, I timidly approached. I mustered the courage to ask her: "Ms. Klaussen, don't you think that writing horror stories is really unhealthy for a person?" I didn't have the courage to say the part about Satan, but "unhealthy" seemed to be close enough.

She stopped erasing the board and turned to me, thinking over my question. Her response was a huge surprise. She said, "For someone like Poe, writing horror stories probably helped him release his inner demons, and that was a good thing."

The thought that writing horror stories could be a good thing sent my mind reeling again. And she said "demons," which made me wonder if she really knew what I was talking about, but I didn't have the courage to ask if she literally meant demons. I didn't realize it at the time, but this was the moment when I became a horror writer; in a sense, Ms. Klaussen gave me the permission to be a horror writer, a permission that I couldn't give myself.

Just like Poe's narrator who had a terrible secret torturing him, I also had a terrible secret that was pounding to be let out (like a murdered heart), and it wasn't my secret fear of Satan coming to possess me; my big secret was that I was gay. Ever since the fifth-grade, I was becoming more and more aware of a strong attraction to the other boys at school, and I was deeply ashamed by this attraction. I had heard my classmates talk about "faggots" and "queers" for years, and I was horrified to think that I was one of those. Just like Poe's narrator, the secret would not let me free—one day I would have to confess.

I told my dad that I needed to tell him something, and I explained all about my fears about Satan, Ouija Boards, and horror stories (I held back the part about being gay, however). I remember sitting on my bed as my dad explained how the Bible guaranteed that Jesus would protect me from Satan, and I didn't need to worry about it all. He showed me a passage from Romans: "For I am convinced that neither angels nor demons, neither the present nor the future, nor any powers, neither height nor depth, nor anything else in all creation, will be able to separate us from the love of God that is in Christ Jesus our Lord." That Bible passage, and most importantly what my dad had said, finally put my mind at ease, and I didn't worry about Satan anymore.

Looking back over thirty years later, I wonder if my fear of becoming possessed by Satan was really about my fear of becoming gay, a fear of losing control of my own identity, becoming something I didn't want to be. Fortunately, being gay turned out to be much better than I imagined, even if it was really scary before I came out of the closet. I would later leave the church behind, but I truly cherish the moment when my dad comforted me and helped alleviate my fears about Satan. It was the one time in my life that a Bible verse had truly given me comfort.

But Satan wasn't finished with me.

THE MYSTERY OF THE WHITE MOUSE AND THE SECRET ROOM

ONE DAY, RIDLEY'S GOLDEN RETRIEVER named Bumpy captured a white mouse under the basement stairs by the Ping-Pong table. Bumpy, a dog with maternal instincts, carried the mouse in her teeth as careful as a snake carries its egg. The mouse was covered in saliva, but safe. Ridley, a pale twelve-year-old with freckles, named the mouse Puff-of-Mist and put him in a shoebox. He showed the mouse to his best friend Grape, a pudgy boy who always wore a windbreaker, and together they showed the mouse to Grape's baby sister in the crib.

"Puff-of-Mist can be the mascot for our club," Grape said. "Definitely better than using my sister."

On the night Grape slept over, the boys played Ping-Pong when Bumpy captured another white mouse in the basement. "Two white mice means a mystery," Ridley said, and Grape agreed. The stacks of boxes in the basement seemed to form a maze that went beyond the reach of the solitary light bulb above the Ping-Pong table. With flashlights, they searched for clues. "I found a clue," Grape shouted. Mice turds next to a stack of boxes, which turned out to be mysteriously empty. Grape pushed the stack aside and discovered the secret door. It was locked.

"You have to promise me you will never go inside that room," Ridley's father said when the boy asked the next day. "It's where I keep my hunting rifles," he explained. Ridley promised.

The next time Grape slept over, Ridley showed Grape where his father kept the key next to a handgun and a stack of dirty magazines in the headboard of his waterbed. "But you promised your dad," Grape said. "I know it will solve the mystery," Ridley said. After inspecting the dirty magazines, Ridley led the way to the locked basement door. Grape followed, wringing his hands. When Ridley opened the door, the boys smelled the overwhelming odor of mouse urine in the darkness. Their flashlights revealed the wire cage teeming with white mice and the massive terrarium overflowing with shadow. The instant Ridley cracked open the lid, the black boa constrictor wrapped around his throat, and Ridley dropped the flashlight. Ridley kicked over the wire cage; the horde of white mice fled across the floor in all directions. As Ridley turned blue, Grape pulled at the thick coils in vain. Bumpy bit the snake's tail, but to no avail. The snake crushed the boy's throat and slithered away into the maze of boxes.

The ambulance took the body away. The police asked their questions.

Between swigs of whiskey and sobs of despair, Ridley's father told Grape the whole story: When Ridley came out of the womb, the umbilical cord was wrapped around his throat as tight as a yo-yo. In her grief, Ridley's mother made a deal with Satan, who loitered in the corner of the delivery room unseen by everyone but her. She offered her life in exchange for her son. Just as Satan froze her heart and scooped out her soul, the umbilical cord uncoiled itself from the baby's throat and transformed into a little black constrictor as tiny as a shoelace. The baby screamed for the first time as Satan dropped the serpent into the father's coat pocket. Of course, Satan added a stipulation. Ridley's father must feed and keep Satan's constrictor in secret for the rest of his days, or else the serpent would claim the boy again. When Ridley entered the forbidden room, the deal was broken.

Ridley's father gave Bumpy and Puff-of-Mist to Grape now that Ridley was gone, and Grape returned home, the front of his windbreaker wet with grief over his best friend. And Satan's constrictor terrorized the neighborhood.

At the nursing home for dementia patients, the attendants didn't believe the residents' stories about the black serpent lurking in the trees outside until Hilda was found in her rocking chair. Little Esther told her mother about the imaginary friend coming over for a tea party in the back yard; it was a ruse of the demonic constrictor that could send messages to children in dreams. A ten-year-old's birthday sleepover in the treehouse turned into a massacre. Blacked out in a puddle of vomit, Ridley's father met the constrictor one last time. All night long, Bumpy guarded Grape's baby sister.

After school, Grape and Bumpy searched the neighborhood. In his backpack, he carried his official Boy Scout Hatchet—to claim the head of the monster. When Grape and Bumpy returned home, they found the baby's crib empty, the monstrous serpent asleep in the nursery, a large bump in its center. Ferocious Bumpy attacked the serpent. Full and sluggish, the snake tried to defend itself. With the snake occupied, Grape hacked away with the hatchet, the snake as thick as a tree trunk. Grape's mother, thinking the baby was taking her nap, rushed into the scene of horror. In a torrent of blood, the baby slid out into Grape's arms; the baby was whole and unharmed.

At last the snake was dead.

Grape's mother called the church's Satan Emergency Hotline, and Father Holworth rushed to the house. With a few prayers and some splashes of holy water, the puddles of snake blood in the nursery sizzled and evaporated. With his extensive boy scout training, Grape erected a funeral pyre in the back yard. Father Holworth offered more prayers and helped Grape burn the foul carcass of Satan's constrictor. Loyal Bumpy at his side, his windbreaker soaked with snake blood, Grape watched the purifying smoke of the pyre and remembered his lost best friend. The priest explained to Grape that the snake was unable to digest his sister because the baby had been baptized, and therefore protected by Christ, but Father Holworth secretly suspected that something else had happened—suspected that perhaps the baby had been born again in darkness.

THE FACE ON THE CHURCH

T HE LITTLE MAN LURED ME away from the train station. He had frightening shoes and a perfect smile, but I followed him for the daisy in his hat and the butterflies he kept beneath his horse-leather coat. I was a little girl with pigtails and a gay checkered dress. When we were alone in the woods, he pulled out his false teeth, set them down on the rotten leaves, and strangled me to death by the roots of a tree.

Just like all the mothers say, a murderer's face is imprinted upon the eyes of his victim, so the killer scooped out my eyeballs with a spoon. Before he could swallow them, the spirit of the tree took pity on my eyeballs and transformed them into angry hummingbirds. They sped away to find the police. The hummingbirds used their wings as brushes and painted the face of the murderer with berry juice and roadkill blood on the side of the church. The church faced the police station, so everyone would know the murderer's identity.

The appearance of the face on the church was miraculous. All of the parishioners and the policemen commented on the handsome visage and the intensity of the eyes: "If only he were our preacher," they said as they passed, "every word of his sermon we would surely follow."

THE BOXES

ONCE UPON A TIME, INSIDE a warehouse as large as a cathedral, there lived a family of boxes: a papa box, a mama box, and a baby box. Vick worked alone in the warehouse, his toupee made from the hair of ten-year-old boys. He kept a box cutter in his tight leather belt and slashed the boxes mercilessly. Some of the boxes said Vick did it just for fun, but the smart boxes knew the truth: Vick was searching for something.

One day, the baby box said to his papa, "I'm afraid the man will slash me while I'm sleeping."

His papa said, "I'll watch over you."

The baby box could see his mama was sick; she had an oily black stain on her cardboard. The warehouse rats eyed the mama box. Meanwhile, psychopathic Vick continued the search for his lost box. He slashed every box that looked about the right size. Every day the mama box grew sicker and sicker. One day, their worst fears came true: Vick spotted the mama box.

"Leave my mama alone," cried the baby box.

The psychopath slashed the mama box wide open—all the way across her belly; her packing peanuts spilled across the concrete floor. From inside the slaughtered mama box, the psychopath removed his prize: the mummified head of his own evil mother, whom he had murdered years ago, but the head had never really died. He held up the head by a fistful of hair, and when he parted the lips to admire the fangs, the undead head bit Vick's finger. The poison went right to Vick's heart, and he fell down dead on the concrete floor. The papa box and baby box wept for the mama box as the warehouse rats converged upon Vick's body and consumed him.

The head rolled away into a dark hiding place where the warehouse rats worshiped it as a god.

THE PICKLE MAKER AND THE DEVIL'S AX

ONCE UPON A TIME, A girl named Petal fell in love with a Pickle-Maker's apprentice.

Every day Petal walked the same path to school, past the Pickle-Maker's plain storefront before turning left down a dumpster-crowded alley on her way to the horrible Catholic High School. She could see the school past the shadows of the alley; it condemned her with its stern cathedral face.

The moment she spotted the beautiful Pickle-Maker's apprentice, a boy named Drew, who wore his pristine white apron as he swept the pickle shop, Petal instantly renounced all plans to become a bride for Christ. Drew sat next to Petal on the park bench, eating his sack lunch with his right hand while holding Petal's hand with his left. She loved to hear him tell about the customers in the shop and his bosses: portly old Luger the Pickle-Maker and his even portlier son, whom everyone called Box. The rest of the day, Petal's right hand smelled of sweet pickles and she covered her nose and mouth with her palm all afternoon in a fragrant daydream.

Then one morning, as Petal meandered down the alley, she heard a strange squeaking voice in her mind, a desperate little voice pleading for help: "Help me miss—please help me," it said. "I'm an enchanted frog and I'm being held a prisoner."

Just as the voice requested, Petal returned with a large bucket of water. The voice emanated from a barred basement window in the shadow of a putrescent dumpster. With a pizza box from the dumpster, Petal brushed away the black widow spider webs and reached through the bars until her hand entered the water of a fish tank next to the window.

"Now I'll swim into your hand, miss," the voice said.

Petal felt a squishy creature, about the size of a baseball, swim into her hand. That must be the frog, she thought, but when she pulled her hand back through the bars, she discovered that she held a small human head with octopus tentacles and long brown hair. Startled, she threw the little octopus head up into the air, but fortunately it landed right into the bucket like a circus diver. The little telepathic head, whose name was Crispin, apologized for claiming to be a frog, but he knew no one would ever consent to picking up a disembodied octopus head through a strange window.

Crispin shared his harrowing tale:

It turned out that Luger the Pickle-maker and his son Box were servants of the Devil, and worse than that, they were the ax murderers who terrorized the city. For years, headless bodies were found on park benches, in elevators, on church pews, even in the Tunnel of Love at the carnival. Their ax murders were as internationally renowned as their spicy and sweet pickles.

The Devil himself gave Luger the enchanted ax in exchange for Luger's soul and the soul of his son Box, and the ax enabled Luger to pursue the avocation of chopping off heads for sport and pleasure. No matter how poor the aim, if Luger swung the ax, the target's head was off; it was a head-collecting ax, crafted by the Angel of Death. But even more miraculous, the ax never spilled a drop of blood. The ax instantly cauterized as it chopped, capturing the soul inside the brain like a pimento in an olive.

While Luger loved the chopping, Box developed a talent for pickling the heads with Satanic black magic. At first, it was quite difficult for the heads to breathe in their pickle jars, but soon they sprouted gills and a nice set of tentacles from the cauterized neck. When the heads were ready, Box put them in a massive fish tank, which he purchased extra cheap from a defunct lobster restaurant.

One day, to everyone's great surprise, one of the heads named Sarah laid some eggs under the model pirate ship; her boyfriend Jack fertilized the eggs (Luger took them together from Lover's Lane); soon little Crispin hatched, but only grew to the size of a baseball, and the telepathy was an unwanted side effect of the black magic.

Whenever Box worked on pickling the heads, he had to endure those squeaky little questions in his mind, which felt to Box just like when he drank a milkshake too fast.

Now shut up there little Crispin, he threatened, or it's into the microwave with you! And then pop!

All the heads lived in terror of the microwave oven.

Luger and Box kept their fish tank and pickled heads in a secret chamber in the basement. They instructed Drew to never go into the basement room, which Drew never even considered; however, he did know which key on the large keyring opened the door.

Fortunately, the tank sat right underneath the barred alley window, which sometimes Box left propped open—black magic pickling smells of strong garlic.

All the while Crispin told Petal this terrible tale, she carried the heavy bucket across the park to the town square where the police station was located, stopping momentarily at the great fountain in the center of the square.

Just as Petal looked around for a policeman, a burly hand grabbed her slender arm. Without stopping to think, she dumped the bucket into the fountain, which was quite deep and blanketed with coins and algae. Then Petal stood face to face with the pickle-reeking servant of the Devil.

Drew ate his bologna sandwich and Fritos on the park bench, looking all around for his sweetheart who never showed up.

With the apprentice at lunch, Luger and Box used an entire roll of duct tape on Petal and dumped her on the floor of the secret chamber. Luger would return with the Devil's ax.

Drew, a very sensitive boy, despaired because he felt certain an intelligent girl like Petal could never love a boy who smelled like pickles, a fault his father berated him for nightly. Besides, he heard a rumor about Petal's calling to be a nun.

As Drew strolled and despaired through the park, only fifteen minutes left of his lunch break, he found himself at the wishing fountain in the town square. This was his chance; he took out a penny, and he asked Jesus to relinquish his hold upon Petal's destiny; he asked Jesus if a lowly Pickle-Maker's apprentice could wed beautiful Petal instead. Then he tossed the penny; a second later, he saw a baseball-sized human head holding his penny in its mouth.

As Petal lay on the floor, she peered up and saw the heads in the fish tank beckoning with their eyes. They recognized her as the girl who rescued Crispin. She managed to climb up a stepladder and jump into the tank. All the heads bit and pulled at the duct tape. Soon her hands were free. Luger marched into the secret chamber with the ax, ready to do his business.

When he saw Petal in the tank, he dropped the ax and climbed the stepladder; he tried in vain to pull Petal from the water. Just as he leaned too far forward, Petal pulled him into the fish tank.

The heads converged upon Luger, biting at his jugular vein and his groin. The thrashing water filled with blood. Petal climbed out of the fish tank; Luger now just floated.

Petal picked up the Devil's ax from the floor as Box walked into the secret chamber. Petal didn't even need to aim. Box's head rolled under the fish tank and Drew rushed in with the police. His frantic kisses tasted like sweet pickles.

At the wedding, Crispin was the ringbearer, holding the golden band between his teeth in the fishbowl by the groom. When the priest baptized little Crispin, his entire fishbowl became holy water, so he never had to worry about servants of the Devil again (and the water in his fishbowl never needed to changed again). Little Crispin blessed the household of Petal and Drew forever after.

AGNES AND THE TREEHOUSE RIPPER

ONCE UPON A TIME, A treehouse Ripper terrorized backyard slumber parties. For years, no one dared to sleep all night in a treehouse. At the annual convention of treehouse enthusiasts, terror cloaked everyone like a pall. A clever FBI agent addressed the convention attendees at a special forum on the Ripper (quite sure the Ripper himself would be in attendance). The agent revealed disturbing aspects of the Ripper's M.O. The Ripper murdered and gutted the family dog at the base of the trunk. The Ripper strung up the children in sleeping bags like pupas in cocoons, but the agent didn't reveal the whole truth (the strange qualities of the silken rope—the lab techs labeled it "insectoid"). And when the authorities cut down the victims, a horrible discovery: somehow the sleeping bags digested the children, the bodies like fresh owl scat inside—just the bones and the skull left—all the children identified by dental records.

The treehouses of America fell into disrepair. After many years, it seemed the newspapers forgot about the treehouse Ripper.

There lived a little girl named Agnes whose father went insane. Her older brother Buzz and his best friend Alfonso teased her constantly about the treehouse Ripper. They downloaded crime scene photos, and pasted them all around her bedroom so she would be forced to see them when she awoke from her Ripper-haunted nightmares. Agnes' father, a well-known expert craftsman of treehouses and author of several do-it-yourself books on the subject, had built three masterpiece treehouses on his large wooded property, but he attended that forum at the convention, heard what the FBI agent said, so he forbade his children to sleep in the treehouses.

Sadly, the untreated shell shock that nestled and festered inside Father's subconscious mind suddenly erupted, and the doctors committed him to a padded room. With Father gone (and Stepmother drunk at the country club most afternoons), Agnes' brother Buzz soon discovered the secret underground room where father kept his strange collection of horrific war souvenirs and contraband weapons.

On the dense, forested property, Agnes, Buzz, and Alfonso played Vietnam all summer with jagged Bowie knives, empty AK-47s, camouflaged helmets, and walk-talkies without batteries, Buzz and Alfonso always Green Berets and Agnes always the Vietcong agent to be captured and tortured for intelligence.

As autumn and the confines of school approached, Buzz hatched his horrible plan: they would all three spend the night in Father's three treehouses—each of them alone all night at their respective treehouse post with only a cell phone to send text messages, the first to go home a despicable crybaby deserter. Buzz and Alfonso tormented Agnes. "You're not a good soldier," they taunted. You're just a girl." Agnes, desperate to show them, desperate to outgrow her little-sister status, committed to the desperate mission with a blood oath.

Death before dishonor, they cried. The Ripper will die by our knives, they pledged.

For advance warning, Buzz had Father's Aleutian seal dog, a breed known for dense coat, fierce devotion, and ability to pull wounded seals from holes in the ice. The dog slept at the base of Buzz's tree. Once they tucked Agnes inside her sleeping bag with her camouflaged pajamas, Buzz and Alfonso cut the ropes of her ladder so she had no way down, except to climb through a maze of sharp branches in the darkness.

In the final moments of twilight, Buzz and Alfonso assumed their posts in their treehouses. Only the chirping of crickets and foraging of racoons in the shadows below.

During the witching hour, the Aleutian seal dog fell into an evil trance that cut the cords of her bark; she lay on her back as a terrible bloody hand popped through the dog's belly like the claw of a crocodile baby through leathery egg skin. According to the ancient laws of black magic, in order to gain entrance into this world, the Ripper must come through the vacant womb of a sleeping dog.

The Ripper himself a horrid imp, thick scabs for armor like exoskeleton, layer upon layer composed of blood from all the children and dogs he murdered for his master Satan. Doubtful even a knife could penetrate the scabs. His front teeth—tiny and sharp for tearing skin when butchering his children. He squatted down. The thick silken rope emerged moist and glistening from his anus—embedded within, he hid spinnerets like a spider.

Moving through the branches like a stealthy demonic gibbon, first he murdered Buzz; next he murdered Alfonso, both of them asleep at their posts. He strung up the boys' bodies in the sleeping bags, chanted the evil incantation to make the sleeping bags digest the boys so they would be reborn in the underworld as horrible insectoid angels for Satan.

The Ripper picked up Buzz's phone and texted Agnes— everything is quiet dear sister—time to go to sleep—it's almost three o'clock in the morning.

The Ripper gave himself away; Buzz only used military time.

Agnes turned up the lantern as the black imp perched itself on the windowsill of the treehouse. A sliver of drool fell from its mouth, and Agnes smirked victorious (deep within Father's forbidden underground room, Agnes had infiltrated the locked trunk where Father kept his collection of hand grenades).

Agnes pulled the pin when she received the imp's text message; Agnes released the handle as the Ripper's drool descended.

At exactly 0300 hours the Ripper leapt upon her as the grenade obliterated them and blasted the treehouse into flying stakes and falling splintered branches. Agnes rid the world of the treehouse Ripper, but uprooted her mortal soul, which wandered from treehouse to treehouse; she became known as Hand Grenade Agnes, a ghastly-pale phantom in camouflage pajamas, who whispers terrible secrets of the charnel house to superstitious adolescent girls at treehouse slumber parties before disappearing in a spectral flash of light at exactly 0300 hours.

THE DARK VENGEANCE OF GUMBO THE GORILLA

ONCE UPON A TIME, AN old vampire drank a baby gorilla. Across from the gorilla exhibit, the vampire nursed on blood all day at the zoo, coiled up in the shadowy bushes by the old drinking fountain. With a sly trick of invisibility, the vampire could strike out like a snake and steal quick spurts of blood from zoo patrons in flip-flops. Lovely veins on the tops of feet he preferred, and the unsuspecting patrons never felt the sting until the numbing saliva wore off hours later.

But then everything changed for the old vampire; the new landscapers uprooted the drinking fountain and planted the humming Aquafina vending machine, part of the renovation to celebrate the unveiling of the new gorilla arboretum, which they built especially for the new baby boy, Gumbo the Gorilla, rescued from the horrors of the bushmeat trade.

Deprived of bare feet in flip-flops, the vampire shriveled, a hunger that burned worse than sunlight. Beneath the full moon, the vampire transformed with black magic, became a liquid shadow and rolled through the bars of the new arboretum.

The blood of the baby gorilla tasted spicy and exotic; vampire hunger outweighed restraint. The beloved baby gorilla, the front page darling, was dead.

Crowds of zoo patrons in flip-flops wept.

The baby gorilla's body laid out on the cold stainless steel autopsy table, the chest was cut open, both halves splayed like rib-cage angel wings, his pink brain in a bucket. While the zoologists took a coffee break at the witching hour, Gumbo's little heart, resting in the silver tray, turned to a poof of spectral mist, which spread and intermingled with the body and the tender brain in the bucket.

The mist slithered out from the secret underground morgue into the forest beyond the boundaries of the zoo. There the mist coalesced. A massive full-grown silverback gorilla appeared, a vampire gorilla, with a full-grown hunger for blood.

The gorilla discovered his uncanny aptitude for vampire black magic.

Gumbo remembered with cinematic clarity: the poachers with shotguns and machetes; first they shot his mother, chopped off her nurturing hands. The poachers collected the baby gorilla and strapped him into a backpack papoose before they removed his mother's head. They kept the baby gorilla in a hut with the mother's remains. They didn't need to tie him. He sucked his thumb and clutched his mother's head, tethered to it by fear and confusion. The vampire gorilla could still see the flies on her silent eyes, could still see the machetes taking her hands. The flies still buzzed in his mind. When the Rwandan park rangers rescued the baby gorilla, they removed his trembling undernourished body from the hut, but deep down in the infant ape-mind, Gumbo remained forever in the hut with the head of mother, his ape-mind now deep beneath his new vampire consciousness, which was born through the mysterious power of black magic.

The zookeepers held a drunken wake for their beloved baby gorilla. As he stumbled home from the bar, Bobby, the primate sign language tutor, sensed something in the eerie mist that crawled from the trees. Bobby was the first to teach Gumbo how to sign "I love you," which the news media loved. It was how little Gumbo greeted Bobby at the start of each signing lesson. His Ph.D. dissertation ruined, Bobby despaired as he walked past the dark windows of the pawn shop. He'd never get another chance like baby Gumbo again, a groundbreaking study of linguistics and primatology, his ambition as dead as precious little Gumbo.

At the downtown pawn shop they kept a secret cabinet of curios, which held the hideous gorilla hand ashtray, the sinister treasure frequently sought after on the black market. From beyond the streetlights, the spectral mist crept through the bars on the pawn shop window. The falling glass sounded the alarm. The vampire could sense that ashtray from across the city. The pawn shop security camera recorded the luminous mist and a blurry, monstrous shadow within.

Amid the wreckage of the pawn shop, the detectives studied the surveillance camera footage; the detectives noted the untouched bills in the smashed cash register, but the entire collection of machetes stolen. The owner didn't tell them about the theft of the forbidden ashtray.

Then the call came in, the first severed pair of hands discovered near the hobo camp in the forested park.

The Medical Examiner scrutinized the hands, deduced by the slice it might be machete. The detectives, in their trench coats and mud-caked wingtips, loitered in the hallway. With nicotine-stained fingers, they sipped hot coffee from Styrofoam cups. Behind the bushy eyebrows of the detectives, procedural machinations tick-tocked.

Could the severed hands be related to the theft of Baby Gumbo's corpse? And what was that shadow on the surveillance tape?

Bobby, the beautiful young sign language tutor, spoke to the news crew cameras outside the primate center, eyes brimming with tears as he told the story of first teaching Gumbo to sign "I Love You."

"My heart is broken," Bobby told the cameras. "It is a tragic day for the whole city. Gumbo belonged to all of us."

Two hobos, Leslie and Alex, passed a can of SpaghettiOs and a box of Chardonnay back and forth by the campfire. They had camped there in the forested park by the zoo all week, just a few hundred yards from the old abandoned mental hospital, but strange rumors of a shadowy creature began to circulate, and many of their friends fled the forested park, but Leslie and Alex knew that hobos were a superstitious bunch. There was always some weird rumor going around, probably just another ploy to oust them from the park.

A vortex of spectral mist descended upon them, the fire snuffed out, the hobos thrown back, femurs cracked, no running away with broken legs.

From out of the mist, the vampire gorilla appeared with his machete. The vampire gorilla held down Leslie's arm and chopped off the hand, stuck the gushing stump in his mouth. He knew all people would do the same to him; he saw the ashtray in the secret cabinet, saw what they did to his mother. Gumbo sucked until the screaming stopped.

The next day, detectives inspected the two new sets of hobo hands in large Ziploc baggies. Hikers had found the crime scene.

In his pajamas, Bobby dumped the overflowing wastebasket of tissues, damp with snot and tears, in the alley dumpster next to his apartment. He had called in sick to grieve his ambition

From behind the dumpster, a strange claw gripped his arm, a sharp claw like gnarled, living black wood, rooted in the stump of the hobo vampire whose transmogrified visage young Bobby now stared into with disbelief and horror.

The rest of the hobo vampires appeared from behind, beneath, and within the dumpster where they waited for Bobby as instructed by their dark master, each with a fang-rimmed maw where once they had mouths, each with tree-branch vampire claws in place of their amputated hands.

"What do you want?" Bobby asked.

"The dark master wants you," one of them hissed.

On the other side of the forested park by the zoo, the abandoned psychiatric hospital loomed, as dead as the moon, as black as the bottom of the sea, waiting to be demolished for asbestos and evil spirits. The hobo vampires carried Bobby right over the barrier fence, like a levitating parade, and his grim entourage became an undertow of shadow that pulled him down the ruined hallways of the hospital to a padded cell. The rest of the night, the ghosts of lobotomized psychopaths paraded up and down the hallway, welcoming Bobby to his new home.

When the sun rose, Bobby screamed for help until his voice was like sandpaper on stone while the hobo vampires slumbered in the black basement morgue. He drank a few droplets of rain water from a crack in the ceiling.

Finally, the sun set again, and the hobo vampires returned to escort Bobby to the courtyard.

Beneath the full moon, Bobby saw the empty courtyard of cracked concrete and weeds. Then the eerie spectral vortex of mist descended on the barren courtyard, and it filled with lush Rwandan jungle. In the center of the courtyard stood an ancient tree, and the vampire gorilla sat in the crook of two massive branches like a throne. The vampires brought Bobby before their master.

The vampire gorilla signed "I love you," and Bobby instantly recognized baby Gumbo in the silverback monster before him.

"It's you," Bobby signed. "How can this be? I thought you were dead."

Gumbo thought for a moment, then simply replied, "I am."

The gorilla gestured to his left and a banquet of food and drink appeared, but the banquet was limited to food served at zoo concessions: hot dogs, cotton candy, popcorn, nachos.

Astounded and frightened, but also starving after his day of captivity, Bobby satiated himself with the delicious junk food created by the gorilla; Gumbo was a genius of black magic.

Bobby sat with the gorilla in the jungle courtyard, complete with bird calls and bug bites. With rudimentary sign language, the gorilla explained that Bobby would teach him like before so Gumbo could understand more about the weird apes who ruled the world with cages and machetes.

So every night, Bobby was brought to the jungle courtyard to tutor the vampire gorilla, and every morning the jungle dissipated into bare concrete and weeds. During the day, Bobby was kept prisoner in his padded cell.

The hobo vampires went out hunting at twilight; they brought back helpless hobos and anyone who lingered too long in the dark city streets where the vampires hunted. They presented the captives to their master, and the vampire gorilla chopped off their hands with the machete just like the poachers chopped off his mother's hands, but the vampire gorilla promised he would never chop off the speaking hands of the young man whom Gumbo loved. Bobby was his tutor and only friend.

The long RV caravan of mercenaries, belonging to a subsidiary of Blackwater that specialized in vampire outbreaks, arrived in town at the behest of the local government. At the command center, the detectives showed the mercenaries the old blueprints of the psychiatric hospital, a big red X on the courtyard.

The mercenaries readied their napalm flamethrowers and wooden stake projectile crossbows; they kissed their crucifixes.

In the tranquility of the jungle courtyard, Bobby signed to Gumbo: "Why cut off their hands? They never hurt you. There are other ways to find blood."

"My anger is a hunger," Gumbo signed and then beat his chest. Gumbo showed Bobby the gorilla hand ashtray that he stole from the pawn shop.

Then they could hear the inhuman screaming of the hobo vampires as the mercenaries incinerated them in the rooms and hallways of the abandoned hospital. The glow of the fires penetrated the mist of the jungle courtyard.

Gumbo sat in the tree throne and waited. He would kill all the people who trespassed. He would use the machete on all their silent hands. His black magic could swallow flame.

Bobby held the gorilla hand ashtray. He knew the vampire gorilla would kill all of the mercenaries, and Bobby silently prayed for Baby Gumbo's lost soul.

Since no one had ever prayed for a vampire gorilla before, the novelty of the situation attracted the attention of the Angel of the Lord. She appeared to Bobby and Gumbo in the form of the martyred primatologist Diane Fossey, who, like Gumbo's mother, also perished at the hands of wicked men with machetes.

As the mercenary team burned their way through the hospital, getting closer and closer to the jungle courtyard, the Angel of the Lord waved her hand and all of the vampire's black magic dissipated. Instead of a monstrous silverback in a courtyard of Rwandan jungle, a little baby gorilla stood in a courtyard of cement and dried leaves. Little Baby Gumbo took Diane Fossey's hand, and the Angel of the Lord delivered him to a jungle where all murdered gorilla mothers wait for their lost children.

Bobby awoke in his apartment as if it had all been a dream, but he still had indigestion from all of the hot dogs and nachos.

He soon abandoned his dissertation on gorilla sign language for a controversial memoir about his experience with Gumbo the vampire gorilla. No one in the news media would believe the truth about what happened, and his books were shelved next to the memoirs of alien abduction; however, a few years later, a collection of 26 pairs of severed hobo hands were stolen from the FBI's secret deep freeze. Even today, if you know the right keywords, you might be able to find a pair on the black market ebay.

At the zoo, an old vampire found a comfortable, albeit chilly, home in an Aquafina vending machine across from the gorilla arboretum, and the zoo patrons only occasionally complained of small nicks when retrieving their water bottles.

COREY GOES TO THE ZOO

COREY HAD TO GUESS WHICH of the three Satanic hags was his true mother, and he hoped he didn't choose the wrong one. It was a simple game.

"Hey, you come to the zoo a lot, don't you?" the nanny said as she held little Forrest up over the railing so he could see the mandrills through the plexiglass wall.

"Yeah, I like it here, especially the monkey house," Corey said.

The other day he had spotted her looking at him when he was crying on Father Lemon's shoulder by the predators of the Serengeti Plain.

"They have rainbow butts," cried out a passing child at the sight of the male mandrill, who had turned away from the plexiglass. Hunter and Forrest, the nanny's charges, giggled at the comment and repeated it.

The nanny gave them a stern glance to behave and then turned back to Corey. She hadn't seemed interested in him until she saw him crying on the priest's shoulder. "Which monkeys do you like the best?" she asked.

"Definitely the mandrills," Corey said. "They're so colorful. I heard that they are the world's largest monkey—or, the male at least. Related to the baboons—I was talking to somebody who works here."

The nanny smiled. "Do you have a favorite one?" The nanny and Corey had seen each other at this exhibit many times. Corey would sometimes hang out at the mandrill's for an entire hour.

Corey nodded. "Definitely the male." The male mandrill was twice the size of the three females in the exhibit, which was filled with various tree branches and ropes for the mandrills to climb and green branches and leaves for the mandrills to eat. In addition to the rainbow hues on the monkey's swollen rear end, the male had a long snout with a red, trumpet-shaped stripe and bright blue ridges on either side. When he yawned, his jaws were truly spectacular. Corey spent more time watching the mandrills than any other exhibit at the zoo. He even had a tattoo of a snarling mandrill on his shoulder.

"Oh, not me," the nanny said. The male scares me. The females are just as pretty and not nearly as arrogant. I love their amber eyes. Delicate too—I feel sorry for the females, having to live with such a brute."

Corey chuckled nervously at this comment. "Oh, he's not a brute," Corey said, feeling shy all of a sudden and noticing that she didn't wear any makeup at all, but her eyebrows were plucked. He had never been this close to her before. "He's really sweet actually," Corey said. "He's just all bluff and swagger."

"What's your name, by the way?" the nanny asked.

"I'm Corey. You?"

"I'm Angela. It's nice to meet you."

He had wondered about her name for months and was too afraid to ask. That nanny sure liked to wear dopey-looking fisherman hats—in all kinds of bright colors, almost as bright as the mandrill butts. The hats made her look a little bit like a tulip, which sort of endeared her to Corey, and Corey's mother was obsessed with tulips.

Corey had wire in his jacket pocket, just in case it came to that. If he guessed wrong and the hags demanded one of the

26

little boys, he could probably handle that with his bare hands, but Corey was still untested

Hunter jumped back when he saw the mandrill yawn and expose its fierce jaws. Corey was alone with Angela and the boys in the alcove, which was part of a dark tunnel with windows looking up into the exhibits for a variety of apes and monkeys, including the orangutans, the chimpanzees, and the mandrills .

Corey felt the temperature drop as the mandrills became visibly afraid. OK—it's time, he thought. The females cowered beneath a horizontal log while the male began to snarl and bristle. They could sense it.

"What's wrong with them, Angela?" Hunter asked.

Satan's mind cloud filled the alcove. Angela and the boys froze with dread. No one would disturb them now until Corey's choice had been made. The cloud would repel anyone coming down the tunnel.

The three naked hags appeared to Corey in the plexiglass.

Corey always took the train to the zoo. That was how he started his day. After all these months of daily visits, his routine became fixed. He began at the Amazon rainforest where he could see the crocodiles both under the water and on the shore. Next he went to the monkey house where he spent hours watching the orangutans and the mandrills. Sometimes, the mandrills just sat there and looked around at the people watching them. In those moments, Corey felt like they had switched places, or that his life had just as much meaning as their lives did. He always finished his morning at the bat house or the painted iceberg where the polar bears lived. For lunch, he always ordered the same thing: two hot dogs. In the afternoon, he walked all through Africa.

Corey tried to look presentable before going to the zoo, shaving off the sparse red stubble from his chin and tucking his wild curly hair in a baseball cap. He did this just in case he got the nerve to speak to her.

She seemed to have a pretty cool job, bringing little Hunter and Forrest to the zoo every day. He guessed Hunter to be about 5 and Forrest closer to 3. He knew their names because the nanny had said them so many times, calling to them or telling them to sit so she could fix a shoelace or something. But he always wondered about her name. He found it pretty easy to get close to her because she texted and talked on her phone a lot. She didn't seem too aware of anything around her, but why would she? She was at the zoo, and of course all the dangerous creatures were in cages at the zoo.

Corey had to mow the lawn for his mother, and in exchange she gave him the annual pass to the zoo and a small allowance. That was pretty much all he had to do to keep his downstairs apartment. That, and he had to see the psychiatrist on Tuesday afternoons and go to Mass with his mom on Sundays.

Twenty-three-years-old and too old to be living in his mother's basement—a total loser, Corey thought.

Corey loved to wipe out the dandelion heads that always sprouted up in the spring. Before starting the lawnmower, he would smoke a little of the medical marijuana that the psychiatrist prescribed, which made the whole process much more relaxed; he didn't worry about the lawnmower escaping from his grasp or running over his foot. With the medical marijuana, he didn't even mind picking up the poop in the yard, but he sure wouldn't want to do that job at the zoo.

He never smoked the medical marijuana before going to the zoo, however. That would be too disrespectful to the animals, and he felt creepy being high with all the little kids running around. He did smoke it before Mass, however. That was when he really needed it because he broke out in hives on his arms and his anxiety hit the roof when he stepped into the sanctuary. The medical marijuana definitely helped, despite the protests of his mother.

Just the night before, Corey threw up after a nightmare about hairy arms and legs rubbing up against his naked body. The marijuana helped to calm him down, but the sound of the vomiting or the smell of the marijuana woke up his mother. He could hear her footsteps on the floorboards above, but she didn't come downstairs that time. Now she knew just to leave him alone.

The clawed hands touched him everywhere in the nightmare, but the worst part was the hot drool and the nauseating dog breath, the kind of nightmare that left cryptic messages in welts on Corey's chest. He put some rubbing alcohol on the words, just in case they got infected, but they would always be gone in the morning. Eventually, Corey went back to sleep.

The psychiatrist seemed to think Corey had a case of Post Traumatic Stress Disorder, which would account for the horrible nightmares, his inability to hold down a job, and his raging temper. Corey didn't know why he had it—not exactly. He wasn't a veteran of any wars or anything. He just knew it had something to do with the summer when he was thirteen. His mom probably knew something more, but she wasn't telling, which caused numerous arguments that ended with Corey punching holes in the drywall upstairs. The psychiatrist was waiting for him to say exactly what happened that summer. But how could he ever tell?

Sitting across from the predators of the Serengeti Plain for more than an hour, Corey felt a gentle hand rest on his shoulder. It made him flinch. Looking up, he saw Father Lemon in his spring windbreaker.

"Good afternoon, Corey," he said, warmly gripping Corey's shoulder.

"Father Lemon! What are you doing here? Did my mom send you?"

"Mind if I join you, Corey?"

"No—of course not." The zoo seemed unnaturally quiet that day, and the remote bench around the corner from the lions provided them with some privacy.

"Your mother is very worried about you, Corey. And frankly, so am I. She said I would probably find you here, and she gave me the GPS code for your phone." Father Lemon wore one of those funny little hats that old retired men always wore. Corey hated the concern he saw in Father Lemon's wrinkled-up eyes. "Now let's have it, Corey. It's me you're talking to now."

"I don't know what to do, Father," Corey said. He felt tears well up in his eyes. "He has me. I can't get free of him. Every night he's in my bed. I feel his hairy legs all over me."

Father Lemon put his arm around Corey and let the young man weep for a moment before he asked more questions.

"Now tell me, Corey, and be honest. Has Satan's mind cloud come over you again?"

"No, Father. Not that. It's just the dreams and the welts."

"The three women?"

"Yes."

"The impure thoughts?"

"Yes."

"Tell me, Corey, what do the welts say?"

"It's that same language. I can't read it."

"What do you remember about when you were a boy?" "Things are starting to come together. The psychiatrist keeps asking me, but I haven't told him anything, really. He thinks I have PTSD or that I was sexually abused or something, but I know it's not that. I know you saved me from him, Father Lemon."

Fragments of memory returned to Corey—faster and faster—how horrible the welts had been, the words all in

Enochian, the preferred tongue of Satan. The vile curses that spilled from his tongue in a dozen different languages. But worst of all, he remembered abusing himself under the sheets and throwing the burning seed of Satan in Father Lemon's face when he came to pray. They had no choice but to use restraints on Corey.

"Tell me about the three women," Father Lemon whispered. They heard the lion roar in the distance.

"They show up in my dreams. Sometimes I see them when I'm awake—in the mirror or in the cages with the animals, but mostly in my dreams. They're old and naked. I can hardly begin to tell you what they look like, Father." The words stuck in his throat. He couldn't continue.

"My boy, remember I have been through the worst of this with you," Father Lemon said.

"Their breasts are huge. They have blood running from their nipples, and their pubic hair is long and dripping wet. They say that one of them is my mother, and I have to guess which one, but that's a lie, isn't it Father? They say I have to guess."

"Do not guess, Corey. Whatever you do, do not guess."

"They say it's just a game for their master." Corey could see the women in his mind's eye, their tongues long and black from rimming the anus of Satan.

"Do not play their game or believe their lies. You know who your mother is, and she is not one of those horrible brides of Satan. Whatever you do, do not play their game. We will go to the sanctuary now and pray together."

"No, I can't go. I'll be sick. I just can't go there."

As Corey cried on Father Lemon's shoulder, the nanny walked by with Hunter and Forrest, maybe on their way to the corral of goats. Those kids loved to pet the goats. She noticed he was crying and looked away.

Karen, Corey's mother, wore her bright white hair in a short, stylish cut. Still in her bathrobe, she fidgeted with the tulips on the kitchen table while Corey slumped against the wall, leaving his breakfast half-eaten. Sometimes she cooked for him before he went off to the zoo, or before he mowed the lawn.

"I just want you to be happy, Corey, and leave the past behind," his mother said. "If that means you need a little medicinal help now and then, well I think that's just OK, even if Father Lemon doesn't approve."

Corey didn't listen. Which of the old hags would he choose next? Which was his true mother? They all looked similar, but for the color of their pubic hair. One with black, coarse hair, the other with reddish tones, the same as Corey. Perhaps that was the clue he needed.

"Where did they find me, mother?" Corey asked, ignoring her endless monologue about the medicinal marijuana.

"Don't start that again, Corey," his mother said. "They didn't find you anywhere. You are my own child, and your father was a good Catholic man until the Lord chose to take him early, and your father's death had nothing to do with the horrible ordeal you experienced as a boy."

"Who are you trying to convince?" Corey said.

"We always loved you and prayed for you. I only wish your father had been here for you as a boy. Maybe things would have been different." She adjusted the tulips in her vase.

Corey picked up the vase and threw it against the wall. His mother emitted a staccato shriek of surprise as glass shattered everywhere, tulips falling to the floor.

"I'm so sick of your lies," he screamed. "I belong to Satan and you know it—even now I feel his claws around my heart. I can feel the taste of his saliva in my mouth. It's time for this game to end."

He snatched his mother's keys from the hook on the wall and ran out the screen door, slamming it behind him. Fuck taking the train to the zoo, he thought. He hopped in his mother's car and sped off.

Corey couldn't move, but he wanted to. He was just as frozen as Angela and the boys and just as scared as the mandrills. All three of the naked hags appeared in the plexiglass. They didn't need to say anything. He knew he had to guess which one of the hideous old crones was his true mother. He reached for some sort of intuition to guide his guess, but none came.

It had descended on them, Satan's mind cloud, which was what Father Lemon called the worst side effect his adolescent possession, much worse than the messages in welts or the cursing in foreign languages. The mind cloud was still with him. Back then, during his eight-week confinement in the hospital, he made the nuns do horrible, humiliating things. Only Father Lemon seemed able to resist him.

Corey had already guessed once—and guessed incorrectly—when the hags spoke to him from beneath the surface of the polar bear's pool. He had guessed wrong. For that, he already owed them one victim. The game was simple. Maybe little Hunter. Maybe little Forrest.

He could crack open the plexiglass with the will of Satan. At that moment, Corey believed that he could. The male mandrill would do his bidding. Corey made eye contact with the huge monkey, and its weird amber eyes could see right through Corey, right through to the presence of his true father, Satan, who filled his whole being.

If Corey guessed wrong again, the mandrill would have to take both Hunter and Forrest.

But suddenly, Corey doubted that he could split the plexiglass at all, even with the will of Satan. He would have to kill both of the children himself.

The sound of a weeping, frantic woman broke Corey's reverie. At the outer edge of the mind cloud, only as far away as the next exhibit in the tunnel, Father Lemon and Karen stood together. They had found him. They could feel the horrible dread of the cloud, could see Angela and the two boys frozen like dummies before the plexiglass wall, and they couldn't get any closer.

While the female mandrills huddled in a group beneath the log, the male mandrill made a violent show of strength: screaming, baring his jaws, and charging the plexiglass wall, but Corey was right; it was just show and bluster. The poor creature was terrified of the evil presence on the other side of the glass.

The evil hags in the reflection all pointed down the tunnel. Corey didn't understand.

"She is the sacrifice that you owe us," they whispered at once. "She is the one, the fake mother—she is the one you owe us." And then they smiled and licked their lips with their black tongues. "But first you must guess again. Which of us is your true mother?"

"No, Corey!" his mother screamed. Karen had broken through the outer layer of Satan's mind cloud. She could see the hags now. The weird pressure of the cloud intensified, tried to force her to the floor, but Karen persisted anyway—pushed through. She wrapped her arms around her Corey, who stood frozen and inert. Satan's mind cloud dissipated.

Angela noticed that the young man she had been talking to was now hugging a crying woman. Hunter tugged on her sleeve.

"The monkey is scaring me," Hunter said.

"Yeah—me too," Angela said. Disoriented, she took both of the boys by the hand and led them away from the mandrill exhibit.

Then, Corey knew the answer. The answer was obvious. Karen, the woman who had raised him, had always been his true mother. Everything else had been a lie and a trick.

"I guess you," Corey said to Karen. "You're my mother, not any of those old hags."

"That's right, sweetheart," Karen said and hugged her son again.

Father Lemon stood behind them, scowling. The time had come. The elderly priest had battled for this young man's soul for almost ten years. Karen stepped away from Corey, and Father Lemon moved in. For the first time, the priest left behind the rites and incantations of the official exorcism; instead, he walked right up and claimed Corey's soul. He hugged the young man, kissed his cheek, and then, as if unwinding a serpent from a tree trunk, Father Lemon wrenched the foul entity from Corey's core. Like Jesus Christ, who had cast the demons into a herd of swine, Father Lemon cast the demon right through the plexiglass wall into the mandrills.

Corey fell to his knees and vomited his hot dogs all over the floor.

Karen helped her son to his feet.

"Thank you, Father," Corey whispered as his mother led her son out of the tunnel.

Father Lemon, however, remained at the plexiglass wall. The male mandrill was perturbed and disoriented, charging around the cage and swinging from the ropes while the females hid beneath the log.

Behind Father Lemon, the janitor arrived, grumbling to himself as he mopped up Corey's puddle of vomit.

The male mandrill finally began to settle down, and before Father Lemon left to catch up with Karen and Corey, he saw the mandrill sit triumphantly upon the tree branch, displaying his jaws and his muscular frame while his three subservient brides, having failed to trick young Corey, emerged from their hiding place to pay homage at the foot of their master.

THE HAIRY WORM OF ROTTENNESS

I BIT INTO A ROTTEN APPLE as a child, and eating apples has never been the same since. I lost my trust for the purity of apples. I know it is true of me too like my father before me: I have been pierced by Satan like the apple core of the earth. My body is as hairy as Satan's body frozen in the ice at the ninth circle. The hairy worm is at my center, but still I yearn for purity with my facade of shiny red skin.

GRANDMA

TED WANTED TO BE THE Headless Horseman for Halloween. His grandma made the costume: with sharp scissors, she cut a black cape, which would billow on horseback while chasing skinny schoolteachers; with a sharp needle and black thread, grandma sewed a winter coat, which she adorned with silver skull buttons that had a bad habit of biting fingertips; with a sharp butcher knife, she carved the cackling jack-o'-lantern, which had twisted carrots for devil horns and a black swollen tongue from a farmyard sow. Ted tried on the costume, but a problem remained: Ted still had a head, so Grandma chopped it off with a sharp firewood ax. Ted won first prize in the costume contest, which was held in the school gymnasium.

BALLOONS

J ANIE HAD A CARNIVAL OF horrors inside a bouquet of balloons. Among them, the orange balloon held the ghost of a rabid wolfman who licked the inside with a hot tongue. The green balloon contained a vampire who turned to mist that glowed like a flashlight in the fog. Inside the black balloon, an unspeakable spirit squirmed—its moans sounded like freight trains in the night. In unison they all said, "When the night goes dark, our balloons will go POP, and when you're sound asleep, we'll eat you up like a cup of pudding." So Janie untied the balloons and released them in the bright afternoon. They floated away into the sky much higher than seagulls.

Killing Rats for Food

I HUDDLE AT THE CORNER ON the wet sidewalk. I beg for pocket change and I beg God too, but God just gives me more pain in my belly, and so I steal from God: the worst blasphemy. I steal his rats from the mounds of garbage in the alley and the dark corners of the squatter's basement. It only takes patience and a quick pop with the rusty hammer for a warm mouthful of flesh and blood. The rats are the most blessed of all God's creatures because only the rats can rejoice and fuck and eat and give birth to babies beneath a mound of garbage, the most common habitat. And I know the rats will long outlive me, but for now it's just another quick pop with the hammer and a wet mouthful.

Zombie Minnows Swim Belly Up

WHEN YOU GIVE A VAMPIRE a blowjob, the sperm will hang upside-down from your molars like bats in a cave. Zombie dogs love Dog Chow, and so do zombies, if you tell them it's crunchy brains. Vampires pull off their long fingernails and lick the blood beneath like children lick cookie batter from beaters. When zombies take showers in locker rooms, they really should wear flip-flops. Dip your vampire's condom in holy water; it provides an extra tingle, and it keeps the sperm from passing through the latex like specters through tomb doors. If your zombies are hungry, give them fetus brains deep fried like clams. They'll thank you for it. It turns out that sunlight doesn't burn vampires to ash, it makes them like disco balls. Zombie herpes is quite aggressive. Vampire eyeballs can live happily in a fishbowl. Just add a pin prick of blood weekly. For your own safety, never make eye contact.

GAME OF LIGHTNING

IN THE SUMMER, THE SKI resort gets as many lightning strikes as a dead whale gets shark bites, something about the configuration of the peaks that traps thunderstorms like fireflies in mason jars. Olympic skiers train there in the winter, but the ski resort hosts very different competitions in the summer: the participants call it Dodging the Frog Tongue of an Angry God. All night long, the players ride the chairlift to the top, their blood heavy with booze, their hearts with despair. Like all existential variations on Russian Roulette, the game is simple: to be or not to be, you know. The objective is to stumble down the mountain without a lightning bolt deep frying your heart like a jalapeno popper, all your iniquities fluttering around you like dragonfly wings in the face of God the Great Predator Frog. The town's only ambulance is nicknamed the Barbeque Wagon. It stays busy all summer. Being struck by lightning is the best way to be clipped short by the judgment of God, even better than riding first class in an airline disaster.

MASKATRON

A NIGHTMARE IN THE FIRST GRADE: Mrs. Hartman gathers the children with the recess whistle, the real Mrs. Hartman strangled beneath the desk. The impostor is the Maskatron, and it sees that I know. I run from the schoolyard; it sees me run.

Kenner released the Maskatron doll in 1976, one of the Six Million Dollar Man's enemies. A foot tall, Maskatron came with three interchangeable human faces to cover his true visage of alien circuitry, all three masks stored in a handy chest compartment. Beneath the Maskatron's street clothes, I discovered cold iron armor for skin and more circuitry panels with removable chips.

I liked to strip off Steve Austin's red jumpsuit, his perfect plastic chest like a Greek statue without nipple or navel, his strange rubber sleeve like a foreskin, which could be rolled back to reveal the bionics in his arm. On Christmas morning, I played with him in a secret spot beneath the Ping-Pong table. Peering through the doll's eye hole, I could see with bionic vision.

On the television show, the reveal was the worst part, when the Six Million Dollar Man knocked loose the face with a bionic punch, and we saw the lifeless puppet eyes in a nest of circuitry, which hummed like bees, an intercom for a voice box

It could be anyone.

After preaching his sermon on Sunday morning, my father took my brother and I for a long drive in the red Chevy Malibu outside town into the foothills. He didn't tell us where we were going. My brother joked that dad was the Maskatron. Father removed his pastor mask.

MOTHER'S DAY

O N SUNDAY AFTERNOON, DAD TOOK mom's head out of the freezer and placed her on the kitchen table by the tulips. She liked the tulips. After she thawed for about an hour, she moved her eyes all around and snapped her teeth. That's when my big brother and I showed her the pictures with smiling suns and green grass that we drew for her with our magic markers after church. Dad kissed her on the forehead and she went back in the freezer, but only after he sealed her up in a large Ziploc bag, to prevent freezer burn.

LIGHTNING STRIKES

I WAS THIRTEEN, IN THE THUNDERSTORM of puberty, just a little pudgy, my hair parted down the center. I appeared to be a placid student because I turned in my algebra homework and sang solos in the church choir. But no one saw my primary defect that ran through my being like a serpentine lightning strike through a tree trunk. One day when thunderstorms boiled, the umpire called off the Little League game. My baseball coach told the team what happens when you're struck by lightning on the field: your fillings melt, blood boils, cleats blown off a hundred yards away, eyeballs run from your skull like candle wax; at the ER, the doctors peel away the polyester jersey fused with blackened skin; your digital wristwatch will never tell the time again, circuits fried the same as your brain. The coach had seen it before in the Vietnam jungle. And if you survive, you forever see the world through queer goggles: ravens note your passing, ghosts know your face, your voice cracks in church solos; no one can see the secret scar that runs from the crown of your head to the sole of your foot like a kite string tethering your soul to electrified mud.

MY HORROR HISTORY

My FASCINATION WITH HORROR GAINED momentum while puberty accelerated, the ninth grade a miserable year for queer teenager anxiety: lust at the sight of boys wearing silky red track shorts and tank top uniforms, a lust quagmire that I attempted to sprint through on hot afternoons when the boys ran without their shirts; I tried to capture mind's eye photographs, which blur in the sweat and sun of my memory. I read Poe's "Tell-Tale Heart" for the very first time. Poe's narrator cannot contain his guilt; he cries out: he committed the foul deed. The tortuous beating heart compels him, and I felt a need building within me to cry out, to release, to confess the desire for boys in running shorts as I ran the 100-yard-dash. I crossed the finish line; I had forgotten to breathe the whole time: pulse percussion thumping and pounding perversity beneath the floorboards of my brain.

KNORR LAKE

D AD PULLED THE CAMPER TO Knorr Lake in our red Chevy Malibu. The driver's window was parted for dad's cigarette. The wasp got sucked in and went right down my shirt in the back seat. I screamed like being electrocuted. At the little roadside store, dad put baking soda paste on the fourteen stings across my chest and bought me a stuffed squirrel to hold in my lap. We got a great spot by the lake, but Dad couldn't get the camper level and he cussed out the infernal little bubble, even though he was a preacher. My brother found the minnows trapped in the creekbed half dried up. I caught one, put it in the dog leash clasp and swung it around my head until the fish came apart. I couldn't undo it. We fished from the edge of the boulders. Dad made me pierce the worms myself. I caught three fish and watched dad's silver knife slice open the bellies brimming with guts, and I folded their clammy bodies in aluminum foil for the campfire, impossible to get all of the bones. On rainy nights we played card games in the camper, and dad pretended to be a bear, clawing and growling outside the window to scare my brother and me. We cremated my father five years ago. He had a heart attack after a hip operation. That summer the rangers discovered the fish in Knorr Lake had parasitic worms. They had to close the campground, the beetle kill threatening to burn.

LAND OF THE DEAD

THEY ALL WEAR FLOWERS ON their hats in the land of the dead. They promenade through the park where ferns and shadows mark the boundary, the concrete fountain a geyser of acid. Of course, the flowers are bright plastic, manufactured in China. As my faithful boyhood dog hobbles by my side, I see sweet Agnes who whispers through her tracheotomy. You don't need lips in the land of the dead. Old Tom always had a laugh until that trio of seagulls made off with his tongue, but he can still curse them. I never expected to see my baby boy here, now an old man. He walks past with his cane, a daisy tucked in his fedora. I had hoped him to be somewhere above on a chaise lounge made of clouds and cherub bottoms, but he is here too, his head a soft purple globe for tangled worms and old lullabies.

TABLE SCRAPS

M Y GENIUS FRIEND BECAME AN Irish Wolfhound—for an experiment.

His long snout wouldn't permit speech, but he raised his bearded eyebrows knowingly. He romped in ponds, chasing frogs. He caught rabbits, forcing himself to devour them to complete the primal experience. Of course, he used the bathroom like a civilized man, finding difficulty with the toilet paper.

He invented cunning games to play with the neighbor boys, but I think he liked it too much when they scratched that irksome spot behind the ear and praised him.

He stared at the TV, resting on lazy haunches, awkward paw on the remote control. He took naps on the lawn, twitching in his nightmares. And then one day I caught him squatting in the rose garden.

He wouldn't behave himself at the dinner table anymore. His eyes became soft and moist like the Alpo I scrape from the can. The children trick him into tail chasing. Now he pants constantly, without dignity, extending a rude, flopping tongue, pissing on mailboxes to mark imaginary territory, forgetting his past identity in anticipation of table scraps from the master.

THE DREADFUL EXCAVATION

A FTER CHURCH, A WEIRD BOY gave me an extra frog that he captured by the lake. I kept it in the deep window well of my basement bedroom where once a Black Widow appeared. I filled the window well with fresh branches from the yard and live crickets from the pet store. On hot summer afternoons, I pulled the jumping legs off grasshoppers, dropping them helpless in the window well. The grasshoppers couldn't escape the precise whip of the frog's tongue. Once, I placed a crippled grasshopper right on top of the frog's head. For a moment the frog looked upwards, and in a tongue-flash, the grasshopper was gone. I got bored with watching the frog devour grasshoppers, and I neglected the frog in the window well as the fall got colder and the grasshoppers disappeared for the season. During the long winter, I thought about the frog every now and then as I worked on homework at my desk. The frog was dead beneath the brown leaves and snow in my window well. I couldn't see it, but I knew its grave was there. In the spring, I couldn't bear to look for the little body beneath the wet blanket of rotten leaves. Every time I looked out my bedroom window, I was haunted by my neglect. I asked my mom for help, and she climbed into the window well with her gardening gloves. I couldn't bear to watch the dreadful excavation for the dead frog. She came back with the frog in her gloved hands. It was alive. I didn't know frogs hibernate.

SPIDER

ON THE DAY I BECAME a spider, I bought the right
toothpaste for fang hygiene—and the right condoms
too, but there's no such thing as safe sex when you belong to
Latrodectus, the genus of The Widow. Soon the arguments
became pointless: all eight of my eyes assumed the correct
point of view. You tried to appease me with your prettiest
compliments, but I sucked them dry, and they dangled in the
bedroom, desiccated. I never forgave you when you walked
through my web on purpose. I know it was on purpose. And
I am waiting up here in the corner by the potted plant. There
are eggs beyond count in my sac. I have to give you credit. You
eventually learned how to pluck my strings. After everything,
you had the skill of a harpist. And I showed you what it really
means to be a spider when I descended in a flash and took you
screaming in the bed sheets: spinning, endlessly spinning.

TIPS FROM A SEVERED HEAD AFICIONADO

O F COURSE IT'S JUST AS much an art form as taxidermy. If you can keep the stump supple, it draws water like a fresh Xmas tree. The heads that fetch the most on ebay display the slice known as the "guillotine clean," so much better than the ragged hacksaw edge. Nothing drives up prices like long luxurious hair, which I keep silky with *Winter Vanilla Cleansing Conditioner* (plus keratin), and at night I keep my heads in an antique ice box, which never dries like the ravages of freezer burn. An inexpensive little secret: cap the teeth with a rainbow of pencil erasers, so the bites only tickle like a teething baby. It's crafty fun for the kids to cover the braids with felt snakeheads, good for a game of "Gorgon Trumps the Kraken." For a night out dancing, I switch out the eyes for little disco balls encased in crystal, which incidentally tell precise fortunes. And with some simple extensions, I weave the hair into a purse strap, and the head faithfully holds my car keys all night with the tenacity of a door knocker.

THE CITY BEAST

IN A CIRCLE OF MOTOR oil like a fairy ring, I stumbled on
that damn stool, all gut rolls and double chins of shit,
rotund segments of a fecal caterpillar, a chain of lumps like
featureless heads all dumped together in a pile on the concrete
lot behind the paint factory. I probed it with the board of a
pallet, gagging to find the wheels of a tricycle inside like rat
bones in owl scat, the snapped beams of a walker, and a slouch
hat for the pennies of a harmonica beggar.

What innards can gestate a miracle like alien forms that
surface in fossils to bungle evolution for everyone? What is this
anal incubus that disturbs my smoke break? I want my fifteen
minutes, not this revelation worse than a footprint the size of
ten potholes in forest mud.

THE HOKEY POKEY

I T TURNS OUT DEATH ISN'T the saddest thing if you turn yourself around, turn yourself around like the Hokey Pokey. Death can be fun, if you try. The titanium cage around your spinal cord replaced the cancer-filled vertebrae—now it's like a jack-in-the-box. Turn the crank. Keep turning to the beat of that manic gay tune, until that happy clown Death goes POP. Titanium hips can be fun for dancing. You can put the right one in. And you can put the left one in. And you can shake them all about. Just like the seizure from the blood clot that killed you first thing in the morning—right there in your La-Z-Boy. And you can put that malignant brain tumor in—just about a handful now—and you can shake it all about. Just make sure not to slip on the puddles of blood there in the gymnasium circle when you turn yourself around. There's an urban legend that says Satan designed the Hokey Pokey as a secret ritual; some say that's what it's all about.

BREAKFAST WITH THE MONSTER

THE MONSTER COMES INTO THE house, slender enough to slip through the open window of my wet dream, so embarrassing in middle age. At the breakfast table its tentacles adorn me like feather boas; its nipples fill my cereal bowl with warm milk. It likes its eggs runny. I'm just trying to read the paper. So many theories about Darwinian evolution. It won't shut up. Its breath makes my bathroom a sauna, and it smells my anus like a poodle. Of course it dries me after my shower, its coat like old terry cloth, and it combs my hair with a severe part down the center like a mother might groom a retarded son. And I throw up just a little when it compliments my hairy back, the true Sign of the Beast, much more potent than eyebrows that meet in the center.

My Encounter with Bloody Mary

I BELIEVED THE BLOODY MARY STORY when my older brother and his friends told me how the mirror witch would appear. I could see her in my mind's eye, a vivid portrait.

The darkened bathroom mirror would light up and she would be there, wet with blood. In my imagination, she never did anything after that; she just stood there like an evil icon, like a Satanic double of the Virgin Mary. In my mind, I made a connection between the two Marys.

My brother and I were over at Scott's house for a birthday party (Scott was a boy from our church), and several more boys from the church were there that night too. I was the little brother, all of the other boys at least three years older. They even called me "little Darkenbrook." I was in the second grade at school.

Sometime after cake and presents, the story of Bloody Mary came up. Scott explained it to my brother and me in a matter-of-fact way, and the story seemed entirely plausible to my young brain. In retrospect, I think my brother was old enough to know it was all just a scary birthday party con, and I'm sure all of the older boys could see that I believed it. Of course, some part of them might have believed it too.

They tried to convince me to go into the bathroom with them, but they didn't force me. Instead, I waited outside in the hallway in terror as the older boys congregated in the second-floor bathroom with the gigantic mirror and no windows.

I could hear the boys chanting "Bloody Mary" inside the bathroom, and when they reached 13 chants, the boys screamed and came running out of the bathroom, all of them swearing that they saw the bloody woman in the mirror.

I completely believed them. I knew part of me wanted to see her too.

I remember telling my mom the whole thing on the way home in the car, and my mom was furious with my older brother for playing that trick on me. It was obvious they orchestrated the whole thing to scare the little brother.

In retrospect, I wonder—I know part of it was to scare me, but I think they all felt a great thrill chanting with their eyes closed in the dark bathroom, holding hands before the mirror. And when they opened their eyes, what did their minds truly show them?

DRACULA AT WALDENBOOKS

I KNEW SATAN COULD HEAR MY thoughts, so I didn't want to read anything about him, which would instantly catch his attention, and there could be nothing worse for a preacher's son. But at the same time I felt drawn to books about darkness and horror.

I walked up to the counter at Waldenbooks and asked the bookseller if he could recommend a scary novel that didn't have anything to do with Satan. I felt certain the bookseller would understand.

He turned around and looked at the Halloween display on the wall behind the cash register. He grabbed the Bantam paperback edition of Dracula and handed it to me. He didn't have to look anything up or even leave the counter.

Dracula is an epistolary novel from the Victorian era, not exactly the perfect recommendation for a twelve-year-old boy in 1985, but I accepted the recommendation.

Cover to cover, Dracula is full of Satan.

Of course, I knew about Dracula—he was ubiquitous. When I was a second-grader, my mom read me an illustrated chapter book, which I picked from a Troll book order at school. It told the story of Jonathan Harker's first encounter with Dracula at the castle. When the count offers up the squirming baby in a sack to his three vampire wives, my mom stopped reading the chapter book, a strange look of disquiet on her face.

And I remembered that part about the baby when I read the first section of the novel, which is composed of letters from Jonathan Harker to his true love Mina as he travels through Transylvania and becomes imprisoned in Dracula's castle. It remains the most suspenseful and riveting thing I have ever read. The dread grows as Harker figures out his true predicament—the count is a monster and the castle is haunted by the vampire wives.

However, once Dracula slaughters all the sailors on the ship and arrives in London, the book gets boring, as most undergraduate lit students will tell you, so I jumped ahead, and I was offended to encounter a scene with Dracula walking around in the afternoon. That broke the rules. Vampires couldn't walk around in daylight. My older brother had told me the entire plot of *Fright Night*; I knew the rules.

Then I hit upon the most disturbing thing I have ever read in any book: in her bedroom, innocent young Mina is caught slurping blood from Dracula's bare chest. The horror and sexual undertones were just too much for my preacher-kid brain.

I handed over the book to my mom and asked her to please hide it in a box, and then stash the box in a secret corner of the basement. I had vampire nightmares for years after that. Thanks for the recommendation, Waldenbooks.

THE QUEST OF THE ZOMBIE SPELLING BEE CHAMPION

ONCE UPON A TIME THERE lived a spelling bee champion who was murdered with a hammer.

Soon the seagulls gathered around the body and took turns pulling bits of brain from the hammer holes. The brain tasted quite delicious since the boy had filled it with beautiful words, which marinated like teriyaki.

Nearby a great fissure opened in the earth, and Satan leapt out of the hole like a rabbit. He shambled over to the boy's body with his long hairy legs. Satan shooed the seagulls away and momentarily extinguished his great beard of inverted flame. He gave the spelling bee champion mouth-to-mouth, but instead of life-giving breath, he opened up a pit of Satanic radiation in his belly and regurgitated some down the boy's trachea.

Satan lit his beard again and shambled back to the fissure.

When the boy found himself fully resuscitated a few minutes later, he was a zombie. He remembered his name was Chad.

"I need to get home—I'm late for dinner," Chad said, but he didn't know that now he spoke the language of the dead, which all scavengers can speak.

"You can't go home now. You're a zombie," said one of the seagulls who lingered in the hopes of more delicious brain. Chad ignored the talking seagull as if it were a dream, and staggered home.

When Chad arrived at the front gate, he found his dog, a shaggy dog named Panda, guarding the gate. He tried to enter, but Panda growled and snapped.

The seagull stood on the fence. "Your dog can't let you in," he explained. "You're a zombie now. It's a dog's job to protect the house from the undead."

His dog had never snapped at him before, and more than anything Chad wanted to cry, but since zombies can't cry, he said instead, "I don't want to be a zombie. I want to be a real boy."

This was what the seagull secretly waited for. "I can help you become a real boy again, but you have to do something for me in return. I want to taste just a little more of your brain. You don't need it now—a zombie can't win a spelling bee."

"But I'll need it later when I become a real boy again," Chad said.

"When Satan grants your wish to become a real boy, he can just give you all the brains you need," the seagull explained.

"Why would Satan grant my wish?"

"He woke you up for a reason, of course."

Then the seagull explained to Chad what he must do to become a real boy again; the steps of his quest were numerous and daunting.

The seagull and all of his brothers carried Chad by the back of his jacket and pant legs and flew across the ocean.

After many days of flying, they spotted a white island. The seagulls set Chad down on the island that was in fact no island at all, but the back of the great white whale, Moby-Dick.

"We have done our part," said the seagull, "we have brought you to Moby-Dick—now you must share a little of your brain for me and my brothers. We're quite hungry after flying for so many days."

Chad knew that seagulls were quite greedy and couldn't be trusted. By the look in their black button eyes, he knew they would gobble up every last piece if given the chance.

As the seagulls began to circle, Chad walked backwards on the whale—he had an idea.

"Stand still so we can land on your head," cried the hungry seagulls.

Chad stopped right next to a hole in the white whale's back. Just as the seagulls closed in, the mighty whale exhaled through his blowhole, breaking the necks of all the greedy birds with his powerful spout.

"Thank you, Moby-Dick," Chad said.

Being part phantom, the whale understood the language of the dead.

"Tell me why I should not crush you with my jaw or smash you with my tale," Moby-Dick said.

"I'm here to help you—to pull out the harpoon," Chad said.

"My body is riddled with harpoons, little zombie."

"You know which one."

"Others have tried to pull it out before, but none have succeeded."

Chad saw the handle of the enchanted harpoon, forged by Satan for Ahab to slay Moby-Dick. It inched deeper and deeper into the whale's hump. One day it would penetrate his heart.

Even though many had failed before, Chad pulled out the harpoon with one attempt—just like Excalibur from the stone.

The white whale rejoiced and gave Chad a glorious ride to the bottom of the sea—zombies don't need to breathe, after all.

Grateful to be free of the enchanted harpoon at long last, Moby-Dick delivered the little zombie to a plague ship on its way to the island of the dead.

On board, Chad found plenty of brains to eat—all boiled by the South Pacific sun in the heads of dead sailors. Chad ate until he could eat no more. It was disgusting, but Chad was a zombie, after all.

When the ship arrived at the island of the dead, a great cloud of ravens greeted them on the deck. The ravens coalesced into a towering figure of shadow and shiny black wings; it was the Angel of Death.

It turns out that the Angel of Death is a huge fan of zombie movies, so he was quite pleased to see Chad on his island.

"For what or for whom do you seek on my island?" asked the Angel of Death.

"I'm looking for an undead boy named Bartholomew of the Scissors," Chad replied, still following the seagull's precise instructions.

"I will show you the way to his cave, but only if you promise not to kill him with that harpoon you carry, for he is like a son to me."

After Chad promised, the Angel of Death pointed the way, and the zombie hiked along the treacherous rocks of the coastline for many hours before arriving at the mouth of the cave.

Deep in the cave, he found Bartholomew sleeping in an aluminum canoe as if it were a Viking grave. Hundreds of shiny silver scissors swirled around Bartholomew like a school of minnows.

"I smell a zombie that's been too long in the sun and brought with him too many flies," Bartholomew said. "Tell me why I shouldn't stab your brain a hundred times or bury you in a cave-in."

"I'm here to challenge you to a duel," Chad said.

"What kind of duel?" Bartholomew asked, sitting up with interest.

"A duel for spelling bee champions." Chad remembered seeing Bartholomew's name engraved on the spelling bee championship cup that stood on his bookshelf at home, which meant Bartholomew had won the cup many years before when still a human boy.

"If you win," Chad explained, "I will give you this enchanted harpoon, which was forged by Satan for Captain Ahab to kill Moby-Dick."

"And if you win."

"You will stab me in the heart with a pair of your scissors."

Bartholomew paused for a moment. "A strange prize, indeed, but I accept your terms."

Chad removed the compact dictionary from his jacket pocket (every spelling bee champion carries one), and they commenced the duel, passing the dictionary back and forth with each turn, both attempting to find the most difficult and perplexing word. The duel went on for days—both of them were spelling bee champions, after all.

Finally, on the seventh day, Bartholomew failed to spell "catafalque," and Chad followed up by spelling "caryatid" correctly.

"You are truly a great Spelling Bee champion," Bartholomew said and, as requested, he stabbed Chad directly in the heart with a pair of scissors (it was the only way to take a pair of Bartholomew's scissors away from the island, which was Chad's plan all along). To Chad, being a zombie, the stab hurt no worse than getting his ear pierced at the mall with a spring-loaded piercing gun.

"Since you have beaten me," Bartholomew continued, "this enchanted canoe will ferry you back and forth between the land of the living or the land of the dead."

With Moby-Dick's harpoon at his side, and Bartholomew's pair of scissors in his heart, Chad wished for the canoe to take him to the seaside mansion of the world's most famous supermodel—it was rumored that she had the most luxurious bathroom mirror in the land of the living.

The seagull had given Chad the secret password to enter the enchanted mansion (for the supermodel was also a powerful witch).

When Chad stood before the majestic mirror, he recited the incantation: *Bloody Mary Bloody Mary Bloody Mary*

Bloody Mary Bloody Mary Bloody Mary Bloody Mary Bloody Mary Bloody Mary Bloody Mary Bloody Mary Bloody Mary Bloody Mary.

Bloody Mary, in a bright sheet of wet blood, lashed out from the mirror and slashed Chad's throat with her long black fingernails. But since Chad was already a zombie, this hurt no more than a paper cut.

"Why do you bother me, zombie boy?" Bloody Mary asked in a dreadful voice.

"If you recite a beautiful poem, I will wash your hair," Chad replied.

"Will you brush it with a hundred strokes?"

"I will."

Bloody Mary perched on the edge of the bathtub and recited this poem:

> *My bosom still drips for the babe*
> *who now moulders in the grave*
> *because you are the greedy bee*
> *that pillages the flower,*
> *and you tore my maidenhead*
> *like the wicked bee*
> *that pillages the flower.*
> *For death is woven throughout*
> *like a gay ribbon*
> *in the braid of a beautiful maiden,*
> *and I was once a beautiful maiden*
> *who fell beneath the galloping horse*
> *of your desire,*
> *trampled beneath the galloping horse*
> *of your desire.*
> *My bosom still drips for the babe*
> *who now moulders in the grave.*

After listening to the melancholy beauty of Bloody Mary's poem, Chad certainly would have shed a tear if zombies could cry.

Chad washed the blood from her hair and used the super model's hair dryer that was gilded with gold. Then Chad began to brush Bloody Mary's hair with the supermodel's brush that was studded with diamonds.

Lulled into a reverie by the strokes of the brush, Bloody Mary began to hum as her attention wandered. Quickly, while she wasn't looking, Chad pulled the magical scissors from out of his heart and cut off a lock of her raven-black hair.

Upon the first cut of the scissors, instead of cutting hair, Chad found himself cutting the dotted lines around a beautiful paper doll of Elizabeth Bathory in her regal finest. She transformed just like the seagull had told him.

Chad tucked the paper doll into his jacket and climbed back into the aluminum canoe. He wished for the canoe to deliver him to the fissure in the earth near the site of his murder.

The canoe flew deep into the fissure, traveling for many days past the boundary of the underworld. The canoe delivered him to Hell's Door, behind which stood Satan's throne room. Just as the seagull had explained, only the Satanic harpoon could fit into the impenetrable lock on the door. Chad inserted the harpoon into the lock. He heard a click, and the door opened.

Chad found Satan, with his beard of inverted flame, seated on his throne next to an empty throne made of virgin's bones.

"Why do you trespass in my throne room?" Satan boomed.

"I've come to return your harpoon that you forged for Captain Ahab to slay Moby-Dick, but more importantly, I've come to return your lost bride who long ago escaped into the mirror realm," Chad said as he offered the folded-up paper doll in his outstretched hand.

As soon as Satan took the paper doll, Bloody Mary appeared next to Satan in royal splendor on her throne of virgin's bones.

"What do you ask in return for these kingly gifts?"

"Only that you make me a real boy again."

"It is done," Satan declared.

Chad found himself standing in front of the gate to his house. He felt his head—all of the hammer holes gone. He was a real boy again. All that remained of his quest were the foul smelling stains on his clothes and a peculiar scar over his heart.

Panda the sheepdog greeted Chad at the gate and rejoiced at the boy's victorious return from the land of the dead.

Meanwhile, in Satan's throne room, Bloody Mary tapped her black fingernails on the armrest made out of a virgin's femur and plotted her revenge against the spelling bee champion.

In the world of the living, a depraved hammer murderer still roamed the neighborhood.

NED AND THE GREAT WHITE SHARK

ONCE UPON A TIME THERE lived a boy named Ned. His best friend was a great white shark. Ned's father got eaten up by cancer, and Ned's mother circled the city all night driving long empty buses and picking up stray riders.

Whenever the moon was bright, Ned escaped under the fence of the trailer park in his sneakers, raincoat, and pajamas. From the rich neighbor's dock, Ned borrowed the aluminum canoe that he rowed out into the freezing waters of the bay. Ned simply wished upon the moon, which called the shark like a doorbell. It was unusual for a great white shark to swim in the bay, but the yearning heart of a lonely boy can attract a shark like ladles of fish heads and chum in the water.

The shark, as big as an empty train tunnel, rose up from the moonlit water, his smile a guillotine. The shark's voice was deep and gravelly like a garbage disposal: "You have come for me again," the shark said. "I have missed you my sweet boy, my heart as heavy as a sea lion without you."

Ned took the boy scout knife from his raincoat and winced as he cut his index finger—just like playing blood brothers. The shark inched closer in anticipation, and Ned rubbed his bloody finger in the shark's weird nostril, which to a shark was better than catnip. The shark's eye shields rolled up with pleasure. "I have a surprise for you," Ned said, and he pulled out the beach ball, still deflated in the store package.

While Ned blew up the beach ball, the shark circled, as excited as a weimaraner. They only got to play fetch for a few throws before the shark punctured the beach ball, but it was worth the $3.99 Ned paid at the drugstore.

After playing catch, Ned dangled his hand in the cold water and meditated upon the moon as the shark swarm circles and caressed the boy's hand with his passing dorsal fin. Unable to resist any longer, the shark rose from the water. "Come and swim in the water with me, I love you so," the shark said. But Ned knew that a shark never confused love with hunger. For a great white shark, they meant the same thing.

"I can't swim with you," Ned explained. "I have to go to school tomorrow."

"But if you come in the water with me, you can be born again as a shark."

Ned knew that all of the world's mythologies agreed upon this point: all shark victims become sharks themselves, the shark's belly a portal to the next life".

The shark said, "You will know the pleasure of hot mammal blood in cold waves, the power to hold a thrashing sea lion in your jaws, and the electric adrenalin of feeding frenzy when the mightiest of the whales offers himself in a great banquet of death."

"But I can't," Ned said. "I have a geometry test tomorrow."

Dejected, the shark started to swim away towards the moon, but Ned took off his sneakers and raincoat and pajamas and jumped into the water of the bay, which was as cold as a sodapop.

Ned thrashed in the water. "Come back," he shouted, his teeth chattering.

In the distance, Ned saw the dorsal fin turn and go under.

Ned screamed when the shark's jaws chomped down as fast as a mousetrap, the boy engulfed in a cloud of blood, but then it was over. The shark ate the boy with the skill of a dentist pulling a tooth.

Ned's legs and arms and torso sloshed around with all of the sea lion flippers and surfboard chunks in the cold soup cauldron of the shark's belly, but the shark left Ned's head behind to bob up and down on the surface of the water as Ned watched and waited for the moon to split open like a birth canal.

The Zombie and the Mouse

ONCE UPON A TIME, A mouse made a house in a zombie's empty eye socket. The zombie, who lived in an alley with many garbage cans, gave the mouse all the bits of cheese that he could find. The zombie didn't mind all the broken fingers from springing the mousetraps. With his good eye, the zombie watched the mouse in a discarded bathroom mirror, which was propped up against a garbage can, and the zombie uttered his soft giggles. The zombie gave the mouse a soft tissue for his nest and a cigarette butt for a pillow.

A famous writer lived in a beautiful house with a garage door that opened into the alley. While taking out his garbage, the writer discovered this special friendship between zombie and mouse, and he wrote a picture book about them. He drew the zombie with a tattered cap like an old-fashioned bus driver and the mouse with a dapper suit and bowler hat.

The book became a beloved classic with children everywhere, the writer made a small fortune, and the sale of pet mice spiked, but life in the alley didn't improve much for the zombie and the mouse. Zombies suffer from dementia, and one day the zombie fished the mouse out of his eye socket and crushed him to death with his teeth.

Menacing Shadows

IN THE STIFF TUXEDO, BAKER paced back and forth in the foyer of the condo. His co-workers, Alex and Agnes from corporate headquarters, still adjusted their makeup and evening gowns in the upstairs bathroom. When the doorbell rang, Baker instantly pulled on the oak door without checking the peephole, the accumulation of ice causing the door to stick for a second before cracking and giving way. The driver stood on the frozen landing, silent in the shadows against a backdrop of towering evergreens. Baker had neglected to switch on the porch light, and he felt an odd shiver at the presence of the man.

"Sorry, we're not quite ready. The ladies will be down in just a moment," Baker explained.

"No problem sir," the driver said. "I'll be waiting in the car."

Baker watched as the driver, dressed in a heavy black overcoat, walked down the stairs with caution, the steps still slick despite a layer of salt. Baker noticed the driver appeared to be too muscular for the size of his overcoat. A weightlifting enthusiast, perhaps, Baker thought. He prided himself on noticing the little details about people. Little details about people and little details about numbers made him a sought-after accountant, despite his young age.

The business retreat marked Baker's first visit to White Crag, a world-renowned ski resort where movie stars could be spotted on the slopes and many Olympic athletes trained for the Winter Games. He heard that the mild November left the slopes light on snow so far this season, almost delaying the opening of the resort, and the clear sky offered no hope for new snow that night.

In the doorway, Baker gazed up at the brilliant full moon that gave patches of snow an eerie glow and cast long skeletal shadows, the stars above shining much brighter than back home in the city. Baker considered giving downhill skiing a try while visiting the resort, somewhat afraid of embarrassing himself on the bunny slope. He might just stick to drinking cocktails in the hot tub.

Baker heard Alex and Agnes coming downstairs from the upper floor.

"You're going to freeze to death if that's what you're wearing," he said. Both of the women wore sparkling formal gowns with open backs and high heels.

"We're only walking from the door to the car," Alex said. "I'm more worried about slipping on the ice in these heels."

With the assistance of the driver, Baker managed to help the ladies down the icy stairs and into the toasty town car idling in the driveway. Alex took the front passenger seat, Baker and Agnes the back.

Although somewhat accustomed to the upper echelons of the corporate world, Baker felt a little out of his depth with these two glamorous women. Agnes, probably in her forties, had a practiced elegance about her that Baker found intimidating. Baker guessed he might be closer to Alex in age, but her stunning beauty made Baker feel as nervous as a schoolboy at the fall dance.

Baker took it as a sign of confidence that the upper management trusted him to escort these important women to a social function and share a condo with them during the business retreat. He had heard rumors about the company's luxurious business retreats to White Crag for years, but they had never invited Baker or anyone from his accounting team before. Quite a bit of mystery surrounded the opening night gala, and Baker could see that Alex shared his intense curiosity.

"Have you ever been to one of the company's winter retreats?" Baker asked Agnes.

Agnes gave him an odd, knowing smirk. "Oh yes. I've been going for years. It's a night you will never forget."

Baker smiled with nervous anticipation and glanced up at the driver who watched them in the rearview mirror, noticing the driver's crooked nose and thick scar that divided his eyebrow, and Baker also noticed that the driver wore an earpiece like a secret service agent.

Apparently, their condo was located very close to the mountain facility, the location of the mysterious corporate gala, because they arrived in less than five minutes.

"I think we could have walked," Baker joked, but neither of the women seemed to hear him as they stepped out of the town car in their precarious high heels.

Astonished at the brightness of the full moon above the facility, which looked more like a concrete military bunker than the location of a formal gala, Baker looked all around at the dense forest surrounding them and the dark shadows cast by the eerie light from above. He felt a strange shudder of fear.

The driver seemed to read his mind. "Don't worry sir," he said, "we'll keep you safe," gesturing toward the illuminated path to the front entrance.

Baker smiled. "Of course," he said, but it seemed to Baker like a very strange thing for the driver to say.

Once he stepped inside the ultra-modern foyer, all sleek concrete, mirrors, and abstract art, the ominous feelings dissipated as many well-known co-workers greeted him, everyone sipping cocktails and dressed in formal wear. He had never seen so many vice presidents of the company together in once place, and had never seen them so merry, a stark contrast to how they conducted their grim business meetings. Baker realized he had truly achieved a measure of success if they were bringing him into this elite inner circle. This was much more than a business retreat, clearly a reward for service and loyalty to the company.

Once everyone had arrived, the attendants corralled all of the guests into a banquet room where the company treated them to a sumptuous feast with a choice of salmon or steak, and of course more cocktails. Some of the vice presidents delivered half-sober speeches about the efforts of the many unflappable corporate teams, the stratospheric profits with foreign infrastructure projects and manufacturing, another successful luxury resort launched in the Caribbean, and of course the vast humanitarian outreach in war-torn countries. Then the evening's primary entertainment began.

All of the guests, about thirty people in all, filed into a series of interconnected rooms with dim lighting and floor-to-ceiling one-way mirrors. On the other side of the mirrors, they could see a large forested enclosure like an exhibit at the zoo. Baker stepped close to the glass and looked for any sign of an exotic creature like a lion or a tiger. A zoo exhibit was certainly a strange way to end the evening. Perhaps the exhibit contained a specimen of local fauna inside like a bear or a wolf.

Baker noticed some small monitors up in the corners by the ceiling. The monitors played what looked like surveillance footage with the green tint of night vision, and the monitors showed the same scene, sped up in time lapse, over and over in a loop. It appeared to be a man curled up in a ball on the floor of a padded cell, but then something bizarre happened. He ripped out of his clothing and transformed.

"Is that something from a horror movie?" Baker blurted out, realizing he had too much to drink and spoke too loudly. Agnes stood nearby in the cluster of guests, and she only gave him a weird, knowing smirk in reply.

The monitors went dark; staff members wheeled in carts with enough night-vision goggles for everyone. Some of the drunk guests giggled in delight as they set down their champagne flutes and tried to put on the goggles, adjust the straps, and turn the power on. As Baker put on his goggles, he noticed his driver standing in the back corner of the room, and the man nodded at Baker as if to say, go ahead—you won't be sorry. All of the lights went dark.

With the night-vision goggles, Baker could see quite clearly inside the forested enclosure. He assumed whatever was inside couldn't see them as they crowded at the one-way glass for a glimpse. At first, Baker couldn't believe how bright everything looked with the green night-vision, and then he realized that the enclosure had an open roof, and the brilliant full moon hovered above.

The spectators emitted some scattered nervous laughter when a small hatch opened and a fawn traipsed into the enclosure. The little creature ran back and forth in front of the windows, and then stopped dead in its tracks. There was something else in there with the baby deer, and the poor thing appeared to know it.

Baker didn't know if the werewolf had been there all along, hiding in the shadows, or if the creature had slipped inside the enclosure through an unseen door. Had it not been for the fact that Baker focused his attention on the fawn, he might have missed the event altogether—the beast moved that quickly. And then the fawn vanished, swept away in the creature's fangs. The drunk guests applauded at the feat of predatory skill, as if watching a stunt at the circus, or a vanishing act at a magic show, but they also felt a sense of genuine awe and reverence at what they witnessed.

Baker felt like he wanted to vomit. What ungodly thing had he just seen? And who was he really working for? He stumbled back from the window. He felt a sturdy hand on his shoulder—it belonged to the driver.

"Are you okay sir? Can I get you anything? I know it's a lot to take in." The voice sounded friendly, but Baker sensed something menacing underneath the tone.

"No, I'm good," Baker said. "It's just so... awesome... I'm in awe."

Apparently, this was the right thing to say because the man squeezed his shoulder warmly. "You've got that right, sir. He is awesome indeed. And now I think you could use a refresher on that cocktail."

Baker stepped shakily back to the window. He didn't think anyone else had spotted it, but Baker prided himself on noticing the little details. It was difficult to spot because, with the night-vision goggles, it blended in with the leaves and shadows of the undergrowth. Just a few feet from where the fawn had stood, Baker saw the unmistakable form of a severed human hand.

"Buddy's going to sleep over tonight," Neal said to his twin brother Michael. "Is it okay if we use the bunk beds?"

Michael looked up from his algebra notebook, scowling. "Well that would mean I have to sleep on the couch."

Neal leaned against the doorframe of their shared bedroom. "I know," he said. "I'd do the same for you if you had a friend sleep over."

"I never have friends sleep over," Michael said, turning his attention back to the algebra equation. "So the answer is no."

Neal's cheeks flushed bright red. Michael knew exactly how to get to him. For a moment, Neal looked outside the window at the gloomy November twilight. The previous night had been clear and bright with the full moon, but it looked like storm clouds had moved in, good news for the ski resort. "Well—I mean—we can all hang out all together if you want. I just thought..."

"Yeah I know—you just thought why would I want to hang out with that chubby idiot." Michael didn't even look up from his desk.

"Come on, Michael. He's my best friend."

"Yeah I noticed that I got replaced quite a while ago."

"It's not like that. You're my brother. Besides, when do you ever want to do stuff together like friends?"

"Oh just forget it," Michael said. "If you give me your game time after school this week, I'll sleep on the couch tonight."

"Mom doesn't let us trade game time—you know that."

"I'll pretend to be you—duh. She can only tell us apart when we talk." It was true; the two were truly identical twins, both a little skinny for eighth-graders and both with messy brown hair, freckles, and crooked teeth that their mother couldn't afford to fix with braces, especially not two sets of braces. "And if we get caught, so what. What's she going to do?"

"Okay—it's a deal, but if you get caught with the game time, it's on you."

"And you have to change the sheets after chubby boy sleeps in my bed."

"Why do you have to be such a jerk, Michael?"

Neal left his grumpy brother in their room, ran down the stairs, and skated across the living room in his socks to build up some static electricity. He went past the fireplace and mantelpiece that displayed their fractured family history in framed photographs. The father, the infamous Jack Mercy, was nowhere to be found in any of the photographs, having been locked away in maximum security prison for almost a decade, and locked away forever, they hoped. One photograph showed the twins together, hugging each other and smiling in their swimming suits at the lake, but that happened three summers ago before adolescent rivalries bitterly divided them.

The oldest son, Jimmy, only appeared in the group photo. Fourteen years older than the twins, Jimmy had troubles with drinking and severe depression. They hardly ever saw him, but they knew he still occupied the family cabin in the mountains where his father used to take him when Jimmy was a boy.

The mantelpiece also displayed several photos of Maddie and Meghan, both in high school, Maddie a senior and Meghan a sophomore. They both had long brown hair, their noses dotted with freckles like their brothers, but the sisters were spared the crooked teeth that all the sons shared with their father. The sisters, close friends with perfect grades at the high school, appeared to be the most well-adjusted of the Mercy clan, but the public and private shame of their father's crimes also weighed heavily on them.

Sarah Mercy could be seen in most of the photographs with her children. Her round, warm face belied the heartbreaking conflicts of the past decade. She worked as a veterinary technician in the affluent ski resort town, tending to the pampered pets of the wealthy residents, including the toy poodle of a famous movie star. Sarah rented a townhouse for her family, just a twenty-minute bus ride away from the heart of the ski resort.

Having built up enough static electricity with his socks on the carpet, Neal shocked his sister Meghan by touching the back of her neck.

"Ow! Cut it out, Neal," she cried out.

It was late Saturday afternoon, which meant homework deadline time. All homework for the weekend had to be completed by the time their mother returned from the veterinary clinic, or else it meant being grounded on Saturday night and Sunday. Along with after-school restrictions on video game time, their mother strictly enforced this rule. At the large dining room table, Maddie, Meghan, and Neal had their homework all spread out, a chaotic mess of textbooks, notebooks, worksheets, and pencils. Michael used to join them at the table, but now he preferred to do his homework alone at the desk in the bedroom—fewer distractions, he claimed.

Neal completed his algebra equations and reading questions about *Lord of the Flies*, so he started to pack up his school bag with his notebooks and books.

Maddie still worked on her chemistry while Meghan drew in her sketchbook for art class, which assigned numerous sketches throughout the week like a journal. She could draw whatever she wanted to earn the sketchbook points. Neal looked over her shoulder.

"Well that's a weird thing for you to draw, Meg."

"Yeah, I know," she said. "It just came into my head—must be those horror games Michael's always playing."

"Maybe you were thinking about Dad," Neal said.

"That's not funny, Neal," Maddie scolded, looking up from her chemistry textbook.

"You're right—I'm sorry," he said. "Oh—is that supposed to be the well by the old cottage," he added, trying to lighten the mood.

"Yeah, exactly."

The drawing showed a typical Hollywood werewolf with claws raised under the full moon. A dead fawn dangled from its drooling jaws. She didn't know why she drew it or why she added the old well by the abandoned cottage, which stood just a short walk from their home through the woods. When younger, Maddie and Meghan played there frequently before life got busy with high school, even though their mom told them the well was dangerous.

"That's an awesome werewolf, Meg," Neal said. "I think the deer needs some work, though."

"Yeah, it's supposed to be a fawn—a baby deer."

"Hey Neal," Maddie said from the other side of the table. "Did I hear you say that Buddy is coming over tonight?" She started to pack up her schoolwork too.

"He should be here in a few minutes."

"Once we clear off all the school stuff, it's your job to set the table before mom comes home from work, so make sure to set a place for Buddy."

"Okay I will."

As soon as Neal finished setting the table for six, the doorbell rang. When Neal opened the door, Buddy stood on the porch struggling to hold on to his sleeping bag and backpack at the same time. The early fall darkness had arrived, and the snow began to fall in earnest.

"Ooh, it's really snowing," Neal said, grabbing the sleeping bag.

"Yeah—it hasn't started to stick yet, but it will, and then the snowboarding will be awesome," Buddy said, stepping inside and stomping his boots, his sandy-colored hair disheveled as he pulled off his ski cap, his round cheeks bright red from the cold. Buddy had a season pass for the ski slope, and snowboarding was Buddy's primary passion, but Neal's mom couldn't afford passes for her kids, so Neal had to save up his allowance in order to go snowboarding occasionally with Buddy. Fortunately, Buddy had an extra snowboard that Neal could use.

"Did Michael say we can use the bunk beds?" Buddy asked. He didn't have any siblings, and he got really excited about sleeping in the bunk beds.

"Yeah, let's take your stuff upstairs. Why did you bring a sleeping bag?"

"I know Michael hates it when I sleep in his sheets."

Michael was clearing off his desk when they entered the room. "Yes, yes, I'll get out of here," Michael said, clearly irritated.

"Hey Mike," Buddy said. "How's it going?"

"Yes, you can sleep in my bed," Michael said as he stormed out of the room.

"You should hang out with us later," Buddy called after him, but Michael didn't respond. "Twins are really weird," Buddy said to Neal. "I don't get it. What did I ever do to make him hate me?"

"Don't worry about it," Neal said. "Michael's just pissed off at the world."

"Why's that?"

"Probably because our dad is a serial killer."

"Oh yeah—I guess that would explain a lot," Buddy said, throwing his duffel bag on the bottom bunk.

"So did you finish reading *Lord of the Flies*?"

"I did. I hated it," Buddy said.

"Really? Why? I thought it was awesome."

Buddy laid back on Michael's bunk, kicking his shoes off. "I was pissed that they killed off Piggy. Why do they always have to kill the fat kid?"

"If he wasn't so fat and slow, maybe he could have dodged that rock," Neal said, and then tried to grab a handful of Buddy's belly fat.

"Cut it out—I'm too ticklish," Buddy screamed, laughing hysterically as Neal pounced on top of him. Neal bonked his head on the top bunk as Buddy tried to flip him over, a move he learned in the first week of Junior High wrestling before he dropped out. "Cut it out or I'll crush you!"

They calmed down and sat on the edge of Michael's bunk. "No, seriously, you didn't like *Lord of the Flies*?"

"Well, I can see that it's a good book and everything, but it really creeped me out the way they started killing each other. To tell you the truth, I think that's what really happened to Bobby Fletcher."

"What do you mean?"

"The police always talked like it was an adult that kidnapped him or that he got lost in the woods or something. But I think he got killed by some of the other kids at school—you know, some of those super-rich kids at school are really weird and fucked up—at least as fucked up as the kids in *Lord of the Flies*."

"Why do you think that?"

"I don't know. Just a hunch."

Bobby Fletcher was one of their classmates who had disappeared the previous school year. His parents were still married, so the police didn't suspect a custody battle kidnapping, and they never found any sign of his body. Most likely he got lost in the woods; the forest at their doorstep was vast, but the search dogs never found any scent, even after they switched to dogs trained especially to find cadavers. The police had interviewed Neal, Michael, and Buddy, but they hadn't seen him on the day he went missing.

"You don't suppose your brother is a serial killer?" Buddy asked.

"What?" Neal asked with a surprised laugh.

"With your dad being a serial killer and everything. I thought maybe it could be a genetic thing. I mean—I know you're not a serial killer because you're my best friend and everything, but Michael is just different, you know."

"Well, don't let Michael hear you say that. He gets seriously mad whenever anybody talks about my dad."

"I guess that's the thing that really creeped me out about *Lord of the Flies* because the evil kid reminded me of your brother a little bit."

"Nah, my brother's okay—he's just an asshole because he represses all of his feelings." All of the siblings had seen various psychologists over the years after their father had been arrested and sentenced.

At that moment, they heard the garage door opening, Neal's room being directly over the garage. His mom had arrived home, and that meant time for dinner. A moment later, she came into the kitchen with two big buckets of fried chicken that she picked up at the drive-thru after closing up the veterinary clinic.

Sarah really liked her son's best friend, and Buddy loved to tell her stories. All through dinner Buddy showed off, attempting to make Sarah and the sisters laugh. Neal was laughing too, but he had heard all of Buddy's stupid stories before. It always amazed Neal how much Buddy could talk and still stuff his face with fried chicken. Only Michael remained stone-faced and sullen.

After dinner, Neal and Buddy cleaned up because it was Neal's turn to set and clear. Meghan and Maddie got ready for a double date at the bowling alley while Michael snuck out to the garage where he continued with a woodworking project. Sarah let Michael back the car out of the garage as long as he promised to bring it back in so it didn't get covered with snow.

As Neal and Buddy washed and dried the dishes, Buddy brought up the subject again. "It's creepy how he does that woodworking stuff out there all by himself on a Saturday night," Buddy said. "Does the FBI ever include woodworking in their serial killer profiles?"

"Shut up—Michael's always liked that woodworking stuff. He used to get badges for that in boy scouts, and all of the tools and stuff in the garage used to belong to my dad."

"See what I mean," Buddy said, and Neal scooped up a handful of dishwashing suds from the sink and threw it at him.

Buddy drooled slightly on the pillow in Michael's bunk when someone shook him awake at a quarter after 3:00 in the morning.

"What's going on?" Buddy mumbled. By the light from the hallway, he saw Neal standing over him in the dark bedroom, his best friend dressed in his army-green winter coat with a furry hood and an orange ski cap. He pointed a flashlight right at Buddy's face.

"Come with me," he whispered. "I have a big surprise for you."

He pulled Buddy, still sluggish from sleep, out of the sleeping bag and pushed him through the bedroom doorway into the dark hall. With the flashlight, he led Buddy down the stairs to the coat closet by the front door.

"Be extra quiet or else you'll wake up my mom."

"What's this all about, Neal?" Buddy asked.

"Put on your shoes and coat and I'll show you—I've been planning this for weeks. You're going to love it."

Buddy was in his bare feet and pajamas, but he did what his best friend said. He pulled on his waterproof boots without socks and threw his long, red puffy ski jacket over his checkered pajamas. He pulled on his hat as Neal carefully opened the front door and led the way outside.

It was a gorgeous winter night. The storm had dumped a few inches of fresh snow and then kept moving to the East. The sky had cleared and the moon shone especially bright because the full moon had been the previous night. They didn't even need the flashlight.

Without any further explanation from Neal, Buddy followed him across the yard and past the small parking lot for the complex of townhouses, leaving fresh footprints in the sparkling layer of fresh powder. On the far end of the parking lot, Neal walked into the shadows of the towering pine trees with the flashlight beam showing the way.

Buddy felt a jolt of fear at the thought of going down the path into the forest. "We can't go that way," Buddy said. "We'll get lost in the dark."

Neal didn't stop walking, but just called back over his shoulder: "We won't get lost. I know the way."

With the flashlight and the bright moon, they could see the snow-covered path snaking through the trees, but the forest on either side of the trail overflowed with shadows. Buddy had a mortal terror of getting lost in the woods, but he trusted his best friend with his life.

"Are we going to the abandoned cottage?" Buddy asked, a place, almost like a secret fort, where they had spent many hours playing together, but they had never gone there in the dark before, and why did Neal say "I know the way" when of course they both knew the way.

"I have a cool surprise for you there."

Having been roused from a deep sleep, Buddy realized he didn't even know what time it was. He reached into his jacket pocket for his cell phone to check the time, and he discovered that his pocket was empty.

"Oh shit," he said. "I don't have my phone."

"It's okay," Neal said without stopping. "It's probably in the bedroom or something. I have mine."

Buddy knew he had never taken his cell phone out of his coat pocket. A sick feeling of unease began to roll around in his stomach. And then Buddy figured it out. He couldn't believe that he didn't see it before. Obviously, Michael decided to play a cruel prank on Buddy by pretending to be Neal. While Neal and Buddy slept in the bunk beds, Michael must have put on Neal's coat and hat, removing Buddy's cell phone from his ski jacket where it hung in the closet and getting Buddy outside before he was fully awake, the real Neal still asleep in the upper bunk the whole time.

The feeling of fear and unease switched to anger. Did Michael really think Buddy was that stupid? In that moment, Buddy decided to be bold and play along. He wasn't afraid of Michael; Buddy could expose the trick at the last minute and make a fool of Michael. Not only was Michael a bully, but he was a bad brother and mean to Buddy's best friend Neal, so Buddy kept the secret and continued to follow Michael down the trail.

They had walked for about ten minutes when they arrived at the abandoned cabin, once a forest getaway in the '40s and '50s before the massive ski resort arrived in the '60s, the cabin totally neglected since then. The cabin had a solid concrete foundation, but the sunken roof had large holes where the rain and snow came through, and the windows and front door were open to the forest. Even the old dirt road that once led to the cabin had been blocked with fallen trees and become overgrown. Between the abandoned cabin and a ruined, leaning outhouse on the other side of the clearing, there stood an old stone well, something much older than the cabin. A large piece of particle board, spray-painted with a warning, covered the well to keep anyone from falling to the bottom. The old well, dried-up for decades, was an older remnant of a settler's cabin from the previous century. The older structure had been completely removed to build the more modern cabin in the '40s.

Michael got ahead of Buddy, and when Buddy rounded the corner to the front side of the cabin, he saw Michael standing by the old well, clicking his flashlight on and off, signalling someone in the forest.

Buddy stopped before he reached the well. He couldn't wait any longer to expose the fraud. "You're not Neal at all, are you?" he said. "You're Michael."

Michael looked back at Buddy with an expression of pure hatred on his face while he continued to signal with the flashlight. No one had ever looked at Buddy like that before. When he saw Michael's face, he knew this was much more than a simple bully's prank.

"Is this what you did to Bobby Fletcher?" Buddy asked, his voice shaking all of a sudden. "Did you trick him into coming out here too?"

Before Michael could answer, a deep, bestial howl ripped through the freezing darkness. Michael stopped signalling with the flashlight.

Buddy knew he had made a terrible mistake underestimating Michael.

A jolt of terror shooting through his body, Buddy turned and ran to the other side of the cabin to go back down the trail the way they came. He didn't have a flashlight to guide him, the moon bright enough for him to see.

But it was already too late.

The massive werewolf, half in shadow, blocked the trail. Buddy couldn't see the beast clearly, but he could see the unnatural orb-like eyes that glowed with cold moonlight, not a reflection of the moon, but an eerie spectral light issuing from within. A warm stream of urine flowed down Buddy's leg.

The horrible truth struck Buddy: Michael had lured him out here to feed him to a werewolf. All of the darkest rumors about Neal's father were true, and Michael was a psychopath just like him.

Michael had already vanished into the woods.

Buddy turned and ran with all his strength for the well, the only refuge close enough. The creature, right at his heels, leapt at Buddy, falling just short, a single claw catching on Buddy's calf muscle and ripping it wide open. Screaming, Buddy fell forward and slid across the snow to the well. He pulled himself up, grabbed the piece of particle board that covered the opening and turned around to face the beast, holding the piece of particle board in front of him like a shield. As the werewolf hit the piece of wood with its weight, Buddy flew back, flipping over and falling head first down the well. His echoing scream snapped into silence as the bones in his shoulder and neck shattered at the bottom.

The werewolf, his long snout shoved into the well, smelled Buddy's wounds in the darkness far below while a long sliver of drool fell all the way down the well and landed on the side of Buddy's face, the other side pressed into the rotten mud. The werewolf stopped for a moment, perhaps considering the level of difficulty in retrieving his meal from the bottom of the well. Instead, the creature withdrew his head, carefully replacing the piece of particle board over the mouth of the well.

Jimmy made the coffee while looking out the kitchen window at the snow-covered forest outside. Only a few inches fell, but he knew that the ski resort would be thankful for anything. He opened up the back door to blinding sunshine. Just like he thought, he discovered tracks from the forest that led right up to the back door. Of course, he didn't really remember what happened—just nightmarish flashes—but he knew that the other one would remember.

Just like the townhouse that his mother Sarah rented for his sisters and twin brothers, Jimmy also had a fireplace with a mantelpiece, and just like his mother's house, the mantelpiece displayed family photos, but unlike his mother's house, his father was not absent from the photos. In fact, Jimmy's father appeared in all of them, the photos having been taken before Jack Mercy's arrest, conviction, and multiple life sentences.

Jimmy didn't even remember how many life sentences they gave his father. It obviously didn't matter.

In the photos, Maddie and Meghan were just little girls, the twins just toddlers. Jimmy was a young teenager then. His parents had taken most of the photos right there at the cabin and the nearby ski slopes that Jimmy could see from the front drive. He also had framed photos of his parents together, and the photos proved his parents had been in love once, at least the photos proved it to Jimmy. He knew his mother had eradicated all signs of his father in her townhouse, but in the cabin, Jimmy's father was everywhere.

The coffee finished brewing, and Jimmy poured himself a cup, adding just a dash of whiskey to get himself going. He felt exhausted.

Jack and Sarah Mercy built the cabin as a family retreat when Jimmy was just a little boy, years before his sisters and twin brothers arrived on the scene. The ski resort on the adjacent mountain was a lot smaller back then, and the land a lot cheaper.

Unlike the ruined cabin where his twin brothers liked to play, this cabin was equipped with plumbing, a septic system, and its own generator. His father had continued to work on the cabin all throughout Jimmy's childhood, up until he was taken away. It had taken a lot of work to restore the place after the authorities had ransacked the property and then scrutinized every inch for any scrap of evidence they could find to put Jack Mercy away forever.

The cabin had one bedroom, so when the whole family had stayed there, Jimmy and his kid sisters would sometimes camp in a tent out back, but they always ended up sleeping on the floor by the fireplace for fear of black bears. There were so many fond memories, it felt as if his father could walk through the door any minute.

Despite the whiskey in his coffee, Jimmy just couldn't seem to warm up, so he decided to build a fire. He had a huge pile of firewood out back. Jimmy worked on chopping the stack all throughout the summer. Jimmy knew that most people considered him to be a crazy, drunk mess, the worst of the serial killer's children, but at least he was an excellent outdoorsmen. His father had taught him well. Jimmy noticed those paw prints again as he went out back to gather up the logs. Just as he finished building the fire, and the initial flames consumed the newspapers wadded up at the bottom, Jimmy sensed that the other one was in the room.

The demon always announced its arrival in Jimmy's mind with the peculiar sensation of altered perception—what Jack Mercy called the "Satanic mind cloud"—a warm mental fog, just a little bit unpleasant, that softened the edges of the mind and made Jimmy more susceptible to the demon's influence. Jimmy knew that he was the only one who could hear the voice, which sounded like a young boy, a hallucination of his cursed mind, but that didn't seem to help Jimmy very much. It certainly didn't make the demon any less real to Jimmy. The demon never spoke right away. It began to whisper with its sharp, electric voice, easing its way into Jimmy's reality.

"Good morning, Buzz,"

"Good morning, Jimmy," the voice said.

Jimmy sat cross-legged in front of the fire to get warm while he sipped his coffee. He could feel Buzz in the armchair behind him, even if he couldn't see it. His "imaginary friend" had been appearing to Jimmy for many years, ever since Jimmy was sixteen-years-old. Jimmy finally turned around to face the empty armchair.

"So what happened last night, Buzz? I saw the tracks out back."

"Michael tried to collect another soul for the master. He is so eager—just like his father. Your day will be so much better if you don't know what went wrong."

"Today, I'm feeling brave—just give it to me straight."

"Okay, but perhaps your coffee should be stronger."

Jimmy walked over to the coffee maker, poured himself another cup with double the amount of whiskey.

"It happened at the well. You scratched the boy. He didn't die."

"Oh no." Jimmy put his head in his hands.

"It's not like that, Jimmy—everything will be just fine," Buzz said. "He escaped down the well. He's down there right now."

"It's worse than I thought. We should go and get him."

"No," Buzz said. "I see a different path for this one."

Jimmy started to take another sip on his coffee when the front door burst open. Buzz vanished from Jimmy's mind and he nearly spilled the spiked coffee on the floor. It was his brother Michael, wearing Neal's coat and hat, his face bright red from the cold.

"Thank God you're here—I hiked all the way here. It all went wrong last night, Jimmy." It looked like his little brother was about to cry. "I'm so sorry."

But Jimmy knew that Michael didn't really cry—he only faked it when he needed to.

Neal woke up. Bright sunlight reflected off the snow outside, lighting up the bedroom and the disarray of dirty clothes, shoes, and school books scattered across the floor. It took a second before Neal was awake enough to remember that Buddy had slept over.

"Wake up sleepyhead!" Neal cried out. "For once you didn't wake me up with your snoring." Neal hung his head over the edge of the upper bed, surprised to see the bottom bunk empty. Where was Buddy? Buddy always woke him up in the morning when he slept over. He must be having breakfast with my sisters, Neal thought.

Downstairs, Neal found his mom on the couch with a cup of coffee watching cable news.

"Where's Buddy?" Neal asked.

"I don't know, honey—I thought he was still sleeping in your room."

Sarah saw the look of panic cross her son's face. "Don't worry—I'm sure he's here, Neal."

Neal inspected the pile of shoes by the front door and saw that Buddy's boots were gone. He opened the coat closet—Buddy's red ski jacket was gone too. Neal ran back up the stair to his bedroom. On the floor of his room he saw Buddy's jeans, underwear, socks, and T-shirt. He picked up his cell phone that was charging on the desk. No messages. He called Buddy's phone—nothing.

"I think I hear his phone," Sarah called from downstairs. They found Buddy's phone at the bottom of the coat closet, buried underneath some extra winter gloves and scarves.

"Where is he, Mom?" Neal shouted. "Buddy never goes anywhere without his phone." He ran up the stairs and burst into the bedroom his sisters shared. They were both still asleep in bed.

"Get out of here, Neal—I'm trying to sleep," Maddie said. Neal turned and ran back out again.

"Is Michael in the garage?" Neal shouted from the top of the stairs.

"He was already gone when I got up—I assumed he was out shoveling." Sometimes Michael earned extra money by shoveling driveways in the neighborhood.

He had to find Buddy. Neal opened the coat closet again, and he began rummaging through all of the coats, but discovered that his green winter coat was gone too. And then he saw it—Michael's black and gray coat was still there. A terrible thought jumped into his head. The twin brothers had played games with switching identities many times over the years. Neal quickly put on Michael's coat, hoping that his mother didn't notice.

"I'll call Buddy's mom to see if he's home," Sarah called from the kitchen.

"Okay—I'm going out to look for him," Neal said. "I've got my cell."

Terrible, dark suspicions were building in Neal's mind. His brother had played some kind of a terrible trick on Buddy.

Neal was in luck. Since the snow had stopped falling late last night, there were only two sets of footprints in the yard. Neal followed the tracks to the parking lot. For a moment, he thought he might lose the trail because some of the residents had walked across the parking lot and driven their cars away that morning, but then Neal picked up the trail on the other side of the parking lot, the footprints heading into the forest. Neal guessed that Michael had taken Buddy to the old ruined cabin—going to the cabin was the only reason they ever used that trail.

Buddy awoke in total darkness, curled up in a ball on the frozen mud at the bottom of the well. He tried to sit up. Shivering with cold, he had never felt so sore in his entire life, especially his shoulder and neck. He winced at the pain of his calf muscle. The ripped pajama pants were crusty with blood.

He was still in a mental fog from a deep sleep, and it only seemed to get worse. Confused and disoriented, he slowly remembered that Michael had tricked him. Somehow he had fallen down the well. And there was something else—a monster, a horrible monster. It was a werewolf. Everyone knew that Jack Mercy the serial killer was in league with Satan, but there were many unproven rumors about werewolves too. Buddy had read about all of it online.

Buddy tried to reach into his pocket for the cell phone to call his mom, but then he remembered that Michael had taken the phone out of his pocket.

Looking up at a few slivers of light leaking through the board that covered the well, Buddy began to cry.

"Help me!" he screamed. "Somebody please help me!"

But soon his cries dwindled. He had played with Neal at the abandoned cabin many times. Dense forest surrounded the remote cabin; it didn't have neighbors, and Buddy had never seen another person there.

Buddy realized that he had landed on something. Too dark to see clearly, he felt zippers and straps—some kind of a book bag or a backpack.

He felt a strange, fuzzy sensation fill his mind, but this wasn't the fog of sleep or shock; it was the arrival of the mind cloud.

"Buddy! Are you down there?" a strange electric voice echoed through the well. It sounded like the voice of a young boy, and it didn't just echo through the well—it seemed to echo through Buddy's mind too.

"I'm here!" Buddy screamed, looking up, but the board still covered the top of the well. "Get me out of here!"

"I'm sorry, Buddy, but you're going to have to climb up."

"That's crazy—I can't climb all the way up there. You're going to have to lower a rope. Call the fire department. They can get me out."

"I can't lower a rope or call the fire department. You have to climb out."

"What are you talking about? That doesn't make any sense. I can't climb—I'm injured."

"I know you're in pain, Buddy, but I think you'll discover that you can climb. It might seem hard to believe, but I know you can climb."

"Just help me," Buddy pleaded.

"No. Climb, Buddy. You're stronger than you know."

Still holding the bag he found beneath him, he carefully looped his arm through the strap and tried to stand. Buddy's entire body, stiff and sore and frozen, slowly returned to life—Buddy had no idea that he had been dead for several hours. Once he finally managed to stand up in the well, he leaned against the cold stone and tried to catch his breath. He discovered that he could move his arms and legs, even his neck and shoulder, despite the pain, and the intense soreness seemed to lessen with every movement as life fully returned to his limbs.

"Climb, Buddy!" the voice commanded.

He tried to find an edge to pull himself up or a good foothold, but all he found were small cracks in the stone.

"Take off your boots, Buddy," the voice said.

Buddy did as the voice commanded, untying the laces and pulling off his boots.

Even though his fingers only found small cracks and creases in the freezing stone, he discovered that he was able to pull himself up. Strangely enough, with his toes as well, he was able to push himself up with a barely a crack in the stone.

"Climb, Buddy!" the voice shouted with encouragement.

Buddy's heart pounded in his chest. Not being a very athletic boy, other than snowboarding, Buddy had never attempted to climb like this, but the harder he worked, the more progress that he made. The grip of his fingers only seemed to grow stronger.

Before it even seemed possible, Buddy knocked the board off the top of the well and climbed out. Once he pulled himself up and over, he collapsed by the side of the well in the snow. He looked around for the boy who encouraged him to climb, but Buddy was completely alone.

Buddy pulled himself up, using the well for support, his bare feet freezing in the snow. He looked at the the claw marks across the piece of particle board. He looked at the tracks and the blood in the snow. His calf muscle covered in dried blood, Buddy could see where the monster ripped it open. The muscle was terribly sore and sensitive to the touch, but the long red wound had completely closed, and Buddy could walk with a limp.

Bare feet or not, he wasn't going to just wait there all day. He had to walk. He figured if he stopped frequently and tried to warm his feet, he could possibly make it back to Neal's without getting frostbite.

Neal had started running down the path toward the abandoned cabin, the footprints from Michael and Buddy clear in the fresh layer of snow. Neal was breathing hard, his side hurt, and he thought that he might puke, but he kept running down the trail.

And then there was Buddy—limping down the trail coming toward him.

"Buddy!" Neal screamed, and the sight of Buddy confirmed his worst fears. His best friend's face was covered with mud, one leg of his pajama bottoms shredded, and his calf caked with dried blood.

Neal ran to Buddy and hugged him tight. Even though the hug was painful for Buddy's sore shoulders and neck, he held on to Neal and squeezed him back. Buddy began to weep with large intakes of breath and broken sobs.

"Thank God I found you, Buddy. I was so scared," Neal said. "We need to get you to the hospital. You don't have any shoes!"

"It's okay, I can keep going," Buddy said, wiping the tears and snot from his face. "I feel the cold, but it's not too bad."

"Oh God, you probably have frostbite already if you're that numb."

"No, no—it's okay."

"I'll try to call the ambulance with my cellphone—if I can get a signal," Neal said.

"Let's just go back to your house—please. I'm really okay. I'm just so glad to see you."

They made their way through the snow back to Neal's house. Neal was so worried about Buddy's feet, he didn't even ask Buddy any questions about what happened.

When they made it through the front door, Sarah screamed at the sight of Buddy.

"I'm going to call the ambulance right now," she said.

"You can't do that, Sarah," Buddy said. "You're a doctor for animals—you can clean me up, right?"

"What do you mean, Buddy? I'm calling the ambulance right now—don't be ridiculous."

"But if you call the ambulance, I'll have to tell the police."

"Tell the police what?" Sarah asked.

"I'll have to tell the police that Michael tried to murder me."

Judging by the amount of blood on Buddy's pajamas, Sarah was convinced that his calf would require stitches at the emergency room, but to her great surprise, once she wiped away some of the blood with a warm washcloth, she only discovered a long scratch. Despite his horrific appearance, he really did seem to be okay. When Sarah wiped off some of the mud from the boy's feet, they appeared to be pink and healthy, no signs of frostbite.

Of course Sarah knew that she needed to call the ambulance or take the boy to the emergency room; of course she knew that the boy should tell the police about what Michael did, but she also knew what would happen next, knew all too well how the media frenzy would descend upon them if serial killer Jack Mercy's son was accused of attempted murder, and she remembered how last time they wanted to implicate her. She remembered how last time she almost lost her children as a result.

Neal and Sarah helped Buddy into the shower, but Buddy insisted that he could manage on his own. Sarah waited in the hallway just in case he needed any help. As she waited, her cell phone rang.

"Hi Mom," said the voice on the other end.

"Oh my God!" she exclaimed. "Jimmy! I haven't heard from you in so long. Is everything okay?"

"Yeah, Mom, everything's fine. Are you okay? You sound upset."

"We've got a situation here, unfortunately," Sarah said.

"I think I know all about it. That's why I'm calling, actually. Guess who showed up at my door this morning?"

"Is Michael there? How did he get there?"

"He walked, apparently."

"Is he okay? I'm going to kill him."

"Mom, he's totally fine."

"Do you know what he did?"

"I don't want you to worry about him," Jimmy said, "but he is going to stay with me for a little while."

"What?" Sarah shouted into the phone. "That child of mine has a hell of a lot of explaining to do. It's a miracle that Buddy wasn't killed."

"A miracle?" Jimmy asked. "So you're saying Buddy's there?"

"I'm driving up to the cabin to get Michael as soon as we get Buddy back home."

"Don't come up here, Mom," Jimmy said. "At least not today, okay? Give me a little time with him."

"Have you been drinking, Jimmy?"

"Give me a few days with him—at least don't come up here today. I know I'm not his dad, but I am his big brother—I'm dealing with it, okay—just give us some space."

"I don't know about this, Jimmy. I have to go—call me later."

The water in the bathroom stopped. Sarah rushed in with an extra towel and a warm bathrobe.

"I'm still naked, Mrs. Mercy," Buddy protested.

"Give me a break, Buddy," Sarah said. "Has all the feeling returned to your toes? Did you feel dizzy or anything in the shower?"

"I feel just fine, really."

After drying off and getting into the robe, Buddy sipped a mug of hot chocolate while Neal, Sarah, Meghan, and Maddie all sat around the big dining room table. Buddy tried to tell his story. He didn't get past the point where Michael tricked him into going outside before Maddie interrupted.

"What the hell was Michael thinking?" Maddie blurted out. "I can't believe he pulled that off." She turned to Neal. "You didn't hear anything?"

Neal shook his head.

"And you never guessed it was really Michael?" she asked Buddy.

"Not right away," Buddy explained. "It was dark and I had just woken up."

"Plus Michael is getting really good at impersonating Neal," Meghan added. "I think he practices at it—all those little mannerisms and voice inflections that only we would notice."

Buddy told them about what happened at the well, all of them gasped when he said the word "werewolf," all of them having heard the rumors too.

"I'm so sorry this happened to you," Neal said, big tears welling up in his eyes. "I can't believe my own brother would do this to you. I can't believe he would betray me by hurting you, Buddy."

"Not to contradict Buddy's story or anything," Maddie said. "I mean to say, I totally believe you, Buddy. It's obvious that Michael lured you out there to play a prank on you, but how do you know Michael planned that a werewolf would be waiting for you? Sure, it looked like he was signalling someone in the woods, but how could Michael arrange for this thing to be there—that doesn't make any sense. Maybe it surprised Michael too."

"Maddie," Sarah said. "It must be starting over again. Michael must be communicating with your father—or his followers."

"Don't say that, Mom," Maddie whispered, a teardrop running down her face.

"What do you mean?" Buddy asked. "What's starting over again?"

"When my husband was convicted for those murders," Sarah said, "there were some more unexplained bodies— more murders that the police never solved. They could never tie them to Jack with hard evidence, but everyone was pretty sure that Jack was involved somehow—because of some circumstantial evidence. The bodies all looked like they had been torn to pieces by some kind of wild animal, but worse than that—a monster. The word 'werewolf' was used more than once."

"But that was over a decade ago," Maddie said. "Dad's been locked up this whole time."

"And then there's the backpack," Buddy said. The muddy backpack was sitting on the floor next to Buddy's chair. He picked it up and handed it to Sarah. "I found it at the bottom of the well."

Sarah opened it. She only had to look at the name on the notebook inside. She stood up and walked over to the sliding glass door with a view of the back yard and the forest beyond, rubbing her temples. "We can't go through all of this again," she said. "If they have to arrest Michael..."

"Can you imagine what the media will do if they think Michael has inherited something from dad?" Maddie said.

Buddy looked over at Neal, and the look on his best friend's face terrified him. "Don't worry," Buddy said quickly, trying to calm everyone. "Maybe there's another way—without the media finding out. We haven't even heard Michael's side of the story yet. Maybe Maddie's right and he didn't know about the wolf, and he just ran away to Jimmy's house because he got scared."

"But this is the missing boy's backpack," Sarah said. "I don't want the media to find out either, but can you imagine what this boy's mother has gone through. We have to give it to the police."

"Okay, but that's all," Buddy said. "Here's what we'll tell them: Neal and I were playing by the abandoned cabin in the snow like we always do. I climbed down the well on a dare. We'll say Neal was holding one end of a rope and I climbed down. That's when I found the backpack. We'll leave Michael out of it, so it can be sorted out."

"That's a really good idea, Mom," Meghan said.

"I know it might seem dishonest, Buddy," Maddie said, "But you don't know what it was like last time. The reporters hounded us for years. They camped outside the house and watched us every second."

"You don't have to explain," Buddy said.

Sarah remained silent for a moment, staring out into the yard. "Why don't you want us to call the police Buddy? Tell us the truth."

"There is something else," Buddy said. "Something we haven't talked about yet."

"What?" Maddie blurted.

"I should be dead."

"Well thank God you're not," Maddie said.

"Let me finish. A werewolf slashed my leg and I fell down a well—a deep well—and I landed on my head. And now I'm just fine!" Buddy's face turned bright red as he tried to hold back a sob. "Don't you see—I might be a werewolf now too. We can't let the police find out—they'll kill me. Werewolves aren't too popular around here after what happened with your father all those years ago. The police will act like they don't believe it, but they'll come for me just the same."

"That's just crazy, Buddy," Sarah said, trying to comfort the boy. "Listen to all of us, talking as if werewolves are real. No one is going to come for you, Buddy, and you're most certainly not a werewolf."

Sarah pulled Buddy close and held him, but an icy, terrified silence descended on the room.

The rest of the day was filled with the police and an endless series of questions. Neal and Buddy walked a pair of police officers out to the abandoned cabin and showed them the well. Buddy wasn't sure that they convinced them at all.

Before they called the police to tell them about the backpack, leaving out everything about Michael and the werewolf, Buddy and Neal brought a rope out to the spot and ran around the well to erase the wolf prints with their snow boots. Buddy made some snowballs out of the bloody snow from his calf wound and threw them into the trees.

And then they remembered Buddy's boots—still at the bottom.

"We can say I had to take them off to climb back out of the well—for better footing," Buddy suggested.

"I guess that's true, actually," Neal said.

At the well, Buddy could see the officer was skeptical that Buddy was physically able to climb down on the rope, and he didn't seem to fully believe Buddy's story about leaving the boots at the bottom because it was easier to climb back up with bare feet. The well was dark and deep and formidable for any climber. Buddy didn't exactly look like a cave diver.

"You say you went down there on a dare?" the officer asked.

"That's right," Buddy said.

"Must've been some dare."

"I want to get my rope climbing badge in boy scouts," Buddy told the officer.

Within a few hours, the scene swarmed with forensic technicians who came up from Denver on a police helicopter. A specialist climbed down into the well to retrieve more evidence, a task that made Buddy's climbing story look even more unlikely.

Buddy knew the detectives would find his blood down there at the bottom, but how could they know the blood belonged to Buddy; he didn't have injuries—not anymore, at least.

That evening, Neal went back with Buddy to his house to stay the night. Neal didn't want to leave Buddy alone. The story dominated the news: a big break in the disappearance of Bobby Fletcher. Neal and Buddy watched the coverage in the living room with Buddy' parents, Walt and Angela. Fortunately, the news focused on the story of a local boy discovering an important piece of evidence at the bottom of a well, but they didn't make any connection to Neal's family or Neal's infamous father. Buddy wondered if it would stay that way.

"You really climbed all the way to the bottom of that well, Buddy?" Walt asked his son. Walt, a balding tax lawyer, had made a successful career helping White Crag ski resort negotiate their complex tax liabilities, later working as an independent consultant for a number of Colorado ski resorts.

"Sure I did," Buddy said. "I practiced a lot on that camping trip with the scouts."

"Well I'm really impressed, son. I didn't know you had it in you."

Later that night, after playing cards with Walt and Angela, both of the boys glum and silent, Buddy and Neal lay awake in Buddy's bed, which had plenty of room for both of them along with Buddy's golden retriever, Champ.

"I saw those prints in the clearing," Neal said.

"Yeah—they were really big."

"Do you feel different?"

"What do you mean?" Buddy asked.

"Do you feel weird or anything?"

"I feel pretty weird, I guess, but not physically—just weird like the whole thing seems like a bad dream. Do you really think I should be dead?"

"You saw how deep that well was today. You fell all the way down, and it's like you're totally fine—you didn't even break a single bone."

Buddy whispered, "Do you think I'm going to turn into a werewolf, Neal?"

"I don't know, Buddy. People don't really believe in werewolves—not for the most part," Neal said.

"Yeah, not for the most part," Buddy said, "but what do you think? What do you really think?"

"All I know for sure is that we have some time. The full moon was just two nights ago, so we have almost a month to the next one."

"Oh shit! You really do think I'm going to turn into a werewolf!"

"Keep your voice down, Buddy. I don't know—I really don't. It's just that I haven't told you all of the details about my dad."

"I know. You don't have to. I read a lot of stuff online. I could tell that you didn't want to talk about it."

"Did you read about the people who were torn to pieces?"

"I did, yeah, but like you said, they never proved for sure that your dad had anything to do with that. But a lot of people say online that it was werewolves—so those people believe."

"My dad was really into werewolves, Buddy. I mean, nobody would say that my dad figured out how to turn people into werewolves—only that he worshiped the devil and he murdered a lot of people. That's bad enough. There's no doubt he murdered all those children, and there's no doubt he worshiped the devil—like really worshiped the devil, but the whole werewolf thing—that's just another level, you know. There's still plenty of doubt about that."

"Yeah, maybe," Buddy said, "except for the fact that I saw one with my own two eyes, and it attacked me. It definitely wasn't any kind of a normal animal that pushed me down the well. I know I should be dead, but I just want to live my life, you know. I don't want to be like that thing that I saw last night."

"You won't, Buddy, I promise. If my dad figured out a way to turn people into werewolves, then we can figure out a way to un-turn someone. We have plenty of time to figure it out."

"What are we gonna do next?"

"We'll have to find my asshole brothers. Obviously they know something."

At the end of a long gravel drive, the black town car pulled up to the front door of the cabin. Jimmy peeked out through the curtains. It had started to snow again, not a blizzard, but heavy.

Michael played a video game on Jimmy's console, wrapped in a blanket in front of the fireplace. Jimmy didn't get any TV reception or cable at the cabin, so neither of them had seen the news reports about Bobby Fletcher.

"Hey Michael, I've got to go out for a little bit," Jimmy said.

The boy paused the video game and looked back at his big brother, an expression of worry on his face.

"It's fine. You've had your dinner and everything—you just play that video game until you're tired and go to sleep on the couch there. I laid out a sleeping bag. Don't forget to add more wood to the fire. It's a really cold night."

"How long are you going to be gone?" Michael asked.

"Not long at all. It's just some business."

"Come back soon, okay?"

"Yeah—I'll be right back, I promise."

Jimmy pulled on a coat and walked out the front door— he almost never locked the front door because of the remote location in the woods, but he locked the door that night with Michael alone inside.

Jimmy got in the passenger seat of the town car.

"You got someone in there?" the driver asked.

"Yeah, it's my little brother—nothing to worry about, Reggie."

The driver didn't respond, but started the car down the gravel drive.

Baker waited in the foyer of the condo. They told him to be ready at 10:00 p.m. With his coat and boots on, he was ready, but he was nervous. At almost 10:30, Baker continued pacing in the foyer, waiting for the driver. His coworkers, Alex and Agnes, had flown back already with the rest of the group, the business retreat having concluded the previous day, but the boss informed Baker at the last minute that they changed his flight, that they wanted him to attend another social function, an intimate gathering of an elite circle of investors, some more bigwigs for him to meet. It turned out that the retreat had been packed with meetings and activities; however, Baker found some time to enjoy the skiing at White Crag, but he didn't make it past the beginner slopes, it being his first time on skis, and he fell down—a lot.

When the town car pulled up, Baker went right out, and he met the driver on the stairs.

"Nice to see you again, sir," the driver said.

"You too. By the way, I never got your name."

"My name's Reggie, sir."

Reggie drove Baker the short distance through the snowy forest to the compound where the company had held many events during the retreat after the opening night gala. This time, Reggie drove Baker to a different entrance that Baker hadn't used before.

The snow was really starting to pick up, and Baker brushed the large fluffy flakes off his coat sleeves once Reggie opened the heavy metal door with a key and led him inside. Baker noticed a small reception area inside the door with a concierge's podium and small coat closet, but there was no one else in sight. Reggie hung up Baker's coat and led him down a long white corridor. Baker's feelings of nervousness amplified as they went deeper into the facility; after all, Baker had glimpsed what resided there. He noticed that Reggie didn't wearing an earpiece this time, and he sincerely hoped Reggie wasn't some kind of hitman for the company, in addition to being a driver.

Almost as if in response to these doubts, Reggie said, "The meeting room is just down here. The rest of the party will be joining you shortly."

They turned a corner and went past dozens of white doors down another long hallway. They finally arrived at a door with a small placard: "Meeting Room 15B." Another door marked "15A" stood right next to it, and Baker thought he heard some voices coming from inside.

However, once Reggie opened the door with a key and turned on the lights, Baker found 15B to be completely empty, a gigantic room with rows of small, atmospheric lights embedded in the ceiling.

Baker definitely had an uneasy feeling; his instincts rarely let him down. Only a small catering bar stood in the far corner of the large carpeted room, not a single piece of furniture, and floor-to-ceiling one-way mirrors lined the walls on either side. Baker looked around the room. He didn't see any cameras, but that didn't mean there weren't any.

Reggie seemed to be trying to calm Baker's uneasiness, but without much success. "How about I mix you a vodka martini?" Reggie asked, stepping behind the bar. It was what Baker had been drinking throughout the retreat, although he wasn't sure how Reggie the driver knew this.

"Thanks, Reggie, but I think a whiskey neat would hit the spot. Can't seem to get the chill out of my bones."

"It's a very cold night, sir."

Reggie handed Baker the drink, and then surprisingly poured one for himself. Taking it even further, the driver lit a cigarette, sat down on a short stool concealed behind the small bar and began reading a newspaper. When he noticed Baker staring at him, he said, "Hope you don't mind the cigarette—things aren't so formal tonight."

"I noticed," Baker said.

"Do you want one?"

"I think I better."

Reggie handed Baker the cigarette he was smoking and then lit another.

As Baker turned around and dragged on the cigarette, he noticed that the lights came up on the other side of the one-way mirrors, and he could see the forested enclosure again, but from a different vantage point than the exhibition on the night of the opening gala.

"Oh shit," Baker whispered under his breath. "Not this again." He could see the snowfall coming in from the open ceiling, but he didn't see a fawn this time. He wasn't exactly looking forward to seeing the werewolf kill something else. He downed the rest of his whiskey and took a deeper drag on the cigarette.

He went to flick his ashes in the ashtray that Reggie set out on the bar, but instead he stubbed it out when he saw the lights come up behind the one-way mirrors on the other side of the room.

Behind the mirrors, he saw about a dozen people, mostly older men in dark business suits, all holding drinks and conversing. These must be the voices he heard in the hallway. He recognized a few of the vice presidents and some others he had noticed during events at the retreat, but he also noticed a group of elderly men watching him with malevolent intensity. They did not converse like the others. He had never seen them before. Reggie watched Baker with an air of faintly curious amusement.

Finally, one of the vice presidents spoke through an intercom. "You've had it, Baker," he said. "We found out you've been feeding information to Dirk Magill. You're not that clever, you know."

A look of shocked astonishment crossed Baker's face and he hurried over and put his hand on the glass as if reaching out to his accuser. "There must be some mistake," Baker shouted at the glass. "I did speak to Magill once, but I didn't feed him any information—not about the werewolf or about Jack Mercy—nothing important."

"They can't hear you," Reggie said, the cigarette dangling from his lips.

"Can you get them back on the intercom?" Baker asked.

Reggie didn't answer, but pointed at the forested enclosure. Baker turned around.

The werewolf stood on his hind legs behind the glass, watching Baker and breathing a patch of fog on the glass with the hot breath from his snout. The creature was excited, a long line of drool fell from his jaws and his eyes gleamed with desire. Baker could see now that it was a foul thing, not an animal of the world.

Reggie pressed a button behind the bar and the glass panel slowly retracted, the freezing air from the enclosure quickly filling the room along with the horrid, musky smell of the creature.

Just like when Buddy confronted the werewolf by the well, Baker pissed his pants.

Baker didn't have time to cry out before the creature was on him. The agony of the werewolf ripping him open soon dissipated into numb shock. On his back on the floor, staring up at the group of spectators upside-down, the werewolf digging around in his belly, Baker noticed that some of them kept chatting and sipping their cocktails, but not the cluster of old men. They watched the werewolf feed, and they seemed to enjoy it just as much as the werewolf did.

Baker died as the werewolf consumed his slippery liver, which fell out of the creature's jaws twice.

Reggie stubbed out his cigarette and threw back another shot. He whistled sharply.

The werewolf looked up from his meal and growled.

"Go on now," Reggie said, as if speaking to a poodle.

In a flash, the werewolf had retreated with the rest of Baker's remains back into the forested enclosure. Reggie pressed the button to close the glass panel, and the mirrors on both sides of the room went dark.

Despite the size of the room, it turned out to be quite difficult to reach the door on the other side without stepping in blood-saturated carpet or getting gore all over his shoes.

When he opened the door, the cleaning crew was waiting in the hallway, a line-up of carpet shampoo machines.

"Oh Jesus Christ," one of them muttered when he saw the bloody spectacle of the room.

"You guys have fun," Reggie said and headed down the hallway.

After talking late into the night, Neal finally dozed off, and Buddy could hear his best friend snoring lightly as Buddy stared at the glowing red digits on the alarm clock. He tried not to think about the horrible experience in the well—and tried even harder not to think about the unspeakable thing that sliced open his calf.

The boy felt himself slipping deeper into despair, but the only thing that kept him afloat was what his best friend said: if someone could figure out how to turn a person into a werewolf, then it seems logical there would be a way to "un-turn" them, something to solve—like a mystery, Buddy told himself, not like a curse—nothing like the old black-and-white werewolf movies he had watched on the classics channel.

It was almost 4:00 in the morning when Buddy started to drift off to sleep. That was when he heard the voice again.

"Buddy," it whispered. "Come and talk to me."

Buddy recognized the voice instantly, the voice he heard at the bottom of the well, the voice that encouraged him to climb, and his mind filled with that peculiar, foggy sensation. He didn't forget about the voice, but he didn't tell anyone about it either, not even Neal—it seemed like just another part of the nightmare, but the voice scared him more than anything.

Buddy considered waking Neal, but something prevented him, intuition perhaps, or the influence of the Satanic mind cloud, so Buddy slipped out of bed and followed the voice out into the hallway and down the stairs. Buddy felt sure nothing bad could happen in his own house—he wouldn't let anyone lure him outside again, though.

"This way, Buddy," the voice whispered.

The boy looked all around, not sure which direction, but then he heard it coming from the stairwell into the basement. He paused for a moment, and he seriously considered going right back upstairs and putting his head under the covers until the voice simply went away, but then he remembered the plan treat the whole thing like a mystery. Someone who solves a mystery would follow the voice, he thought to himself. Or maybe a dumb sucker that gets killed would follow the voice.

"Come downstairs Buddy, I have answers for you."

It seemed like the owner of the voice could read his mind, and of course it could. Then Buddy remembered that the voice saved him once before, so maybe he should trust the voice.

Buddy followed the carpeted stairs down to the basement. There the carpet stopped. He stepped on the cold cement floor in his bare feet and turned on the overhead light bulb. It was a large, unfinished basement with the water heater and furnace along with a Ping-Pong table beneath the light bulb. Numerous old boxes, some of them as old as Buddy, were stacked against the wall. In the far corner, beyond the Ping-Pong table, Buddy could feel the presence of the thing. He couldn't see it, but he knew it was there.

"It's me, Buddy," the voice said. "I'm the one who saved you from the well."

"I know," Buddy said.

"My name is Buzz, and I'm here to guide you."

"Guide me?"

"Through all of the changes happening to your body."

"What? Do you mean puberty?"

"No, Buddy—not puberty."

"So, you know about it? You know about the werewolf," Buddy said, his voice trembling.

"I know all about it."

"Are you in my mind?"

"Well, that's complicated, Buddy. Hard to explain"

"I think you better try."

"You can hear me and speak to me, and there are others like you, Buddy. They can hear me and speak to me too, and I'm always watching over you. I'm your guardian angel, Buddy. I only want to help you get through this."

For some reason, Buddy's instincts told him to be skeptical of this, but he said nothing—just looked down at the Ping-Pong table and touched one of the paddles.

"Look, Buddy. I know how strange all of this must seem. I don't want you to feel like you owe me, but just remember who helped you out of that well."

"What are you trying to say?"

"You were dead, Buddy. You hit the bottom of the well and your neck snapped, spinal cord severed. You were dead, but I brought you back."

"What do you want from me?" Fear almost choked the words in Buddy's throat.

"Nothing. I just want to help you. I just want to guide you. You want to solve the mystery, right?"

"That's right."

"Here's something I need you to do. When Michael took Neal's coat—when he was pretending to be Neal—he left his own coat in the closet. So now Neal is wearing Michael's coat."

"Okay—so what?"

"There's a secret pocket on the inside of the coat next to the zipper. Inside the pocket, you will find a key to a post office box. I want you to go back upstairs to the kitchen and write down this number: 4759. Do you have it?"

"4759," Buddy said.

"Think about it for a second, do you really have it?"

"I got it—4759."

"Next, I want you to get the key from Neal's coat in the hall closet. Neal doesn't need to know about this yet. In fact it would be safer if he didn't know."

"Safer?"

"Safer for him, Buddy."

"I understand," Buddy said.

"It's a clue, Buddy—your first clue. I want you to trust me—consider it a token of trust."

Buddy turned away from the presence and went back up the stairs to the kitchen, where his mom left a light on over the stove. He found a note pad and wrote down "4759." He crept over to the hall closet, opening the door carefully because his mom was a light sleeper. He easily found the key inside

Michael's coat. He put the key and the note in his dark orange ski jacket from last year that hung in the back of the closet. This year's coat was in the garage, still covered with mud from the bottom of the well.

When Buddy got back to his room, Neal was awake.

"Are you okay, Buddy?" he asked.

"Yeah, I'm okay," Buddy said as he crawled under the covers. "Thanks for being here, Neal."

At the breakfast table, Buddy's parents and Neal could see that something was troubling Buddy. His mom asked her son what was wrong, and Buddy told her that finding Bobby Fletcher's backpack gave him nightmares.

After breakfast, the boys changed out of their pajamas in Buddy's room.

"I have something to tell you, Neal," Buddy said.

"What is it?"

"You're not gonna believe this."

At the post office, Neal stopped Buddy before they went inside. They walked from Buddy's house to the small strip of touristy downtown businesses where the small post office stood between a bar and a store that sold ski equipment. The post office, closed on an early Sunday morning, was completely empty, but the door to the rows of post office boxes remained open to allow customers to pick up their mail.

"Thank you for telling me about this," Neal said. "I know the guardian angel—or whatever it is—told you not to tell me, and you could have come over here by yourself, but I just want you to know that it means a lot that you told me."

"Yeah—thanks, Neal. You're my best friend. I'm not going to start keeping secrets from you."

Inside, they easily found box 4759. Buddy handed Neal the key.

"Well, now I guess we find out if the guardian angel really knew what it was talking about," Neal said.

Neal put the key in the lock and turned. It opened. Inside the post office box they found a letter. The envelope was marked with a notice that the letter had come from an inmate in a correctional facility.

"Oh my God, Buddy," Neal said. "This letter is from my father."

The two boys sat down on a bench by the window.

Neal was about to open the letter when Buddy interrupted him.

"Are you sure we should open it? I mean, it is addressed to your brother."

"Are you kidding?" Neal said and ripped open the envelope. It looked like a piece of paper from an ordinary notebook. For some reason, he thought it would be special prison stationary. The handwriting was meticulous, elaborate cursive. It certainly didn't look like the handwriting of a mass murderer.

Since, they were alone in the building, Neal read the letter out loud:

Dear Michael,

Thank you very much for your letter. I am very pleased to hear that you are enjoying the art of woodworking. It certainly brought me many hours of pleasure over the years. I am excited to hear that you are building something for me, and I look forward to seeing photographs of the finished product. I am very sorry to hear that you have not been getting along with your brother. I hope you will keep trying. The bond between brothers is very important and very strong. Be patient with him and remember that he is being misled by the treachery of his mother. Remember that you can never blame

115

a boy for following his mother, even if that happens to be misguided and regrettable. Your sisters and your brother Neal have always been closer to her and turned against me by her. But don't blame them. Continue the valuable work you are performing for our Master and Lord. Remember to follow the guidance of your older brother, Jimmy, for he is very special in the eyes of our Lord. I continue to find many brothers and followers of our Lord here in the prison, which provides me some comfort in these miserable circumstances. I want you to remember that we are not alone, even if it feels that way sometimes. There are many brothers and sisters out there who serve our Lord, but beware of anyone who might try to deceive you. If anyone approaches you and claims to be a friend of mine, tell your brother Jimmy right away. I am always with you, my son, and so is our Lord. You are precious to him. I hope to see you face-to-face very soon.

Love,
Dad

Neal set the letter down in his lap and pulled his hand away, as if he might be contaminated by touching it.

"This is much worse than I thought, Buddy. For so long I've thought that all of this was over, but it's not. I can't believe he's brought my brothers into this."

"It sounds like he really doesn't like your mom," Buddy said.

"That's an understatement."

"When he talks about the 'Lord' and all of that business, do you think there's any chance he's talking about Jesus. Maybe he's a Christian now. A lot of people convert in prison, right?"

"There's not a chance, Buddy. My father is talking about Satan, and it sounds like my brothers worship him too, or at least they're following my father."

"I hate to say it, but your dad sounds really crazy, Neal."

It was a school night, so Neal had to come back home at dinnertime, and he dreaded seeing Michael again—if Michael dared to show his face—but it turned out Michael didn't come back home. Maybe he never would. Right before dinner, Neal heard his mom arguing on the phone with Jimmy. At first it sounded like she demanded that Jimmy bring Michael back home, but then it seemed to shift to demanding that Jimmy drive Michael to school on Monday.

All afternoon, Neal and Buddy had talked about whether or not Neal should tell his mom about the letter. His father was right—Neal was very close with his mother, especially after everything they had been through with his father's trial and the media circus in the aftermath. He knew his mother very well, and he knew she would be devastated if she read the letter. It seemed pretty clear that Michael and Jimmy had betrayed her, at least that's what it looked like.

Meghan and Maddie cooked dinner that night, a tuna casserole with a salad. Neal helped a little bit by setting the table and chopping up some tomatoes for the salad.

During dinner, the family ate in tense silence. Despite the high emotion in the room, they managed to put a big dent in the casserole and finished off the salad. Maddie asked if she could be excused, but Sarah said they all had to talk. First Sarah poured herself a cup of decaf coffee.

"As you probably heard, I've been on the phone with Jimmy. He's not bringing Michael back yet, which is probably best for the moment, but you're going to see him at school tomorrow. I hate to say it, but I'm not interested in keeping secrets after what we've been through as a family. I think we have to consider the possibility that Jimmy is serving you father, and Michael is helping out too."

Neal couldn't believe it. Even without showing her the letter, his mother had figured it out.

"What do you mean by 'serving' our father?" Maddie asked.

"They're in a conspiracy together. I've known for a while that Jimmy has been visiting your father regularly in prison, and I've always feared something like this would happen," Sarah explained. "Your father has an almost hypnotic charisma. I'm afraid he's converted your brother and probably Michael too."

"What are they going to do?" Meghan asked.

"I don't know, but I don't think we're safe. I'm not sure who to turn to about this."

"I think I do," Maddie said. "Dirk Magill has been sending me emails again."

Dirk Magill was in his early sixties and he looked as rugged as White Crag mountain, his skin weathered and leathery, his hair thick and wavy, but solid white and combed back neatly. He walked into the all-night diner wearing blue jeans, hiking boots, a flannel shirt, and the best mountaineering parka money can buy. He gave Sarah a grim smile, took off his coat, and joined her in the booth by the window.

"I went ahead and ordered you some coffee," Sarah said.

"Thank you," he said.

"Look, Maddie gave me your number. I think it's rotten that you talked to her behind my back, but that's beside the point now. I need your help, and I'm wondering if your offer still stands."

"Slow down, there, Sarah. Let's take this from the top. Something must've happened."

Dirk Magill was once a killer. He served as a sniper in Vietnam. In addition to being an expert marksman, he killed plenty of the enemy close-up, sometimes with a knife, and even a few times with his bare hands. His father had been a successful industrialist, the owner of an airline parts factory back east, but Dirk shunned the elite lifestyle his father's wealth offered him. Instead, Dirk joined the marines. It was his calling, and he was good at it.

After the end of the war, Dirk had a brief career in law enforcement, but after being sickened by the bureaucracy, he became a private investigator and security expert. He had a wide array of clients over the years, from wealthy friends of his father to poor families who could never pay him. In his fifties, he discovered a new, unexpected hobby: writing. He started with some of his war memoirs, and using his expertise in crime, law enforcement, and weaponry, he began to write books about true crime. He was looking for a new project when the news broke about Jack Mercy's arrest.

Ever since then, Dirk had worked on a book about Jack Mercy, but Dirk was never satisfied with the book, still too many unanswered questions. A big missing piece was the family. He wanted the family's participation in the book, and he needed them to tell their story. He wasn't in any hurry to have the book published. If he died that week, his editor had enough to put the book to press, but Dirk wanted more resolution for the story, and Dirk certainly didn't need the money.

After all these years, Dirk couldn't believe his luck when his cell phone rang and Sarah Mercy was on the other end. Dirk was there in White Crag doing more research and hoping to interview some of the children. He began by reaching out to the oldest siblings: Jimmy and Maddie. Jimmy told Dirk to go to hell, and Maddie basically said the same, but he could tell the girl wanted to tell her story, and Dirk knew she only held back out of loyalty to her mother.

Sarah drank her coffee, ate a piece of pie and told Dirk Magill everything that had happened with Buddy and her sons. She left nothing out.

"So I want to hire you, but not as a writer. I want to hire you to protect my family from what is happening. Once it's all over, I will give you my blessing to publish your book, and I will help you with any information I can. But first, you have to make sure my family is safe. I can't really afford to pay you..."

"Say no more about that, Mrs. Mercy. It's a deal. I am going to text my security team and instruct them to get on the next plane out here to White Crag. In the meantime, I will personally guard you and your family tonight."

"Thank you, Dirk," she said, a tear running down her cheek. "And you can call me Sarah."

At first, alone in his bed, Buddy had a terrible time falling asleep, thinking over everything he had discussed with Neal and worrying what that weird "guardian angel" was going to say next.

Finally, exhausted, he did fall asleep, and he slept soundly until almost 3:00 in the morning, and then he had a whopper of a nightmare.

He was back at the bottom of the well—looking up, and he could see the moon in the sky above, hovering perfectly over the circular opening of the well. He had Bobby Fletcher's backpack with him.

But then he felt water beneath him. The well wasn't dry after all—it was beginning to fill. And it wasn't water. The well filled with blood. Buddy stood, but soon the blood rose all the way to his waist. He tried to climb up like he did before, but the thick coating of blood made his hands too slippery. The blood filled up the well past his shoulders and then over his head. He tried to stay afloat, but he started to feel tired, treading "water" becoming more and more difficult. Up above he could see a ring of people, reporters and policeman, circling the opening of the well, but none of them would help. They only took pictures, the flash bulbs blinding him. And then he saw Bobby Fletcher among them.

Buddy jerked awake in bed, his pillowcase damp with sweat, the mind cloud waiting for him.

Buzz was there in the shadowy corner of the bedroom, invisible but present. Champ had climbed down from the bed, and he started into the empty corner, a slight rumble of a growl in his throat.

"What the fuck do you want?" Buddy said, on the verge of tears again.

"Don't worry. I'm not here to harm you, Buddy. I am you. Don't worry about telling Neal about the key. He is our best friend, after all. I thought it best not to tell him, just for his safety, that's all. You saw how upset he was. But that's not why I'm here."

"Why are you here, then?"

"I want you to meet someone—someone who can help you."

"What are you talking about? It's the middle of the night."

"He's outside, and he wants to talk to you. He wants to explain things, and he wants to apologize for how everything turned out so far."

Buddy jumped out of bed and looked through the blinds. Beneath the streetlight on the snowy sidewalk, a man waved as soon as Buddy looked through the blinds. "Who is that?"

"Don't you recognize him, Buddy?"

Buddy looked again, and then he did recognize him. It was Neal's older brother Jimmy, the one who was serving Jack Mercy.

"Mom! Dad!" Buddy screamed. "It's him—it's the killer."

"Keep your voice down," Buzz hissed.

"Come quick," Buddy screamed.

As soon as Buddy's dad burst into the room, Buzz had vanished, and Jimmy took off down the street away from the light. Walt could just see him before he turned the corner and vanished from view.

Buddy was hysterical, and after talking it over, Walt and Angela decided to call the police—just in case.

It was almost 4:30 when a policeman knocked on the door. Buddy explained that he saw a man standing under the streetlight. The man watched Buddy's bedroom window, and he waved at him. Buddy was absolutely sure it was the killer out to get revenge because Buddy found the backpack. Buddy was careful to make sure everything he said fit with what he had previously told the police. Of course, he couldn't say the name of the man, couldn't say that he recognized him.

Angela insisted that Buddy go back to bed and try to sleep. The police officer and Walt spoke privately away from Buddy, the officer assuring Buddy's father there could be no possible way that Bobby Fletcher's killer knew Buddy found the backpack. The officer thanked Walt and Angela for Buddy's help in finding the backpack, which was a major breakthrough in the effort to find justice for Bobby Fletcher, and apologized for any psychological distress the situation caused the boy. The officer emphasized that Walt and Angela could call the police again at any time for peace of mind. Despite the assurances, Walt had a terrible feeling that somehow the killer did know his son found the backpack.

Neal and Buddy ate lunch together in the far corner of the school cafeteria. The line of students waiting to be served in the kitchen dwindled, but still no sign of Michael. As always, the cafeteria was a cacophony of students shouting and laughing, but Neal and Buddy ate their chicken fried steak and mashed potatoes in silence, a stark contrast to their normal animated conversations about movies and video games. Neal scanned the cafeteria for his brother, and Buddy watched Neal's face closely when Michael finally entered through the double doors across the cafeteria. Buddy could see Neal's face tighten with stress and anger.

"OK—here we go," Neal said as he got up from the table.

Buddy looked over his shoulder to see Michael standing in the line of students, but he didn't want to make eye contact with him.

At first, Michael turned away as Neal approached, as if he didn't see him, but then he faced his twin brother. Neal was surprised to discover that Michael looked sad, almost ashamed of himself, a subtlety that only a twin brother would recognize.

"I've only come to switch coats with you," Neal said, removing his brother's coat and handing it to him. Michael did the same. Once they exchanged coats, they looked at each for a second before Neal spoke again: "Do you have anything to say for yourself?"

"I know you don't get it, Neal," Michael said. "I'm doing the best I can—really. I wish I could say more, but I can't. Maybe one day you'll understand." Michael always said the right thing to manipulate his brother's emotions.

"Just stay away from Buddy, Michael. And when you come back home, I'm really going to kick your ass."

Michael made a face as if he doubted this.

A few of the other boys in the line heard Neal say this and realized this could be the start of a fight, which would be quite an attraction in the middle of the cafeteria, two identical twins punching it out, but Neal turned away and marched back to the table with Buddy. Michael watched him go, feeling the secret pocket to see if the key to the post office box was still there, and it was.

"Come on, let's go," Neal said to Buddy, and the boys abandoned the rest of their lunch on the table, not even returning their trays to the dishwashing station.

"Where are we going?" Buddy asked as Neal led him outside into the schoolyard. Most of the students gathered in the gym after eating because of the freezing temperatures.

"I have to tell you something, Buddy," Neal said. "I've stolen my mom's credit card number, and I bought a couple of bus tickets."

"What?" Buddy exclaimed.

"I have to find out more. I'm going to the prison—to see him. I'm not sure what I'm going to say yet, but I'm going to pretend to be him, to be Michael, to see if he'll say anything."

"Do you think your dad will be able to tell that you're you and not Michael?"

"He barely knows us—he's been in prison since we were three. I'm sure he can't tell. I'm going to try, anyway."

"But what if he finds out—he could still hurt you, Neal."

"I know I can't ask you to do this, but will you come with me."

"Of course, when do we go?"

"But what about your geometry test?"

"Give me a break, Neal—I haven't even studied," Buddy said, which was a surprise to Neal. And then Neal noticed that Buddy looked tired in his eyes—this was taking a toll on the boy, his sleep and his studies.

"We have to go now if we're going to catch the bus. Do you have your cell phone in your coat?"

"I do," Buddy said.

"You'll have to call your parents later—make up some excuse and say you're with me because we won't be back until really late."

The two boys ran along the side of the building where a footpath was already worn into the snow, the way to the secret smoking spot beyond the gym in a little grove of trees. A group of ninth-graders hid their cigarettes as Neal and Buddy ran past. They came upon a fence with a loose board, slipped through the fence into an alleyway behind some stores. They were only a ten-minute walk from the bus station.

A man in a car watched the boys make their escape from the school grounds. He spoke into his phone: "Dirk, this is Quigley. One of the twins just ditched school. I think it's Neal, but I'm not completely sure. Do you want me to follow him?"

Jimmy looked at his buzz cut in the bedroom mirror one more time before pulling on his stocking cap. The duffel bag, sitting on the bed, was all packed and ready to go for the weekend hunting trip with his father at the cabin. Jimmy's mom Sarah stayed behind with his baby brothers, Neal and Michael, and Jimmy's younger sisters. Jimmy's father declared that this was going to be an important father and son weekend, just Jack and Jimmy. Sarah realized that the twins had taken up a lot of the family's attention lately, and Jimmy felt neglected. The teenager had recently turned sixteen-years-old.

After saying goodbye, Jack and Jimmy climbed into the four-wheel drive pickup and pulled out of the driveway. It was a beautiful September evening in the mountains with a crisp fall edge to the breeze, the aspen trees turning beautiful shades of yellow and gold, the sun just going down as they departed. To Jimmy's surprise, instead of going directly to the cabin, Jack drove the truck toward downtown.

"Why are we going this way, Dad?" asked Jimmy.

"I have a special surprise for you," Jack said. "It's just a quick little errand and then we'll be on our way."

At the end of the downtown strip of shops and restaurants, primarily catering to the tourists during the ski season, stood a sports bar called The Black Bear, a popular spot for the locals to do their drinking. Jack pulled the pickup around to the back of the bar where a blond woman in blue jeans, a jean jacket, and snow boots waited for them by the rear entrance near the dumpster. She stubbed out her cigarette and climbed into the pickup. Jimmy scooted over, sitting between his father and the woman.

"How are you doing on this beautiful evening, Nancy?" Jack asked.

"Just fine, Jack. Are you bringing your kid up to the cabin too?"

"Absolutely. It's going to be a special father and son weekend, isn't it Jimmy?"

Jimmy smiled uncertainly at his father and then looked over at the woman, noticing her bright lipstick. Her jean jacket was unbuttoned at the top, and Jimmy could see her ample cleavage.

"I hope you're not planning anything weird, Jack," Nancy said. "He's just a kid." Nancy rubbed Jimmy's flat-top haircut. "No offense, kid."

"You have nothing to worry about, Nancy," Jack assured her, but then said nothing more about it.

Jimmy didn't understand why the woman with the heavy perfume and the fake blond hair was coming along. He thought they were going hunting for jackrabbits and deer, but the boy knew better than to question his father.

It was dark when Jack pulled up to the cabin at the end of the dirt drive, several cars and trucks already parked there, and all the lights in the cabin illuminated.

"Oh wow—it looks like there's going to be a party," Nancy said.

"That's right," Jack said.

As Jimmy stepped out of the pickup, he was shocked to see his grandma Betty, Jack's mother, come out the front door of the cabin, her long iron-gray hair tied back in a braid. Jimmy was very confused—he thought this was a father and son weekend, not a party with his grandma and a prostitute from the bar.

Jimmy met the rest of the people on the front porch of the cabin: a mysterious man named Reggie with rugged looks and an elderly couple named Nan and Clive, who appeared to be the rich tourist types that always vacationed at the growing ski resort. The adults stood around for a moment having everyday small talk about the upcoming ski season and the weather—nothing to indicate the true purpose of the gathering. When Jimmy found a moment, he whispered to his dad, "Are we still going hunting?"

"Of course we are, son. I know you must have a lot of questions, but we are going to try something new. It's going to be a very special weekend."

"A very special weekend, indeed," his grandma said, eavesdropping, and she rubbed his buzz cut, which Jimmy was beginning to regret if adults were going to rub it all of the time.

"Seriously, Jack—we should talk for a sec," Nancy said, and she stepped a few feet away from the porch and lit a cigarette.

They talked in hushed tones for a moment, and Jimmy tried to listen to what they spoke about, but all he heard was his father say. "Don't worry, Nancy—the boy will be with his grandmother the entire time."

Later in the evening, after a big steak dinner that Reggie prepared for the group, they all sat around the fire, and the adults had more boring adult talk, discussing the growth of the ski resort, local gossip, and the problems that always go along with a large, transient tourist population. Nancy looked as bored as Jimmy felt, and she definitely looked just as confused.

Everyone drank red wine from large glass goblets. His father said that Jimmy was old enough to have some. The wine tasted terrible to Jimmy—he couldn't imagine how they could sit there, drinking it all evening. Jimmy told his dad and grandma that he didn't like the wine, but his dad made him drink the entire goblet, even though the taste made him want to gag. A few minutes later, Jimmy started to feel very strange. The last thing he remembered before blacking out was hearing Nancy ask, "What did you put in this wine?"

When Jimmy came back to consciousness again, it was only for a moment. He felt like a rag doll, aware that Reggie and his grandmother dragged him across the floor, and both of them completely naked with strange symbols drawn on their bodies in bright red blood. He thought he heard Nancy crying as they put him in the closet.

"Don't be frightened dear," his grandmother said, her braid loosened and her hair wild and disheveled. "It's the full moon tonight. It's your special day."

They shut the closet door and locked it. Jimmy always thought the lock on the closet door was to secure valuables when the cabin was empty, but now he discovered it had a much more sinister purpose. The fungal hallucinogens in the glass of wine pulled his primal nightmares to the surface. In the darkness of the closet, it felt like he was perpetually falling down a well into a black cavern.

Jimmy heard the Satanists in the bedroom, chanting in ancient Enochian as Jack presided over the foul ritual. He heard Nancy screaming intermittently between the melodic chanting and his father's muffled, rhythmic voice.

Jimmy felt two strong hands grip him and hold him, and he no longer felt like he was falling into the abyss. A boy's voice whispered in his ear. "Don't struggle—you're safe. Just let it flow through you—don't resist."

"Who are you?" Jimmy asked in his delirious state.

"I'm Buzz—I'm your guardian angel."

"What is happening to me?" Jimmy muttered.

"It's glorious, Jimmy. Your father has called upon me and now I am with you. Behold, the full moon."

As if he left his body behind in the closet, he floated weightless above the cabin. In the middle of hallucinogenic ecstasy, the glowing full moon above was the most glorious thing he had ever witnessed. He always heard of the "man in the moon," but as he gazed at the beautiful lines on the face of the moon, it seemed like the craters and canyons rearranged themselves again and again into a multitude of faces.

The vision ended as the closet door opened, and Jimmy was confronted with the nude figures of his grandmother, father, and the rest of the Satanic participants, all adorned with streaks of blood. They stripped off Jimmy's clothing. Reggie kept him from falling over as his grandmother painted Satanic symbols on Jimmy's chest with a basting brush dipped in a cup of blood.

When it seemed that Jimmy could manage to walk on his own, the group, singing a strange hymn, pushed Jimmy into the bedroom and closed the door behind him.

Inside, Jimmy witnessed a strange and horrifying sight. By the light of what seemed like hundreds of candles, he could see Nancy tied to the bed, completely naked and covered in blood, and she watched him with terror. Jimmy quickly covered himself with his hands. He noticed a dead lamb in the corner of the room, in a puddle of its own blood, its throat slashed—the source of the blood that covered everyone, what the Satanists used to paint their symbols.

Jimmy had never seen a naked woman close up before. She had a piece of duct tape over her mouth, so she couldn't speak, but the look in her eyes pleaded with Jimmy to help her. A powerful sensation began to arise from the depth of Jimmy's being. He began to tremble and retch. He fell to the floor of the cabin, at first unable to move, but then unable to control the violent shaking and shuddering of his limbs and body.

He then realized that he didn't want to have sex with the woman tied to the bed. He wanted to eat her.

While Jimmy was locked in the closet, Jack Mercy and his Satanic followers had conjured up an ancient werewolf demon that now possessed his son. Jimmy writhed on the floor. The full moon above, although unseen to Jimmy inside the bedroom, seemed to pull on the core of his soul, as if the core was encased in a shell that must violently hatch.

Jimmy screamed and screamed until he thought his voice would rupture, but then his screams became howls. The black claws ripped his fingers open as they emerged. He had the horrible sensation of drool and blood flowing out of his mouth and down his throat as his teeth erupted into canine jaws. The more the teeth hurt, the more he wanted bite down on the woman quivering before him. His skin burned like fire as the unnatural hair sprouted across every inch of his body.

No longer a human being, Jimmy stood before Nancy and regarded his prey.

The creature that Nancy watched with horror was not the same fully-formed werewolf that attacked Buddy by the well or that Baker watched through the one-way mirror. This was just the first stage of the werewolf, a wolf-boy hybrid, but just as hungry.

Jimmy tore Nancy open and fed.

Over a decade later, Jimmy remembered that night, the first night he turned into the creature, the night he made his first kill, and the night he met the werewolf demon named Buzz.

That first night haunted him the most, although he had killed countless people since then. He stood in the doorway to that bedroom and thought back to that night when his father was still on the loose and committing his crimes, including the crime of turning his own son into a foul, unspeakable creature.

For some reason, he felt bound to the cabin in the same way he was bound to the curse. In many ways, Jimmy would love nothing more than to run away and never come back, run away from the cabin, run away from Buzz, run away from his family, and run away from the secret organization that ran the compound and compelled Jimmy to perform for them—and kill for them, but Jimmy knew he could never escape the curse, and he knew hope was lost. He would kill and kill until he was destroyed, and Buzz the werewolf demon would take him down to hell. Jimmy would never find redemption.

The werewolf hierarchy was simple: Jack Mercy, although not a werewolf himself, acted as the Satanic ringmaster of Jimmy and all the werewolves beneath him. All of the werewolves were bound to Jack, and he could turn them simply with his will, full moon or not. For a long time, Jimmy was a hybrid wolf-man who only turned, against his will, whenever the moon was full, or whenever his father wanted him to turn. But once Jimmy passed the curse on to others, he rose in the hierarchy of the pack and he became a full werewolf, an alpha wolf. As an alpha wolf, Jimmy could turn into a full werewolf, much more powerful than a wolf-man hybrid, whenever he chose to, as long as the sun had gone down.

Jimmy knew he had created a new one—he had passed the curse to Buddy on accident—he had meant to eat him and to offer Buddy's soul to Buzz. Now Buddy would turn into a wolf-boy hybrid at the next full moon.

Buzz, the werewolf demon, seemingly did the bidding of Jack Mercy, but the demon had a claim to all of the werewolf souls, even Jack's, for all eternity.

Jimmy poured himself another whisky, despite the fact that he needed to drive to town to pick up Michael from school.

"So how are you feeling, Buddy?" Neal asked as they rode the bus to the maximum security prison, about an hour into their journey with another hour to go.

They had arrived at the station with plenty of time to catch their bus. The ticket agent and the driver both gave them weird looks, assuming that the boys should be in school and not taking bus trips without parental supervision. Sometimes, the truth just worked the best, and when Neal told the agent and the bus driver he was traveling to visit his father in prison, they gave him sympathetic looks and didn't ask more questions.

Buddy thought about it for a moment, staring out the window. "I'm not sleeping well. I can feel the curse inside me—it grows a little bit every day, sometimes by the hour. I find myself yearning for the full moon, as much as I'm afraid of the full moon. That probably doesn't make sense."

Neal didn't know what to say. As he looked at his best friend, he realized that the Buddy he knew before was gone forever, and it was his fault—or, at least, his family's fault. Somehow he would have to make it right.

From the bus station, they took a cab to the prison. At first, he didn't think the cab driver would accept his mother's credit card, until he explained that he was visiting his father in prison, and sympathy won out again.

Once they arrived at the waiting room, Neal thought he might throw up or pass out; he had never been so nervous in his entire life.

Buddy stayed behind in the waiting room when the guard called Neal's name and led him to the visiting booth with the shatterproof glass and the old-fashioned telephone receiver to communicate. When the boy saw his father sitting there in the orange jumpsuit, Neal started visibly shaking, and he felt sure he would cry and pee his pants, but he did neither.

Neal knew that this was his father. He had seen a lot of stuff online about him and on television too, but Neal had been too young to develop any real memories of his father before they sent him away, so it felt like looking at his father for the first time, and Neal had a terrible realization that the man could see right through him. He would never be able to maintain a facade that he was Michael.

His father's gaze was intense, a combination of warmth, concern, and just a hint of suspicion. His father had black, slicked-back hair with a pronounced widow's peak and a little gray at the temple, his beard stubble much whiter than his hair. His thick eyebrows met in the center, and his green-brown eyes reflected all of his brilliance and betrayed none of his evil.

"Hello there, son," Jack said when Neal picked up the receiver.

"Hi Dad," Neal whispered, a single tear running down his cheek.

Back in the waiting room, Buddy began to sweat. Being in close proximity to the master of the werewolves was having a strange and powerful effect on Buddy's physiology as the Satanic mind cloud took over and the sickly sweet voice of Buzz the werewolf demon sounded in Buddy's mind.

"What's going on?" Buddy said, rubbing his temples. He could feel a tremendous headache coming on.

"It's your master, Buddy. He's here. Don't you want to meet him?"

Buddy hated himself for saying it. He even hated himself for thinking it, but he whispered, "I do—more than anything."

Michael checked the post office box, surprised that he hadn't received a letter from his father, his older brother Jimmy waiting outside in the car. Jimmy kept the car running for the heat because an arctic cold front had moved into the mountains. The sky was clear and blue, but the temperature had dropped drastically. Michael ran from the post office back into the warmth of the car. When he got back in, he was struck by the sour smell of alcohol coming from his brother.

"Anything from Dad?" Jimmy asked.

"No, nothing," Michael said. "He should've written by now. What else does he have to do?"

"Don't worry, kiddo. Who knows what he has to deal with in there."

"Neal and Buddy are with your father now. They won't fool him," Buzz whispered inside Jimmy's mind.

Jimmy's stomach churned with nausea as he thought about everything that was happening. He tried not to swerve too much on the icy street as he headed back toward the cabin, hoping he could keep the pickup from going into the ditch, the icy road conditions worsening with the sudden temperature drop.

"So are you about ready to go back to Mom's?" Jimmy asked his brother.

"I can't go back. They think I tried to get Buddy eaten by a werewolf, and they think I'm with Dad."

"Well, those things are true, Michael, but it's our family. They'll think you've fallen under Dad's influence. They won't blame you."

"Not Neal, though. He'll blame me."

"Neal might come around too. At least Mom and Maddie and Meghan will think you've been led astray by me and they'll do everything they can to get you back on Mom's team."

"But I can't betray Dad," Michael said.

"Look, I know it's really complicated. It's not a black-and-white thing at all. Dad won't think you betrayed him. Lots of kids keep a relationship with their mom and their dad both after a divorce."

"But nobody has a dad like our dad."

"That might be true. You can't stay with me at the cabin forever. You're going to have to go back and face them. Let's just be thankful they didn't tell the police what really happened at the well."

"I thought you said the organization owned the police here."

"Well, that's true, but it could have been a mess. These aren't the kind of people that you want to inconvenience. Even now, they're going to have to come up with something about Bobby Fletcher, something that doesn't lead back to you and me."

"Can I ask you something, Jimmy?"

"Of course—anything."

"I've been thinking about it for a while, but I never asked. Do you think that Dad is going to want me to become like you, to become a werewolf?"

"That's out of the question, Michael. Believe me, you don't want to be like me, and I won't let it happen. Not Neal, either. I don't want my brothers—or my sisters—to have to go through what I've gone through. No, this is my curse. It doesn't matter what Dad wants."

"Why have you come to see me, Neal?" Jack Mercy said to his son.

Neal felt a weird tangle of emotions. He at once realized that he could never fool his father into believing he was Michael, but the feeling of embarrassment about being caught in his deception mixed with outrage that his father didn't adopt a tone of contrition with Neal. On the contrary, his father seemed stern.

"I found Michael's secret post office box, and I read the letter you sent him," Neal said, choking back his grief.

"Son, you could have sent me a letter at any time, and I would have received it gladly."

Neal had planned to fool his father and find out information, but now that he sat opposite him, he was reduced to a raw nerve of pain and sadness. "How could you say those things in the letter? Aren't you sorry for what you've done?"

"Son, I want you to know that I respect you for coming here and asking me those questions face to face—like a man. I can see that it is difficult for you to understand. I serve a difficult master, and sometimes I have to do difficult things for him, but he is also a glorious master, Neal. Your brother Michael is only just beginning to discover these things."

"Michael tried to kill my best friend, Dad—why did he do that?"

"No. That's not what happened, Neal. Your brother simply led Buddy to the well."

"How could you know what happened. You're in here."

"I do know, Neal. I did see. Like I said, I respect you for coming here and confronting me face to face, so I also respect you enough to tell you the truth. You are my son, and I love you more than you know."

Neal broke down into a sob, half grief and half anger when his father said this.

Jack continued, "A werewolf needs to feed on human flesh, Neal. I know that it's a difficult reality. A werewolf can hunt deer and rabbits—that meat can fill an empty stomach, but it's not what the werewolf demon craves. The werewolf demon must have souls. By bringing offerings to the well, your brother was serving me, Neal. I know that's not what you want to hear."

"But the werewolf didn't eat Buddy."

"I know—Buddy's here right now. In the waiting room."

"How can you know that?"

"I feel him, Neal. Things didn't go as planned that night, but things happened as they were supposed to happen. Believe me when I say that things happened as our master and lord wanted them to happen."

"How can I free Buddy from the curse, Dad? He's my best friend."

"You can't free him. He is part of my family now. He is part of our family now."

"Please set him free," Neal said, crying bitter tears.

"Go to you brothers, Neal. I know you feel at odds with them, but they will welcome you with open arms when you tell them about your visit today. It might be hard for you to believe, but that is the best way that you can help Buddy. Go to your brothers, Neal. Remember that I love you, son."

Neal couldn't look into his father's eyes again. He hung up the phone and turned away. He couldn't hide his tears, and the guard in the room patted him on the back and said, "This way, son. You're a brave young man."

Neal followed the guard into the hallway. "Why do you say that?"

"I've worked here for many years," the guard said. "I've seen many evil men come and go, but your father—your father is the devil."

"I don't understand how you could be so irresponsible," Buddy father's said into the phone.

Buddy stood in the far corner of the bus station on his cell phone, away from the chairs and the rest of the people waiting. "It's not like that, Dad," Buddy said.

Neal, who sat with the other passengers waiting to board the bus, occasionally looked over to see how Buddy was doing.

"You tell me what it's like," Walt said. Buddy had never heard his father so angry before.

"He's my best friend, Dad. He needed me to come along—you know, for moral support. He's never seen his dad before—not ever."

"Well, I can understand that," Walt said, softening. "But that doesn't mean you just leave school without permission and get on a bus without telling your mother and me."

"You're right, Dad. I'm sorry. It just all happened so fast."

"I'll get into the car as soon as I hang up the phone. I can be there in a few hours."

"No, it's okay Dad, really. Neal has bus tickets back for us. We're already at the bus station and we're going to board in just a little bit. Everything is taken care of. If we run into any trouble, I have my cell phone, and I've been charging it here in the waiting room."

"I guess if you and Neal have managed to get this far, you can manage to get yourselves home, but I want you to promise to call me as soon as you arrive at White Crag, and I'll pick you up from the station."

"I promise, Dad. I'll keep you updated if anything happens, and I'll call from the bus. And I'm sorry Dad—really, I won't ever do anything like this again."

After ending the call, Buddy went back over to where Neal sat in the bus station waiting area.

"Is your dad pretty mad?" Neal asked.

"Yeah—he's pretty mad alright, but it's going to be okay. I think deep down he understands. He had a best friend once too."

This made Neal smile, but a deep sadness showed in his eyes.

"Tell me what really happened in there, Neal," Buddy said.

"Well, like I said in the cab, it was a huge mistake and a waste of time. I didn't fool him for a second and I didn't learn anything."

"Come on, Neal. There must be more. Look on the bright side, you got to meet your dad for the first time—that's gotta be worth something, even if the guard said your dad is the devil."

"At least now we know what we're up against."

"What do you mean?"

"You're right—I didn't tell you everything in the cab. I don't think there's going to be an easy recipe for reversing the werewolf curse. I don't think it's really like that at all. There's a demon—a werewolf demon. To break the curse, I think we need to kill the werewolf demon somehow."

"Buzz. The demon calls himself Buzz. I hear his voice in my head—he makes me feel like I'm in some kind of fog. He pretends to be a guardian angel and my friend, but I know he's not. I don't think we can kill him, Neal."

Walt hung up the phone and found his wife loading the dishwasher in the kitchen.

"Well, did you talk to him?" Angela asked, betraying a sliver of panic in her tone.

"It's okay, Angela. I talked to him and he's fine."

"Where on earth is he?"

"You're not going to like this, but he's at the bus station in Fort Chester with Neal. They have tickets and they're on their way home right now."

"Fort Chester? Isn't that where they have the maximum security prison?"

"It is indeed."

"Oh my God," Angela said, dropping a coffee cup in the sudsy water. "They went to visit that boy's father."

"Now, don't overreact, sweetheart," Walt began calmly. "We've known for a long time who Neal's father is, and that boy has been nothing but a great and loyal friend to our Buddy. After everything that has already happened this week, I don't know why Neal chose today as the day to visit his father for the first time, but Buddy just went along for emotional support."

"But without telling us! God knows what Buddy was exposed to in that place."

They heard the sound of scratching at the back door. Buddy's golden retriever, Champ, wanted to be let back in from the cold. Walt started toward the door.

"And don't tell me our son actually met that monster," Angela continued.

Walt stopped, trying to think of what to say next to calm his wife. "Angela, please. Buddy was just there to support his friend. He didn't go in with Neal."

The scratching grew louder and the dog began to whine.

"What has gotten into that dog, tonight," Angela said. "Earlier he wouldn't stop barking."

"Maybe the coyotes are back," Walt said, opening the back door and letting in a wave of freezing mountain air, but to his surprise, the dog wasn't there at the sliding glass door. "Champ?" he called.

Champ's severed head flew directly into Walt's chest, knocking him back and spattering fresh blood all over his face.

"Walt!" Angela screamed.

Walt took a few steps back in shock, but then he saw the luminous eyes of the creature in the back yard. Walt stumbled forward and pulled the sliding glass door closed and locked it.

He wiped his hand across his face and looked at the blood on his palm. "Angela, call the police and tell them..." Walt began to say as the sliding glass door exploded into the room. The creature was a black blur as its body crashed through with the force of a runaway car. With a quick slash of its claw, the werewolf disemboweled Walt, sending entrails and blood across the room. Angela approached momentarily to see if she could help her husband, but turned back as the werewolf removed Walt's head with its powerful jaws.

Her glasses and white apron covered in arterial spray, Angela bolted from the kitchen into the garage, slamming the door behind her. Too frightened and shocked to scream, she desperately scrambled into the front seat of the SUV and hit the button for the garage door opener, but she had the horrible realization that she didn't have her keys for the ignition. The keys were sitting on the kitchen counter next to her cell phone—in the same room where a werewolf was eating her husband.

For a moment, there was total silence, and Angela could barely breathe as she tried to think of what to do next.

The door to the kitchen slowly opened a just a crack.

Angela screamed when she saw the demonic eye peeking into the garage.

The door whipped open and the werewolf leapt upon the hood of the SUV. Angela had only a moment to take in the terrifying majesty of the creature before its right claw shattered the windshield and removed most of Angela's face with a powerful swipe.

The werewolf got down on its haunches, pulling the best pieces of Angela's body through the hole in the windshield. It had a little trouble reaching over the steering wheel to get at the liver. The werewolf loved the liver most of all. After eating its fill of Angela, the werewolf returned inside the house where it finished Walt's liver before dragging away the remainder of his body into the yard.

Dirk sat at the kitchen table with Sarah, waiting for the bus with Buddy and Neal to return to White Crag.

"Do you want any more coffee?" she asked.

"No, I think we should get going. My associate just texted to say the bus is about to arrive. I want you to be there when Neal and Buddy get into the terminal."

Earlier that afternoon, when Sarah heard from Dirk that Neal and Buddy had skipped school and boarded a bus for Fort Chester, she knew immediately that Neal was going to see his father. At first she wanted to intercept him at the prison and stop him from seeing that monster, but Dirk talked her out of it. Her deepest fear was that Jack would get inside her son's mind. It might already be too late for Michael and Jimmy, but she always had a special bond with Neal. She knew that Dirk was right—forbidding Neal to see Jack would only make it worse. She thanked God that Dirk's associate had been there to alert her about this situation. Now she could at least deal with the emotional fallout of Neal seeing his father for the first time. Otherwise, the boy might have kept it a secret from her, afraid the visit would appear as disloyalty to his mother.

Dirk convinced Sarah to let the boys complete their journey to the prison. After all, his associate would be there to watch out for them, even if the boys didn't know that he was following and watching.

When Dirk and Sarah parked at the bus station, Dirk let the car idle in view of the entrance. Dirk's associate, Quigley, approached the driver's side. Dirk rolled down the window, the night shockingly cold.

"The bus is just unloading now, boss," Quigley said.

"We'll wait here if you want to go ahead," Dirk said to Sarah.

On the other side of the building, Neal and Buddy got off the train and entered the warmth of the terminal.

"I don't get it," Buddy said. "My dad hasn't responded to my texts or answered my calls."

"Maybe he's already here waiting for us."

"Have you heard from your mom yet, Neal."

"No, she must've had an emergency at the vet clinic or something. Maybe there's a chance I can still get away with this."

"Oh shit, I don't think so," Buddy said, pointing toward the door of the terminal.

The boys saw Sarah enter the front doors of the bus terminal. It only took a second for her to spot them, and she walked toward them through a small group of people heading to the parking lot.

As she approached, Neal couldn't tell if she was furious or about to cry. She didn't say anything at all when she reached the boys. She just bent down and gave her son a big hug.

Buddy stepped back and could see that both of them were crying.

"You went to see him, didn't you?" Sarah whispered.

"I'm sorry, Mom."

"It's okay, baby—it's okay. There's nothing to be sorry for. You could've told me. I completely understand that you would want to meet him. Just next time you can ask for my credit card," she said. Sarah pulled back from the hug. "Let's get Buddy home and then we can talk."

"Hi Mrs. Mercy," Buddy said, awkwardly.

"Thanks for going with him, Buddy," Sarah said. "I can imagine that your parents aren't too pleased with you right now."

"It's weird, my dad is supposed to pick me up, but I can't get him on the phone."

"Well, we can drop you off."

Outside the bus terminal, Buddy looked all around for his dad's car, but didn't see any sign of him, so he followed Sarah and Neal.

Neal was surprised to see a strange car, and then he recognized Dirk Magill when he got out of the driver's seat. The large man walked around the car to greet Neal and Buddy with handshakes.

"Boys," Sarah explained. "Dirk is going to be helping us out for a while—just until things settle down a bit."

Neal and Buddy were both gravely silent, unsure of the implications of this. Before, Neal had only heard his mother speak of Dirk as someone to be avoided.

"Come on, I'll take you boys home," Dirk said.

As soon as Dirk pulled the car into Buddy's driveway, he could see that something was terribly wrong. For a freezing cold night, it was strange for the garage door to be wide open, and then the headlights illuminated the unmistakeable color of blood on broken glass.

Buddy, about to say goodbye to Neal before getting out of the car, suddenly sensed something amiss, and he bolted from the back seat, leaving his book bag behind.

"Come back here, son," Dirk said, but Buddy was already running across the ice-covered driveway to the garage.

Dirk quickly put the car in park and went after the boy, but not before Buddy saw what was in the garage, half-illuminated by the headlights from the driveway.

Buddy didn't know exactly what he was looking at, but he could see the shattered windshield and half-eaten body parts strewn across the hood of the car. Buddy stood frozen like a statue, and Dirk put his arms around Buddy's chest, picked him up, and carried him back to the driveway where the boy began puking into a snowbank.

Seeing this, Neal and his mother rushed out of the car to Buddy's side. Another car pulled into the driveway, and Quigley quickly joined Dirk at the open garage.

Neal's attention was focused on his friend, but Sarah noticed the two men draw guns before heading into the house.

Dirk hadn't seen carnage like this since Vietnam where he witnessed fellow soldiers obliterated by hand grenades and landmines. This time, however, explosives were not to blame for how this body had been simply torn to pieces, a large portion of the internal organs removed and strewn about, and the severed head on the passenger seat.

"What the hell is going on, Dirk?" Quigley asked his boss, fighting back the urge to vomit like the boy in the driveway. Quigley had also seen carnage in combat, but this was another level.

"It appears that Jack Mercy is back with a vengeance."

Neal was getting really scared. From where he knelt next to Buddy on the frozen driveway, he couldn't see what Buddy saw in the garage, but his best friend was out of mind. Steam rose off the puddle of vomit as Buddy cradled his head in his hands.

To Buddy, it seemed like time had stopped completely, he felt the hands of Neal and Sarah rubbing his back, but it felt like he watched the whole thing from three feet above, disembodied, and then he felt the mind cloud pierce the shock and heard the voice of the demon.

"Now you must understand, Buddy," the demon said. "You have no mother and father. Now, there is only us. We are your mother and father. We are your family. You belong with us, Buddy. Now, there is only the pack."

"Buddy, snap out of it," Neal said, shaking his friend. Buddy seemed to be in some kind of trance.

"It was the werewolves, Neal," Buddy said, collapsing on the driveway, oblivious to the ice. "The werewolves have come for me. You have to kill me, Neal—somehow you have to kill me. My poor mom and dad—I didn't warn them. I should've warned them. I don't want to be a werewolf, Neal."

"Help me get him up," Sarah said, and the two of them managed to get Buddy into the back seat of Dirk's car. Buddy lapsed in and out of coherence, muttering to himself and crying.

"What are we going to do, Mom?"

Buddy slept in Michael's bunk while Neal tossed and turned in the bunk above. Neal thought it strange that Buddy could fall asleep at all, but when Buddy slept for fourteen hours solid, Neal realized that his best friend slept off the shock of seeing what the werewolf did to his mother.

Sarah let Neal take off school to stay with Buddy. Neal was already falling way behind with his homework, but he didn't care. When it came time for her to go to work at the veterinary clinic, Buddy still slept in that deep coma-like sleep. She thought about calling in sick to work, but Dirk assured her that Quigley would watch the house while the boys were at home.

Neal was downstairs in the kitchen, heating up a pizza pocket in the microwave, when Buddy finally woke up around 3:00 in the afternoon. He could hear Buddy crying after the microwave finished its cycle.

Neal abandoned the pizza pocket and crept up the stairs. He stopped just outside the bedroom door, which he left ajar. The blinds still drawn, Neal could hear Buddy muttering in the dark bedroom. At first Neal thought Buddy was just talking to himself after waking up, and Neal almost went back downstairs to give Buddy some privacy, but then Neal realized that Buddy was talking to the thing, the werewolf demon.

"I know I'm in the pack now," Buddy said. "And I know there's no hope for me. Just leave Neal out of it. I'll be Mr. Mercy's son now. Just leave Neal alone."

Neal mustered up his courage to charge into the bedroom, pull the blinds open, and tell Buddy everything was going to be okay, but all of a sudden the dark bedroom seemed to be filled with menacing shadows. For the first time, Neal could feel the presence of the thing and the Satanic mind cloud, the sense of dread palpable in the room. Neal almost recoiled from the doorway, but he burst into the bedroom anyway, almost tripping over the dirty clothes on the floor as he went to the blinds and violently pulled the cord, flooding the room with dim winter sunlight. Buddy sat on the edge of the bottom bunk in his underwear, his eyes red and puffy from crying, but otherwise the room appeared to be empty. It still didn't feel empty.

"Get out of here," Neal whispered, his cheeks flushed red with anger. "You can't have him—do you hear me?"

But then the sunlight seemed to have cleared the room of the evil presence. Buddy buried his face in his hands.

Outside the townhouse, Quigley took the last drag from his cigarette, stubbed it out in a snowbank, and put the butt in his pocket. He could see Neal at the window in the upstairs bedroom. He leaned against the passenger door of his car as Dirk drove up in his SUV.

Dirk stopped the vehicle a few feet from Quigley and rolled down the window. "Anything to report?"

Quigley walked over to him. "I think Buddy might be up. I saw Neal at the window, a moment ago, but otherwise all is quiet."

"That poor kid," Dirk said, thinking back to the carnage in the garage. "No one should see their mother like that."

"Should we go in and talk to the boys—see if they're doing okay?"

"No—let's just hang back and maintain a presence outside the house for now. Sarah should be home in a few hours. Just make sure the boys don't go anywhere in the meantime."

"Sounds good, boss. Is something else on your mind?"

"Yeah, the police have already clamped down on the investigation surrounding Buddy's parents. It's weird—something doesn't fit. A small-town police department in a ski town shouldn't be this organized. They've completely shut me out—like they already knew we were here. I tried to ask some questions at the crime scene. It seemed like they were expecting me. There were even some veiled threats if I didn't keep my nose out of things."

"Maybe they know about you because of your research on Mercy. You are considered an expert on the subject in the public eye, and the town is probably eager to get past all of that."

"Yeah—that's probably true. I hope that's all it is. The local media is playing off the murders from last night as some kind of home invasion—a burglary gone wrong."

"That's not surprising."

Dirk and Quigley looked up at the townhouse. They could see Buddy at the window. Quigley waved and Buddy waved back.

"It's good the boys know we're here. Keep an eye on them and let me know if anything happens," Dirk said.

It seemed like what Neal said to the werewolf demon actually worked because in the following days before the funeral, Buzz paid no more visits to Buddy.

Almost two weeks passed before the memorial service for Buddy's parents. Once the authorities finished with his parents, they cremated the bodies. Fortunately, they used dental records to spare Buddy the horrific task of positively identifying the remains. In the days before the funeral, Buddy stayed with Neal, sleeping in the bottom bunk, filling the space left open by the absence of Michael, who continued to stay with Jimmy at the mountain cabin. Buddy began to attend school again sporadically, and he only left Neal's side when they had to go to different classes. The boys frequently cut class to hang out by the shopping mall and skating rink at the base of White Crag ski resort. The boys never forgot that Quigley followed, watching them, but they never discussed it, the presence of Dirk Magill's private detective becoming a reassuring comfort.

The boys lived those days in simple, blank denial, pretending that their normal lives still existed, intentionally trying to forget about what happened with Michael, the death of Buddy's parents, the fact that Buddy would soon move to his uncle's home across the country, and the inevitable approach of the full moon. Very soon, the life the boys knew would be over forever, so they reveled in the last chance they had at forgetting.

At the memorial service Buddy looked terrible, his eyes red and puffy, hair disheveled, and he had gained more weight since the murders. He barely fit into the black suit that Sarah retrieved from Buddy's old bedroom once the authorities opened up the crime scene. Buddy sat next to his Uncle Dale and Aunt Midge in the front row of the church. Neal sat between his mother and sisters directly behind Buddy in the second row. Of course, Michael and Jimmy didn't show for the funeral.

The mousy-looking preacher offered paltry comfort for the large turnout from the community, droning on about the painful mystery of God's will and turning to each other for support in times of crisis. Buddy barely heard a word of the sermon. In his mind, he felt certain that God had abandoned him that night he fell down the well, and now he was damned.

After the service, his aunt and uncle placed Buddy in the foyer to meet the tide of people wanting to give the boy their meaningless condolences. That might have been the right thing to do, but Neal snuck up behind Buddy, pulled on his jacket, and led Buddy out the side door of the church.

"Buddy, you look terrible—do you feel okay?" Neal asked, once they got outside in the sun.

"Yeah—I feel okay. I've just broken out in hives for some reason. I started itching as soon as I sat down in the church pew."

Maddie had the car idling at the curb for a quick getaway. Neal and Buddy jumped inside next to Meghan, and they took Buddy away from the horrible memorial service. Of course, Quigley followed right behind them.

Back at the church, Dirk met up with Sarah next to the coat rack in the foyer, which was filled with mourners mingling and socializing in somber tones.

"Do you see that couple there?" Dirk asked Sarah, looking toward a well-dressed couple speaking with Buddy's obese aunt and uncle.

"Sure—who are they?"

"Well, this is going to sound very strange, but I recognize them."

"What do you mean?"

"Since the murders of Buddy's parents, I've had my team following up on all kinds of hunches and suspicions, so I recently gained access to all of the records of who has visited your ex-husband in prison."

"Oh shit," Sarah muttered.

"Exactly," Dirk said. "That's Nan and Clive Hall. They have regularly taken turns visiting Jack Mercy about once a month for the last ten years."

"What do you think it means?"

"I'm going to find out, Sarah. I think the best case scenario is they're misguided groupies who are getting some kind of vicarious thrill from shadowing your family."

"And you think that's the best case scenario?"

"We'll save the worst case scenario for when I have some more information."

"They look so normal," Sarah said.

A few days later, on a late Sunday afternoon, Neal sat next to Buddy on the bottom bunk in Neal's bedroom, Buddy's Uncle Dale and Aunt Midge on their way over from the hotel to pick up Buddy. They were off to the airport to take Buddy back with them to their home to Detroit.

"So are you going to be able get your stuff back from your bedroom?" Neal asked.

"Well, some of it, I guess. My aunt is going to come back and try to sell the house, but who would want to live in a house where that happened. Anyway, she's going to have the movers pack up my bedroom when the house is sold."

"Yeah—you have a lot of cool stuff."

"Do me a favor, Neal. Once I'm gone, go ahead and break in there and take anything you want from my old bedroom."

"What do you mean—once you're gone?"

"Gone to Detroit."

"Oh."

The boys sat in silence for a moment, devastated by having to say goodbye, afraid to discuss the big question on their minds.

"I know we haven't really talked about it much since my parents died," Buddy said. "But the full moon is just a couple of days away now."

"Yeah—I know."

"Well, I'm glad I'll be in Detroit. I mean to say—I'm not glad I'll be in Detroit, but I'm glad I will be far away from you when it happens. Detroit might as well be on the other side of the word. I'm glad you'll be safe."

"What are you talking about, Buddy? Have you seen Buzz again?"

"No, I haven't seen him again, but he hasn't gone anywhere, Neal. He has my soul. I should have died at the bottom of that well, you know, but I didn't die, and now I belong to that thing."

"You don't know that for sure, Buddy. Now you're just talking crazy. Besides, Dirk promised that his men will be there to watch over you."

The boys heard Uncle Dale and Aunt Midge arrive downstairs in their rental car.

"I guess I'll be the werewolf of Detroit," Buddy said, and the boys laughed, despite the sadness of saying goodbye. "Promise me you'll go into my bedroom and take anything you want. Get my ski pass for sure—it's in my desk drawer. My parents had paid for it already. And take my snowboard too. It's not like I'll be doing any snowboarding in Detroit. Here's my key to the house—no one knows I still have it."

The key was on a long white shoelace around Buddy's neck. He took it off and put the shoelace over Neal's head.

"Goodbye, Buddy," Neal said and the two boys hugged. "I love you."

"I love you too, Neal."

Buddy didn't say anything else, he got up and went downstairs where his suitcase and his aunt and uncle waited for him.

Neal stayed in the bedroom, not wanting to see Buddy's aunt and uncle—now Buddy's legal guardians. Neal hated them for taking Buddy away. He curled up in the bottom bunk, listening to the sounds of his mother saying goodbye to Buddy, telling him to be strong, the front door closing, and the rental car taking his best friend away.

A few minutes later, Sarah poked her head in the bedroom.

"Hey there kiddo—I'm going to pick up a carry-out pizza, so I'll be back with food in a few minutes."

"Okay. Thanks Mom," Neal said.

Neal stayed curled up in the bed, listening to the sound of his mom's car drive off, and then to the silence of the house. Maddie and Meghan were gone for a school choir event, so Neal was all alone, thinking about Buddy going to the airport and a new life in Detroit.

It was almost dark in the room when Neal heard the bedroom door swing open, startled to see his brother Michael walk into the room.

"What are you doing here?" Neal said, quickly wiping the tears from his eyes.

"I live here, remember?"

"You used to live here—before you turned into a traitor."

"I'm not a traitor, Neal—we're on the same side. It's your dad. It's our dad. Don't you have any loyalty?"

"You're the one who tried to kill Buddy."

"Yeah, and now he's one of us. We're all in this together."

"What about mom?"

"She'll have to be persuaded—just like you're going to have to be persuaded. Dad won't have it any other way."

"Our dad is the devil," Neal shouted.

As soon as the words escaped Neal's lips, Jimmy walked into the room. The older brother looked pale and thin with bags under his eyes and yellow teeth. He reeked of whiskey and cigarettes.

"I better never hear you say anything like that again," Jimmy said. "Now throw a change of clothes in your duffel bag—you're coming with us."

"No, I'm not!"

"You're coming with us even if I have to punch your lights out, Neal," Jimmy said, making a fist.

Michael and Jimmy made a move toward Neal, who tried to swing at Michael, but missed.

"Grab him," Jimmy shouted.

Neal had been in many fights with his brothers over the years, but they had never teamed up against him like this before. Michael and Jimmy quickly pinned him to the floor of the bedroom.

"Throw some of his stuff in a bag," Jimmy said to Michael while holding Neal's arms. Neal tried to wrest himself from his older brother's grasp, but Jimmy was just too strong. "And hurry—we've got to get out of here before mom gets back."

A few minutes later, Michael came out the front door of the townhouse with Neal's duffel bag, followed by Neal with his older brother's hand on the back of his neck, Neal's nose and lip bleeding. Quigley stepped from behind the garage, pulling back his jacket to reveal a handgun in a shoulder holster.

"Hi Jimmy," Quigley said. "You don't know me, but I'm afraid I can't let you take Neal away from here without your mother's permission."

"Who the fuck are you?" Jimmy said.

"I work for Dirk Magill."

"That's the guy who writes those trashy true crime books and spreads lies about my dad. Fuck Dirk Magill—I hate him," Jimmy said, a low growl emanating from deep beneath the pitch of Jimmy's voice.

Jimmy pushed Neal away from him into the snow-covered yard where Neal fell on his face. Jimmy lunged at Quigley before the private detective could draw his handgun, falling on Quigley with his full weight. They fell hard on the concrete driveway. Neal looked up from the snow to see Jimmy burying his face in Quigley's neck. Quigley emitted a quick garbled scream before a geyser of blood sprayed from his neck across the ice on the driveway. Jimmy looked back at Neal, and Neal could see that the jagged fangs of a werewolf had sprouted in his brother's mouth. Michael stood up against the side of the house, frozen in horror.

Neal jumped to his feet and started to run away from the carnage, but he ran right into a tall man in a leather jacket. He looked up and saw Reggie grinning at him. Reggie simply picked up Neal and threw him over his shoulder, walking him over to the black car that was idling in the street. Neal didn't even think about resisting, something about the man so menacing and powerful.

Now that Jimmy's mouth had transformed into the jaws of a werewolf, Jimmy wanted to halt the process, but that was impossible now. Once it started, he couldn't stop it. Without looking back at his brothers, Jimmy ran toward the trees on the other side of the parking lot. He didn't want to be caught out in the open for the full transformation.

On his back, Quigley clutched at the blood gushing through his fingers. He knew he was finished. In his last moments, he pulled the gun from his holster and fired, hitting both of Reggie's knees and bringing the man to the ground in two explosions of pain. Reggie dropped Neal on the sidewalk.

Neal saw his chance. Just as he got up and started to run, Neal was sprayed with blood. Quigley had put a bullet in Reggie's brain. Neal ran as fast as he could—in the opposite direction of the werewolf.

Neal had slept on the floor of Buddy's walk-in closet for three nights. He found Buddy's sleeping bag and he took some of the pillows off the bed, afraid to sleep on the bed in case someone came into the house and discovered him. He felt much safer tucked away on the floor of the closet. Also, he could turn on a lamp in the closet without worrying that someone could see the light from the street, if anyone watched the house.

After the murder of Buddy's parents, the house still contained all of their furnishings and belongings along with most of Buddy's things; fortunately, the gas and electricity were still turned on, but it was way too creepy downstairs where the werewolf had attacked, and Neal never went into the garage.

After Jimmy and Michael tried to kidnap him and Quigley was murdered, Neal ran from the scene until he threw up. Shaking with cold and terror, he hid inside an unlocked tool shed for over an hour until he felt sure nobody followed him. While sitting there in the dark, he remembered the key on the shoelace around his neck. He threw his cell phone off a bridge into a hole in a frozen creek and made his way over to Buddy's house.

It was cold in the house, the furnace turned just high enough to keep the pipes from freezing, and Neal knew he couldn't turn on the television because the house was supposed to be empty, too afraid someone might call the police to report squatters—or even worse, he feared his father's people would be out looking for him.

Alone in the house, with nothing to do but read some of Buddy's paperbacks in the closet and eat canned food from the pantry, Neal's fear and paranoia began to grow, imagining that a powerful Satanic cult must be after him, a cult devoted to his father. Who was that strange man working with his brothers to kidnap him? Something was definitely going on. If it hadn't been for Quigley, Neal didn't know what would have happened or where he would be.

Every time Neal went to get another can of ravioli or a box of cereal from the pantry, he saw those horrible blood stains and the boarded-up doorway to the back yard. He tried not to think about what happened there.

On the second day at the house, he heard someone enter downstairs, but whoever it was stayed for only a few minutes and left again. It could have been a realtor or a carpet cleaner doing an estimate. The whole time Neal stayed hidden under a pile of blankets in the walk-in closet. Whoever was there never entered Buddy's room.

Neal knew that his mother would be worried sick about him and that Dirk Magill was probably out searching for him, but he also felt sure that his father's cult would be searching for him too. Perhaps Magill thought he did get kidnapped. He knew he couldn't hide in Buddy's closet forever, but maybe just a few more days until he figured out what to do. He could eat for weeks on the cans in the pantry, but the boy began to feel desperately lonely.

Neal was eating another cold can of ravioli and considering the risk of taking a shower when he heard someone enter the house again downstairs. Without thinking, Neal set the can on the carpet next to the sleeping bag, and he crawled into his hiding spot underneath some blankets in the corner of the closet. He adjusted the blankets so he could peek from underneath and see if anyone opened up the closet door.

It didn't take long for the intruder to enter Buddy's bedroom. Neal's heart began to pound in his chest, hoping he was safe in the hideout. He knew that no one could detect his presence from looking in the bedroom, but as soon as someone opened the closet door and saw the cans and the sleeping bag, it would be obvious a squatter was living in the house. Sunlight flooded the closet as the door opened.

Neal said a silent prayer that it was just a realtor and not one of his father's Satanic killers. From underneath the blanket Neal was shocked to see muddy bare feet enter the closet—it definitely wasn't a realtor, but who would be out in the winter in bare feet? Was it another squatter? The intruder picked up the half-eaten can of ravioli from the floor. Neal puzzled over this when he heard a familiar voice call his name.

"Neal? Are you there? It's me, Buddy—you can come out."

Neal couldn't believe it. He threw aside the blankets and jumped up to find Buddy, who was covered in mud, but smiling.

"Buddy? What are you doing here?" Neal said as he embraced his best friend, shocked to discover that Buddy was also soaking wet.

"Thank God you're here, Neal. We're in big trouble."

Neal gave Buddy a closer look—the boy wore his winter coat over his pajamas. "What happened to you? Why aren't you in Detroit?"

"It's a long story, Neal. They never took me to Detroit. They paid off my aunt and uncle, but first you have to see what's happening."

"What do you mean?"

"Have you seen the television?"

"No—I was afraid to turn it on."

"There's a chance that the cable hasn't been turned off yet."

Downstairs, they turned on the cable news coverage of the prison break. Law enforcement officials called it the most sophisticated prison break in recent history, coordinating guards, prisoners, and a convoy of vehicles. All of the conspirators wore wolf masks. Dozens had been murdered.

"Those aren't masks, are they?" Neal asked, as the two boys stood in front of the large television in the living room.

"They're not masks," Buddy said.

"Does that mean my father is out?"

"I think so, but they haven't announced it on the news yet. And the full moon is tonight."

"How did you know that I was hiding here."

"You're not going to like this," Buddy said, "but Buzz told me."

"If Buzz knows that I'm here…"

"Then your father knows it too."

"Buddy, what happened to you?"

On the day that Aunt Midge and Uncle Dale picked up Buddy from Neal's house to bring him home to Detroit, they stopped at a local diner before driving all the way to the airport. However, they had a big surprise in store for Buddy.

After eating a cheeseburger and fries, while finishing off a piece of apple pie, Buddy noticed an elderly couple smiling at him as they entered the diner. Buddy's aunt and uncle had been waiting for them.

Buddy's uncle introduced the couple as Nan and Clive. The couple joined them at the table, Clive pulling up an additional seat.

"We have something we need to discuss, Buddy," Uncle Dale said.

Nan reached for Buddy's hand and squeezed it under the table. "There's been a change of plans," she said with giddy excitement.

"Our first priority is for you to be in an ideal environment after this terrible tragedy," Uncle Dale said, "and at this time, we're not sure that Detroit is the best place for you."

"We were very fortunate to meet Nan and Clive at the funeral," Aunt Midge said.

"And they have very generously offered to welcome you into their home, Buddy," Dale said, finishing the thought.

Buddy was shocked and speechless. Almost before he knew what was happening, they moved his suitcases from Uncle Dale's rental car into the huge black SUV belonging to Nan and Clive. The couple ushered Buddy into the back seat of the SUV while his aunt and uncle said their goodbyes. Buddy's head was spinning—he couldn't believe his mother's brother just gave him up to these two strangers. It all happened so suddenly, and Buddy felt sure that something was terribly wrong with the situation.

Nan and Clive had paid his aunt and uncle a hundred thousand dollars to deliver Buddy to them.

Once they buckled Buddy into the back seat of the SUV, the tone completely changed. In the diner, the elderly couple overflowed with warmth and excitement about bringing Buddy into their home. But alone in the SUV, they were icy and silent.

Since Clive drove the SUV away from town, Buddy expected they were taking him to one of the many luxurious neighborhoods built by wealthy ski enthusiasts over the years. Instead, they drove him to a strange building that looked almost like a concrete military bunker.

He parked the vehicle at the curb of a circular drive next to a nondescript entrance. A moment later, a young woman with long brown hair and a business suit met them at the curb. To Buddy, she almost looked like a school principal, and the man that accompanied her looked like some kind of a butler.

She opened Buddy's door. "Come on out, Buddy, and welcome to your new home. My name is Eleanor, and I am going to be taking care of you. But you can call me Ellie. I'm sure you must have all kinds of questions for me."

"What's going on?" Buddy asked. "I thought I was supposed to go home with Nan and Clive."

Buddy took the hand that was offered to him as she helped the boy out of the car. The man who looked like a butler removed Buddy's suitcase out of the back.

"Just wait until you see your new room," Eleanor said. "I think you are really going to like it."

Without another word, Clive drove the SUV away from the compound.

"I'm really confused," Buddy said.

"I know you must be," Ellie said, trying to sound compassionate and understanding. "Unfortunately, we couldn't really tell your aunt and uncle the truth after all."

"The truth about what?" Buddy asked.

The man with Buddy's suitcase stood at the metal double doors, holding one open for Buddy and Eleanor, but Buddy still stood at the curb, preferring to run away into the forest before going inside the compound with these strange people.

"The truth is, Buddy," Eleanor said. "This is really the best place for you now. Here you'll be with friends who understand what you're going through. Here you can be with other people like us."

"Is this like some kind of orphanage?" Buddy asked.

"No, not at all," Eleanor said, laughing slightly. She showed Buddy her palm, which had the outline of a distinct five-pointed star in pink scar tissue. "You see—I'm just like you, Buddy. And there are others like us here too. That's what I meant when I said we know what you're going through."

"What does that thing on your hand mean?" Buddy asked, more frightened than ever.

"Oh that's right—yours probably hasn't come in yet, but it will after you turn for the first time. It's the mark of the werewolf, Buddy."

"Holy shit—you're a werewolf."

Eleanor laughed again. "Of course, Buddy—now come inside and let me show you to your room."

At the end of a seemingly endless hallway, behind a locked metal door, they kept Buddy in his new bedroom. A framed portrait of Jack Mercy hung over the bed, the serial killer and Satanist posing in a sharp suit as if running for mayor. The room, with an adjoining bathroom, was never intended to be a young boy's bedroom, more like an office in the mysterious facility, but they attempted to decorate the room like a boy's bedroom, complete with a roll-top desk and a globe on top of a dresser. Instead of a window, there was a one-way mirror, and the strange group of Satanic old men who watched the werewolf tear Baker to pieces now watched Buddy in the fake bedroom, and they would watch him turn for the first time during the full moon.

The boy knew he was a prisoner.

Eleanor did everything she could to convince Buddy that he was a special guest and not a prisoner, bringing Buddy his three meals a day and chatting with him. Soon, Buddy's education would begin, Eleanor told him. They were in the process of finding a tutor, a special werewolf tutor. It soon occurred to Buddy that they were just waiting for the full moon—that's what Buddy waited for too. He didn't know what would happen after that.

Fortunately, they gave Buddy a television to pass the time.

Buddy woke up in the middle of the night, and he thought that the one-way mirror seemed to glow slightly in the darkness, and he wondered if that meant the people on the other side had a light on, wondered if that meant they watched him sleep. Tossing and turning in the bed, he felt the approach of the mind cloud, and then he realized Buzz the werewolf demon occupied the room with him.

"We're not your enemies, Buddy," Buzz whispered.

"Oh really. You're not my friends, either."

"Why do you say that?"

"Friends don't keep their friends prisoner in a fake bedroom with a one-way mirror."

"Oh Buddy—we're not keeping you prisoner. We're keeping you safe."

"Safe from what?"

"Safe from yourself, of course. Don't you understand yet? You're a monster, Buddy. You're a werewolf and you belong with us. We don't want you out there by yourself. When the full moon comes, you don't want to be out there by yourself."

Buzz faded away, but Buddy couldn't fall back to sleep. A few minutes later, Buddy heard the heavy clunk of the metallic lock on the door and Eleanor came into the room. From the fluorescent light of the hallway, Buddy could see that she wore pajamas too; she must also have a bedroom nearby.

"You okay, Buddy?"

"I'm okay," Buddy mumbled and turned away from her, pulling up the covers.

"A little bird told me you were having trouble sleeping. Try not to worry. Tomorrow night is the night. Everything will be different after the full moon. Believe me, you'll feel differently about everything. A whole new world will be opened to you."

The next day, as Buddy ate his breakfast in front of the television, he saw the news about the prison break. As soon as he heard the name of the prison, he had a terrible feeling that Jack Mercy was behind the entire thing. When he heard the initial reports of prisoners and guards in wolf masks orchestrating the riots and the escape, he knew for certain that Jack Mercy was behind the entire thing.

A few hours after the news first came on the television, a strange man with wide, frightened eyes and dressed in janitorial coveralls entered the room. Buddy had never seen him before. It was the same janitor who had cleaned up the remains of Baker, the same man who had cleaned up after countless werewolf murders in the facility.

The man was clearly in a panic. "Put your shoes on, little boy—quickly," he whispered. "Quickly, little boy—quickly. They're not watching now. They're all watching the television. We only have a few minutes."

Surprised and confused, Buddy, still in his pajamas, threw on his shoes without any socks and grabbed his coat. The second the coat was on, the man grabbed Buddy and pulled him into the hallway.

"Why are you helping me?" Buddy asked the man as they hurried down the hallway toward the door.

"This is no place for a child. This is an evil place—no good comes to anyone here. A child should not be here. You do not know what I have seen here—you do not want to see what I have seen."

The man used his badge to open the door. The man pushed Buddy outside into the snow. "Go now, as fast as you can—through the forest. When you come to the first road, a car will stop for you. Someone will stop for a child. It is all I can do."

"What about you? Can't you come with me?"

"No, no—my soul is doomed, but a child's soul is innocent and clean. God will help you—it is too late for me. I can't watch it happen to a child."

Without another word, Buddy started to run.

A deep blanket of snow on the ground made running difficult. The forest was dense with pine trees, but the undergrowth sparse. Even so, his legs were soon scratched and bleeding underneath his pajamas from sharp branches as he desperately tried to put distance between himself and the facility. Buddy was so scared, he barely noticed the cuts and scrapes.

Then he heard the howling of the beast. One of the werewolves was after him.

Buddy came to the road that the janitor spoke about, but he didn't see any cars. The sound of the howling so close behind him, Buddy had to keep going. If he waited at the road, the werewolf would catch up with him for sure. He crossed the road and kept going.

A few hundred yards past the road, Buddy encountered a shallow creek with a steep embankment. He scrambled down the embankment, but as soon as he stepped on the ice, his shoes broke through and sank deep into freezing cold mud. He pulled his feet free of the mud, but lost both of his shoes. Buddy remembered the last time he walked through the winter forest in his bare feet, so he ignored the freezing cold and kept going. By the time he reached the top of the opposite embankment, his pajamas were covered in mud and the sound of the howling even closer.

Looking behind, he caught a glimpse of Eleanor through the trees. Still dressed in a business suit and covered in bright red blood, she was half-transformed, a snout partially protruding from her face with drooling fangs and the shining eyes of a demonic beast. Buddy guessed that the blood belonged to the janitor. He had given his life for Buddy, and all in vain. Buddy was about to be recaptured—or worse.

In one superhuman leap, Eleanor cleared the creek that had claimed Buddy's shoes. The werewolf closed in on the boy. Buddy ran in blind panic when he heard a loud metallic snap and the terrible squeal of a wounded dog.

When Eleanor didn't overtake him, Buddy stopped and looked back.

Eleanor had stepped into a bear trap, the metal teeth had her leg up to the knee. As she writhed in agony, trying to free her leg with her claws, Buddy could see that the transformation had begun to reverse itself. In a moment, she looked like a normal woman in a business suit—covered in blood and in a bear trap, but the half-werewolf gone for the moment.

Buddy suspected that he didn't have much time before she freed herself, so he backtracked to the road. He noticed a sign warning trespassers that it was private property. Once he crossed the road, he must have ventured into someone else's property, someone who didn't appreciate all of the werewolves in the neighborhood, so the neighbor had put out illegal bear traps for encroaching werewolves.

The janitor was right—the first car that saw the barefoot boy in his muddy pajamas on the side of the road stopped to pick him up and brought him into town.

"What did you tell the man who picked you up?" Neal asked at the end of Buddy's harrowing story.

"I just pretended like I had amnesia. He dropped me off at the emergency room, but he didn't stay. I don't think he was interested in talking to the police. So once he was gone, I left and walked straight here. It wasn't far."

"That's an amazing story, Buddy. Don't you think they are going to come here to look for you?"

"They're going to know where I am no matter where I go—I was hoping to stay a step ahead of them, but I'm out of time. It's going to get dark and it's the full moon tonight. Don't worry, I have a plan."

In the garage where the werewolf killed Buddy's mother, Buddy's father kept an old Toyota four-door around to give to Buddy when his son turned sixteen, the car with his mother's remains taken away and impounded as evidence by the police. With only minutes to spare before sundown,

Buddy and Neal cleaned out the trunk and removed the spare tire, leaving plenty of room for Buddy to crawl inside. They even put in some blankets and a pillow. At the last second, Buddy remembered his father had a bunch of steaks in the extra freezer. He threw in a bunch of the frozen steaks into the trunk.

"Who knows—maybe I'll need something to chew on," Buddy said. Dressed in jeans and a winter coat, Buddy climbed into the trunk. "Do you have the key?"

"I have it," Neal said. "Are you sure about this?"

"Not really, but if I'm going to turn into a monster like the one I saw today, being locked in the trunk is the only safe place I can think of."

"Okay, Buddy. I'll be right outside all night waiting for you."

"Well, if it looks like I'm going to break out of here, don't wait around. Who knows if I'll be in control of myself at all— the last thing I want is to hurt you. It if looks like the trunk isn't going to hold me, promise me you'll get out of here."

"I promise. Do you want a flashlight or anything?"

"No, just close the lid. It's got to be about sunset by now."

"Watch your fingers." And with great reticence, Neal slammed the trunk lid shut.

Sarah and the girls had an emergency conference with Dirk Magill at the kitchen table.

Since Neal had disappeared and Jimmy murdered Quigley in front of the house, Dirk Magill had the house on lockdown. Sarah had called in sick to work and she told the school that Maddie and Meghan were too sick to attend. Dirk called in all of his employees and hired some additional security personnel. As far as they knew, Neal had been abducted.

Sarah insisted that they stay at the house in case Neal or Michael returned home, but after the highly publicized prison escape and the knowledge that Jack Mercy was on the loose again, Dirk tried to convince Sarah that the family needed to go into hiding.

"But we can't go into hiding without Neal and Michael."

"Michael is one of them now, Mom," Maddie said.

"We don't know that for sure," Sarah said.

"I've arranged for a safe house where I can guarantee your ex-husband won't be able to find you," Dirk said, "and I'll have someone watch this house. If by chance Neal returns, we'll know about it."

"But if Jack can escape from a maximum security prison, how can you guarantee our safety anywhere?" Sarah asked.

The question hung in the air for a moment, but Dirk attempted to assure them. "The safe house is tactically more secure. It has total surveillance of the grounds and a panic room in case of emergencies."

But Sarah just wasn't convinced.

Since Neal's disappearance, Dirk and his team worked around the clock to try and find where they took the boy. They had been unable to retrieve him, but they had uncovered many dark secrets about the town in the process.

Dirk now believed the police department of White Crag to be totally corrupt and in the pocket of the shadowy organization that owned the fortified facility just outside of town. They uncovered rumors that the organization was funded by a group of wealthy European Satanists who also owned a controlling interesting in the ski resort, the life blood of the town.

Jimmy's cabin in the mountains had been abandoned, and Dirk's investigators believed all three of the Mercy boys were being held in the fortified facility. Dirk's detective in Detroit reported that Buddy had never arrived there, the aunt and uncle unwilling to answer questions about Buddy's whereabouts.

For a long time, the trunk was completely silent. Bundled up in a warm winter coat, Neal just waited in the front seat of the car in the darkness of the garage. He thought about turning on the radio, but he changed his mind because he wanted to make sure he could hear any movement from the trunk.

Less than two hours after sunset, Neal felt the car vibrating. Neal got out and stood by the locked trunk. It sounded like Buddy was wrestling around in there. Moans of pain and sadness began to come out of the trunk. Neal hated to hear it, not even sure if Buddy was crying from emotional or physical pain. Then, the trunk began to violently rock and Buddy began screaming in agony. For a moment, Neal considered opening the trunk—perhaps being locked in a small space was making it much worse—maybe Buddy needed to be running through the forest, but when the sound of claws on metal began, Neal knew that he couldn't open the trunk. Horrible growls and howls of the beast followed closely behind.

Neal had backed away from the trunk, considering whether or not to run away. It sounded as if Buddy was about the rip his way right out of the trunk when the lights of the garage came on.

Michael stood in the doorway, holding a long sharp dagger.

"What are you doing here, Michael?" Neal said, trapped between his twin brother and the horrible sounds from the trunk of the car.

"Do you hear that, Neal? Buddy belongs to dad now. You're the only holdout left. It's time to make a choice. You can either join us..."

"Or what?" Neal said, his voice shaking.

"This is a special dagger, Neal—it's a relic, brought over here by our benefactors. It was used in Satanic rituals back in the Dark Ages. It's pure silver—you could even kill a werewolf with it."

"So what?"

Michael entered the garage and began taking a few steps toward Neal. The sounds from the trunk intensified. If Buddy didn't burst out of the trunk, it sounded like he would tear himself to pieces inside.

"It's dipped in poison, Neal," Michael said. "All it takes is one scratch and you won't be my brother anymore. You'll drop dead in a second, and then we'll let that werewolf in the trunk eat you."

"You're bluffing," Neal said.

"Jimmy is waiting right outside. Dad wanted us to settle this first—just you and me. What's it going to be, Neal?"

Jimmy was waiting outside the garage door like Michael said. He could hear his brothers talking inside the garage, but he couldn't make out what they were saying over the sound of the werewolf screaming and howling in the trunk. Then the boys went silent, and Jimmy wondered if Michael truly had the nerve to do his father's bidding.

Someone inside hit the electronic garage door opener. As the garage door rose up, Jimmy saw Michael across the garage by the button, and he saw Neal lying face down on the floor of the garage.

Michael had tears streaming down his face.

"Come here, little brother," Jimmy said, and gave his brother a hug.

Jimmy turned over Neal and looked at the boy's face, twisted in the grim rictus of death by poison, a long scratch from the poisoned silver blade across his cheek. Jimmy turned him over again and took a long swig of whiskey from his flask.

"Now it's time to let out the werewolf," Jimmy said. "Close the garage door again." He found the keys in Neal's pocket. The car was still violently shaking when Jimmy opened the trunk.

At first, Buddy just slashed at Jimmy with his claws, but then he jumped out, still in his clothing and winter jacket, but his face fully transmogrified into an unholy beast with sharp fangs and demonic eyes. A normal human would have been torn to shreds, but Jimmy was Buddy's alpha wolf, the werewolf who made him.

Buddy stopped threatening Jimmy, falling under the sway of the alpha wolf's power. Jimmy controlled Buddy, and Jack Mercy controlled them both. Buddy fell to the concrete floor at Jimmy's feet, showing submission, but also still writhing in agony from the transformation.

"Now it's time to do my father's bidding, Buddy. Now it's time for you to kill the traitorous woman. Rise up and go to the Mercy house where you will kill Sarah Mercy and anyone you find there, but leave my sisters untouched. My father will deal with them." Jimmy looked over at Michael who pressed the garage door button again. When the door was only halfway open, the new werewolf scrambled out underneath and ran away into the night.

After watching the werewolf go, Jimmy turned to Michael. "I know it's unbearable, losing both your brother and your mother in one night, but our father is a brutal master—and a vengeful master. We cannot cross him. At least he spared us from killing our mother, even if he didn't spare you the task of killing Neal."

"No, you're not alone, Dirk," Sarah said. "I've developed feelings for you too." The two were alone in the kitchen, the full moon hanging in the cold winter sky outside the window. Dirk set down his cup of coffee on the counter, took a step toward Sarah and tenderly grabbed her hand.

He held her hand for a moment before he said, "Everything is going to be fine. Now that Jack is on the loose again, federal protection is going to be available to you."

"We'll hold off on that option for now," Sarah said. "I've been thinking it over, and you're right about the safe house—I think we should get Maddie and Meghan there as soon as possible. I'll feel much safer there—with you "

"And we'll find Neal," Dirk said. "We won't rest."

"I'll go and tell the girls. We can go first thing in the morning."

"If we're going, we're going now," Dirk said gently. "We're too vulnerable here trying to defend this position all night. We're better off on the move."

Sarah squeezed his hand. "I'll tell the girls to get ready. We can be ready in an hour."

Sarah quickly went up the stairs, her mind flooded with fears and questions, wondering if she should have taken the girls to the safe house when Dirk first suggested it, but she knew Neal and Michael still needed her. She knocked on Maddie and Meghan's bedroom door and went inside, surprised by a wave of freezing cold night air.

"Why is the window open?" she said, at first only seeing Maddie standing in the corner of the room by the closet. Sarah didn't understand what was happening—Maddie, wearing her scarlet-colored sweats for the school volleyball team, clearly terrified and shaking, pointed across the room. Sarah turned her head and saw it. On the other side of Meghan's bed, on the floor by the nightstand, something had its arms wrapped around Meghan, something that was quietly growling. Meghan, on her knees, tried to stay perfectly still because the creature crouched right behind her, the werewolf's long hairy hand around her throat, the tip of a shiny black claw right next to her jugular.

"Don't move, sweetie," Sarah whispered as the demonic eyes of the creature watched her from behind Meghan's shoulder. The werewolf clutched her tighter and growled a little louder this time. Then Sarah noticed that the werewolf wore blue jeans and a winter coat.

"It's Buddy," Maddie whispered.

She was right. Buddy had managed to climb up on the roof without being detected. Meghan, doing her nails by the nightstand, cracked open the window because of the strong smell of nail polish. Before Meghan knew what happened, the werewolf pulled up the window and came through, grabbing the girl and almost biting into her neck, but the commandment from his alpha wolf, not to harm the sisters, came into the werewolf's mind. For just an instant, Buddy woke up from the nightmare of the creature's hunger and instinct. Confused and afraid, the predator clutched the girl tighter, retreated into the corner, and growled in warning. Behind the eyes of the werewolf, Buddy wrestled with his dark, malevolent instincts. Since it was Buddy's first transformation, and the fact that Buddy had not yet killed, the will of the werewolf demon had not completely consumed Buddy—not yet.

"Can you hear me, Buddy?" Sarah whispered, afraid to move.

The werewolf growled louder and gripped Meghan's throat.

At that moment, they heard the bone-chilling howl of a werewolf outside the house; it was close. Buddy looked toward the moon outside the window. Sarah saw it—she saw fear in the creature's eyes. Buddy was still in there.

Buddy returned his gaze to Sarah, pushing Meghan away from him. Crouched in the corner, Buddy tensed his body, about to leap across the room at Sarah and follow his master's bidding. Just as the werewolf was about to leap, Dirk pushed Sarah aside and began firing at the werewolf. Buddy jumped in surprise, landing on the bed.

"No, it's Buddy!" Sarah cried out.

"I know it's Buddy," Dirk said, unloading the handgun into the werewolf who thrashed in agony on the bed. "That's why I'm using regular bullets."

The creature was caught off guard and wounded. Dirk leapt on the bed and wrestled Buddy into a face-down position. The former police officer had a lot of experience with subduing suspects, and he was fast with handcuffs.

"Quick, get the muzzle from my bag," Dirk said to Sarah.

In seconds, Dirk secured handcuffs and ankle cuffs on Buddy. Despite all of the bullet wounds to his chest, the werewolf still struggled. With the full weight of his body, Dirk pinned Buddy to the floor with his knees. In this position, he managed to put the dog's muzzle on the werewolf's snout.

Sarah had her arms around Maddie and Meghan in the doorway. Dirk took a step back, and all of them watched the werewolf thrash around on the floor. Buddy snarled and whimpered, but he couldn't escape the cuffs and the muzzle.

"Look at that," Dirk said, pointing at the floor. "The bullets are starting to come out." They had all heard about the miraculous healing powers of the werewolf, and they could see the bullets collecting on the floor as the wounds healed and the slugs were pushed out.

Dirk had two gun holsters. He returned the Glock to its holster on his left and pulled out the gun in the holster on his right; it looked like an old-fashioned six-shooter. "This one has the silver bullets," Dirk said. "They weren't easy to find, and they don't fit just any gun."

At that very moment, they heard a scream of agony from outside the window. Sarah rushed over and closed the window and blinds.

"Dirk, you're bleeding," Sarah said, noticing a bloody slash on Dirk's thigh.

"It's nothing—I bet you never thought old Dirk could wrestle a werewolf like that," he said, but none of them appreciated the humor. They knew what it meant that the werewolf had scratched him. Buddy was evidence of that.

Sarah brought up Dirk's bag from downstairs, and Dirk pulled another gun from the bag and gave it to Sarah. "Now you watch Buddy and the girls. Don't be afraid to fill him up with bullets again if it looks like he might get loose. You guard this door, and don't let anyone in here but me."

Buddy cowered in the corner and growled, but he had calmed down. Maddie and Meghan got down on the floor next to him—but not too close.

"Come back, Buddy," Maddie said. "We know you can do it—keep fighting."

Meghan touched her hand to her throat, and she noticed a little speck of blood on her finger. She said nothing.

Dirk closed the bedroom door behind him, the six-shooter drawn. He only had six silver bullets, and he feared it wasn't going to be enough.

At the bottom of the stairs, one of the twins ran right into him.

"Where's my mom?" he said.

"Now which one are you?" Dirk asked.

"I'm Neal. Is my mom okay? Buddy's on his way over and he's going..."

"It's okay—your mom's okay, and we got Buddy hogtied. Now tell me—how did you get past my men?"

"All of your men are dead. The werewolves are here."

The first severed human head came crashing through the front window. A second later, another human head flew right through the back window. Dirk grabbed the boy and pulled him behind the stairs.

A chorus of howls followed each human head as the werewolves lobbed them into the house. It sounded like demonic laughter. Dirk had six men watching the outside of the house. A second after the sixth head landed in the living room, a monstrous werewolf came through the back door from the porch. This wasn't a wolf-boy in blue jeans, but a foul beast of pure evil. Dirk wasn't going to wrestle this werewolf into handcuffs. It smashed the kitchen table to smithereens and slashed the couch, filling the air with stuffing as the beast ploughed its way through the room looking for Dirk.

Dirk jumped from behind the stairs, firing; he put a silver bullet right between its glowing eyes. The body of the hairy creature fell right on top of him. The silver bullet killed the werewolf instantly, but the bullet didn't stop the creature's momentum.

In the time it took to get out from underneath the weight of the beast, Dirk discovered it was now just a naked man. It was Jimmy Mercy, Jack's oldest boy.

Neal prepared to run, but then he saw the dead werewolf was his brother. He fell to his knees, reaching out and touching the bright red spot on his brother's forehead.

"You'll be sorry for that, Magill," said a voice behind them.

Dirk and Neal turned around. Jack Mercy stood in the doorway. Behind Mercy, a trio of gigantic werewolves assembled on the front porch, long plumes of steam coming from their snouts with each breath.

"Dad!" Neal shouted. He got to his feet, and he started to go toward him, but then he stopped, uncertain.

"Come to me, son," Jack said.

Neal ran to him, and embraced his father.

Dirk looked over his shoulder, and saw that at least four more werewolves waited on the back porch.

"Dad, my brothers are dead," the boy whispered into his father's ear.

"I know, son. We serve a hard master," Jack said, wiping a tear from the boy's cheek. "Our Lord's rewards are bountiful, and his vengeance terrible."

"Where is he, Jack?" Sarah shouted from the top of the stairs, the gun still in her hand. "Where is Neal?"

"Hello, my dear," Jack said. "It's a pleasure to see you again."

"Tell me now, Jack. What have you done with Neal? Where is he?"

"I don't understand you, dear wife. Neal is right here at my side."

The boy hugged his father tight, his voice muffled by his father's jacket. "You knew it was me?" Neal said.

Only his father could hear the words. "Of course I knew it was you, Neal. I know you, Neal. You are my boy, my pride and joy."

"Get away from him, Neal," Sarah screamed.

"No, mother," Neal said, and the boy looked up at his father's smiling face.

Jack touched his son's cheek and pushed up his chin so he could look Neal directly in the eye.

"I love you, father," Neal said, taking a step back and cutting the back of Jack's hand with the poisoned ceremonial blade, which he had hidden in the sleeve of his coat.

"What have you done?" Jack screamed, pushing Neal away, and the boy collided with the piano in the corner.

As the poison instantaneously took effect, Jack Mercy started to tremble and his face turned purple.

The werewolves swarmed into the house from the front and back door.

Dirk's gun rang out, and he killed two of the werewolves before they even cleared the entryway, but one of them slipped through and leapt upon Neal. The silver dagger still in his hand, he plunged it into the werewolf's heart. The creature fell to the side, turning back into a naked old man, Jack Mercy's servant named Clive.

All of the werewolves who helped Jack Mercy escape from prison waited outside, ready to massacre everyone in the house. Dirk used his last silver bullet as a werewolf started up the stairs to kill Sarah. Suddenly, the demonic power of the werewolves left them—Jack Mercy was dead, his face frozen in an expression of horror and agony, just like Michael's face when Neal had managed to wrestle the blade away from his twin; Neal had killed Michael and swapped winter coats to fool Jimmy.

With the master dead, all of the werewolves that Jack Mercy created, and all of the werewolves that those werewolves created, were divested of the Satanic energy that powered their supernatural transformations and unspeakable hunger. In a few moments, they transformed back to prisoners, prison guards, and followers of Jack Mercy, all naked and disoriented, ripped from the clutches of the demon's possession. Some ran away, some cheered with joy at being free of the curse, while some of Mercy's followers found handguns on the bodies of Magill's headless detectives and committed suicide with a bullet through the brain.

Upstairs, Maddie pulled the muzzle off Buddy's face.

"You're back, Buddy! You're back!"

Handcuffed on the floor, Buddy was disoriented and in a fog. In the corner of the room, Buddy could see a dark shadow twisting like a cyclone—Buzz, the werewolf demon. Before it evaporated with a shrill scream that resounded through Buddy's mind, the veil of the shadow fell away, and for just a second, Buddy could see the true beastly visage of the demon before it disappeared from Buddy's life forever.

Neal rushed into the room. "Buddy! Are you okay?"

"I'm alive, but I can't seem to move."

"That's because you're handcuffed, genius."

"What happened, Neal? The last thing I remember, you locked me up in the trunk."

"Well, just a couple of things happened after that. I'll tell you all about it, but the important thing is you're free. The curse is gone."

"Thank God," Buddy said. "I didn't hurt anybody, did I?"

"No, it turns out you were pretty pitiful at being a werewolf."

Dirk came into the room and unlocked the handcuffs and ankle cuffs, patting Buddy on the back.

"I saw the werewolf demon leave, Neal," Buddy said as he got up off the floor and sat on the bed. "I think it really is over."

Neal sat next to him on the bed. It sounded like hundreds of police car sirens arrived outside the house, even louder than the howls of the werewolves. "It is really over, Buddy," Neal said. "There's no doubt about that, and there's no way you're going to Detroit. You're staying here with me—there's even an empty bunk bed for you." Neal turned to his mom. "Is that okay, Mom?"

"Of course it is," Sarah said from the doorway, holding Dirk's hand.

LUMBER

T HE RAIN PERSISTED ALL NIGHT, turning to feathery clusters of snowflakes at dawn. Lumber slept beneath the discarded pickup shell by the alleyway, undisturbed by the relentless patter of raindrops on the rusty aluminum. The old dog only stirred when the garbage truck roared past and an errant snowball hit the shell. The neighborhood children passed along the alley on their way to school, the old dog emitting a terse growl before returning to sleep.

Lumber liked the smell of the earth beneath the shell where the grass didn't grow.

The man in the house didn't care about Lumber anymore. Sometimes the man remembered to set out food for Lumber in the garage, but sometimes he forgot. For as long as the dog could remember, Lumber squeezed through the flap on the side of the garage to eat his nuggets from the bowl inside, but Lumber never slept there. The garage belonged to the man, and Lumber knew it. Only the shell by the alley belonged to Lumber.

The boy named Toby lived in the house a long time ago when Lumber was a young dog. Lumber could run for hours back then, long before his hips ached and long before he had those terrible seizures. In the dim cavern of his aging canine mind, Lumber knew the importance of a dog belonging to a boy.

Many of the neighborhood children knew about Lumber, the large white shaggy dog that lived beneath the discarded pickup shell. If Lumber's hips didn't hurt too much, he would emerge from beneath the shell. Sometimes they patted Lumber's matted head when he came out to greet them. Lumber never chased the children away from the yard. Lumber didn't even chase the cats any longer. Once Lumber loved to chase all the cats and squirrels, but now the pain overtook him.

The children patted old Lumber's head, but they never tried to bring him home. Sometimes they pulled back the veil of white bangs from Lumber's eyes. No one would want old Lumber anymore. The great shaggy coat reeked of wet dog, and everyone could see he was filthy and uncared for. More than that, they could see he was crippled. Lumber never tried to follow the children, even though he bore no love for his master; he belonged beneath the pickup shell. Lumber's boy had left him there long ago.

The man never patted Lumber on the head. Mostly, the man remembered to leave food and water for old Lumber, but sometimes he forgot.

Once, the man's anger descended upon Lumber. The man cursed and beat Lumber. The dog learned that the garage belonged to the man and not to Lumber, never sleeping there again. However, the man's anger had withered in recent years. Once, the whole house reeked of fear. Lumber's boy Toby was afraid of the man. The boy's mother was afraid of him too.

In the dog's limited imagination, Toby was still a boy, and Lumber could see him in his mind's eye. By now the boy would be in his twenties, but Lumber's mind contained the timeless image of the boy, never to grow up. Lumber still expected that Toby might come back to him, put a collar around his neck again, take Lumber to the park, play catch, and chase him through the maze of the graveyard. Lumber could remember what life had been like.

Now Lumber rested on the cold earth beneath the aluminum pickup shell where the grass didn't grow. Lumber whimpered from the pain in his hip. The brief snowstorm melted and water from the trees overhead pattered the aluminum shell like a drum.

Lumber perceived a flash of red through the fog of his shaggy veil; a red ball rolled down the alley past the opening of the pickup shell. Lumber perked up, raised an eyebrow, but the pain in his hips was too great to leave the shell. Lumber wondered if it could be the same red ball, Toby's ball. The ball rolled past the opening again. Now Lumber's curiosity magnified as he lifted himself off the ground. The past few days Lumber had not left the shell, sleeping in his own filth, too much pain in his hips to get up, and Lumber didn't know how many days had passed since he visited the food bowl in the garage.

Lumber hobbled outside of the pickup shell, the ball waiting for Lumber downhill at the end of the alley. Now it continued to roll again, across the street and down the alley on the next block. It had to be the same ball. A sense of excitement, dormant within the dog for a long time, now rose up again. The old dog started after the ball, despite the crippling pain in his hips. Lumber wondered if Toby waited for Lumber around the corner by the gigantic tree. The boy used to play catch with Lumber in the vacant lot by the gigantic tree.

Lumber followed the ball across the street into the next block, past a row of houses and through a hole in a fence where Lumber saw the massive tree in the muddy trash-strewn vacant lot. Now it was winter, and all the branches reached up towards space like the bones of dead hands, but life still persisted in the massive tree, despite the grotesque, half-exposed base of the root system that appeared like a desiccated wound.

A patchwork of fragmented memories appeared in Lumber's mind, memories of when Lumber belonged to the boy. Lumber could almost hear Toby's voice calling to him, like a faint echo from the cavern of Lumber's memory, but the call seemed to issue from beneath the roots of the tree. Toby never went beneath the tree. Once they lost a ball in the dark crevices beneath, which were large enough for a boy to crawl inside. Beneath the roots, as thick as twisted human torsos, where the rats and raccoons made their nests, Toby was afraid go after the lost ball, pulling back on Lumber's collar when the dog tried to retrieve it.

Lumber heard the boy's voice calling to him from the shadow beneath the roots. The old dog approached, and he smelled something strange issuing from beneath, something Lumber had never known before, stronger and deeper than the smell of the cold sea. The ball was there.

He felt confused and sleepy, and he found himself slipping into the shadow beneath the roots, like rising to the surface of the water from a great depth. Lumber saw the red ball inside the shadow, bright and shining with saliva, as if he had just dropped it. He yearned for the boy. And like a dream, Lumber could see Toby's face beneath the roots, despite the hair covering Lumber's eyes, Toby's face suspended in the shadow, whispering for Lumber to be a good dog and come inside.

Lumber disappeared into the portal beneath the roots of the tree.

It closed behind him.

Lumber awoke, weightless, floating down a long smooth tunnel with veins of green light. A sharp spark of fear caused a moment of panic in the mind of the dog, and Lumber thrashed about in the zero gravity, unable to control his trajectory, but the fear dissipated as a great soothing influence overcame the dog, and Lumber only felt peace as he floated toward the center of The Black Orb.

The Black Orb watched the earth from its orbit, as large as a Gothic cathedral with many labyrinthine tunnels like veins in an eyeball. It wanted Lumber for a purpose.

Lumber released all resistance and peace overcame him as he floated, almost as if the old dog prepared to pass into the next world. If the Black Orb had not planted the hallucination of the red ball rolling past the pickup shell, old Lumber would have perished inside the shell, and now the old dog floated weightless through the innards of the mysterious Black Orb, floating deeper and deeper.

At the center of the Black Orb, Lumber emerged from the tunnel. Like a cavernous sanctuary, the center of the Black Orb contained a perfect shimmering globe of water that reflected the veins of green spectral energy embedded in the black clay-flesh. An unseen force, like an undertow beneath the waves, pulled Lumber toward the globe of water, which looked so refreshing to Lumber after going so long without any water from the man in the house. The globe of water now glowed with silver light, like moonlight, and Lumber perceived visions within, visions of his long lost boy Toby, visions of Toby and Lumber playing catch at the park by the sea. Lumber's snout penetrated the surface of the beautiful water. Lumber lapped up the water, and the water drew Lumber inside.

Lumber emerged from the portal beneath the tree, his shaggy, matted coat running with water. Lumber looked back and could see the rat-infested roots of the tree. The portal closed as soon as Lumber emerged. As Lumber walked through the hole in the fence, ostensibly to return to his shell, the dog became overwhelmed with a new knowledge of himself. During the strange baptism inside the luminous water, the Black Orb had placed something in Lumber's mind, a ghostly life-form that merged itself with Lumber's consciousness, expanding the depth of the dog's understanding, increasing his capacity for awareness.

Inside the water, the Black Orb delivered a life into Lumber's mind: a spectral phantasm. As Lumber stood beneath the tree on the winter morning, the spectral phantasm wrote itself into Lumber's nervous system and the dog's identity. The spectral phantasm became Lumber, and it made Lumber something more than just a white dog.

A few steps past the fence, Lumber noticed that the pain in his hips had vanished. Lumber took a deep breath and felt a thrilling exhilaration like nothing the old dog had ever experienced before. Following the surge of this feeling, Lumber bounded home, and the old dog felt great joy at the crisp freshness of the morning air. Lumber could smell the sea. Lumber could feel the shaggy masses of his matted coat bouncing up and down all around him.

Lumber found himself at the abandoned pickup truck shell next to the alley, seeing the aluminum shell for the first time, even though the dog had lived in the shell for years. Filthy with moss and mud, the rusted aluminum pickup shell now looked nothing like a home. From within the shell came a horrible smell of death.

Lumber jumped away from the pickup shell in horror. It wasn't a dog house; it was a grave. Lumber would never sleep there again.

Lumber had been close to death, and now, after the strange dream of the long black tunnels veined with green light, the entire world was transformed. It seemed as if the shaggy veil had been cut away from Lumber's eyes, but this wasn't true. Lumber's shaggy bangs still blurred his vision, but now Lumber could see in a different way; he could pierce through the shaggy veil.

Lumber felt something stir, something alien, but somehow familiar from the distant past of Lumber's life. Long ago, Toby and his mother had taken Lumber to the horrible place with the silver table where they hurt Lumber, where they had taken away Lumber's sex. And now, Lumber felt an agonizing and wonderful awakening of his sex, as if Lumber had never been lifted upon the silver table. Somehow Lumber's sex had returned, a miraculous regeneration, the neutering reversed.

Lumber thought about his boy from so long ago. He had just seen Toby beneath the roots, but that was impossible. Lumber understood now. Of course Toby would be a man by now. He could be anywhere, but he couldn't be beneath the roots of the tree. Lumber could truly perceive the difference between dreams and reality, but it seemed as if everything might be a dream. Was there really a boy who lived in the house long ago, a boy that played catch with Lumber and let Lumber sleep in his bed, long before the horrible confinement of the pickup truck shell? Yes, he knew a boy named Toby once lived there, and somehow the man had driven the woman and the boy away, and Lumber had to spend all of his days alone in the pickup shell.

It was the man's fault.

Lumber could see the man for the first time, the man who put the brown nuggets in Lumber's bowl, but he was also the man who forgot. He left Lumber's water bowl dry.

Lumber remembered the delicious ball of water at the center of the Black Orb. The thirst surfaced in Lumber, a new thirst. The taste of dog food and the water in the bowl didn't sound good to Lumber anymore. Lumber became aware of something else beneath the revival of his sex, something aching beneath the surface. Lumber needed something, but he didn't know what.

The man in the house was not nice to Lumber.

This fact resounded through the dog's mind, no longer just the mind of a dog. The spectral phantasm had now fused with Lumber's mammalian brain, hardwired itself into the nervous system of the dog, and the spectral eye of the phantasm could see beyond the blizzard of white shaggy bangs; it could see that the man was not nice to Lumber.

Lumber went to the plastic flap at the side of the garage. Strange, but Lumber could barely fit through the dog-door. Yes, Lumber felt larger. The shaggy dog could always pass through the dog door, but now Lumber had to worm through, scraping the matted clumps of his coat against the edges.

No, the man was not nice to Lumber. Lumber saw the thing that the man loved: the motorcycle, which sat in the middle of the garage like an altar, surrounded by the numerous tools to care for it. And it shined; its black surface shined, and

Lumber remembered the shiny clay-flesh of the Black Orb where Lumber floated, and he remembered the old life that now seemed so far away.

Lumber looked at the motorcycle and the tools, looked at the empty bowl of food and the empty bowl of water; the man was not nice to Lumber.

The man entered the garage. Lumber stood between the man and his precious motorcycle, and Lumber understood for the first time that the man loved the motorcycle more than Lumber. The man held his morning coffee, annoyed to see Lumber in the garage. Lumber could sense the chasm of anger beneath the surface of the man. To Lumber, he looked so small now, and the anger inside him so small. Lumber remembered when the man's anger seemed like the wrath of a volcano, remembered when he wanted to please the man more than anything else. As Lumber remembered his fear of the man, a growl emanated from somewhere deep within the shaggy tangles, a new depth inside himself.

The man reared back as if to push Lumber out of the way, but something stopped him. He could see how large the dog had become, and the dog didn't cower. Something about Lumber's posture appeared almost defiant, almost threatening. The man looked at the massive frame of Lumber and felt a surprising twinge of fear. He stumbled over to the garage door opener on the wall as if he couldn't stand to be in a closed space with the dog. With the full light of the open garage door, the man could see something about the dog had changed, but it was undeniably Lumber. He was bigger, but not so much bigger that he didn't recognize his own dog. This had to be Lumber, but Lumber was old and crippled, and this dog looked so massive and powerful. It was impossible.

Lumber couldn't believe how he once feared this man, how the fear of this man had driven his boy away, his precious Toby. Lumber's memory sharpened. Lumber could hear the tirades of the past, and he could hear the cries of the woman and the boy. His mind's eye could now see his memories like they happened in present time. Lumber could remember the bruises. Lumber could remember everything.

Eyeing the dog, the man pushed the motorcycle into the driveway, started the engine, and rode away.

Lumber walked to the curb and breathed the morning air. With each deep breath, Lumber expanded and expanded until he thought he might actually rise to his feet like a person.

Lumber noticed a couple of children on their way to school. The neighborhood children always patted Lumber on the head. When these children saw the massive shaggy white dog in their path, they crossed to the other side of the street. Lumber could feel their fear. No one feared Lumber before. Lumber could feel that the man was afraid too, and Lumber knew that he liked it.

When the man returned home, it was in the late afternoon twilight. Winter darkness arrived early in the Pacific Northwest. The man pulled the motorcycle into the garage, noticing that Lumber's food and water bowls were smashed to pieces. Someone had been in the garage when he was away, he thought. Normally, he never worried about that sort of thing. Most of the people in the neighborhood left their front doors unlocked.

He saw the flyer. Someone had been in the garage and left an orange flyer on the door to the kitchen. He would have to see if they stole any of his tools. The flyer was rolled up lengthwise and placed between the doorknob and the doorframe where it partially unrolled and stuck in place. He wondered if the same kids who smashed Lumber's bowls placed the flyer in here. He unrolled the flyer and saw that it advertised a church. Someone else must've smashed the bowls, he thought. No one passing out flyers for a church would vandalize a garage.

The man hated churches. Every time he went to a church, the people always wanted to meddle in his affairs. Lots of nosy people go to churches. His ex-wife always wanted to make him and his son go to church. The man read the flyer. A new congregation had moved into the old church at the end of the street, about two blocks away, the one with all the new construction. That church had changed congregations more times than he could count. The man didn't care what the orange flyer said.

The man pulled the covers up over his shoulders; the winter night had violated his bedroom. He often had trouble sleeping in the early hours of the morning after a night of heavy drinking.

He could smell something in the house. He knew what it was: the smell of wet dog. The man didn't know how Lumber could possibly be inside the house.

Earlier night, Lumber entered the garage through the dog door, squeezing himself through. It seemed even smaller than before. Despite the total darkness of the garage and the thick hair over his eyes, Lumber could see everything perfectly: the motorcycle, the tools, the pieces of the bowls that Lumber had smashed.

Lumber felt confused, but driven forward by the hunger that burned inside him. Lumber stared at the doorknob. He knew he didn't want to scratch at the door or whine—that was the dog's way. Lumber didn't have to scratch or whine like a dog anymore. Lumber understood about the purpose of a doorknob now. After all of these years, he understood for the first time. Lumber lifted his paw and yearned to open the door.

The doorknob turned. Lumber stood inside. Lumber looked down at his paw. It didn't look like a paw anymore. It had become something else, something like a hand. In another moment, Lumber's paw was just a dog's paw again. Lumber licked the paw just to make sure. It didn't hurt at all.

The man never let Lumber inside the house anymore. Lumber had lived in the house once when Toby and the woman still lived there. The memories of Toby flashed in Lumber's mind as he walked through the familiar rooms.

Now that it was night, Lumber was hungrier than ever, and he had a growing intuition about where to find the sustenance he craved.

The spectral phantasm in Lumber's brain filled Lumber's consciousness with new instincts. The phantasm guided Lumber's paw when he opened the door, and now Lumber found himself standing outside the bedroom door where the man slept. Lumber wanted something inside. Lumber could smell something inside the bedroom; he could smell the man's fear.

The bedroom door swung open. Lumbered entered and stood by the nightstand, watching the snoring man sleep, unsure of what to do next. Almost an hour passed before the main stirred, pulling the covers up to his shoulders and then looking around the room in confusion.

From the red light of the electric clock, the man could see the massive white head of Lumber. The dog looked larger than ever, more frightening than ever in the red-tinged darkness, and it was just his stupid old Lumber who lived under the pickup shell in the back yard.

"Lumber, old boy, is that you?"

The man, shaking, reached up and turned on the bedside lamp.

"Lumber, what are you doing in here? How did you get inside?" And now a small surge of anger filled the man, having his sleep disturbed like this in the middle of the night. What had gotten into that dog? Now with the lamp on, he didn't seem quite so big; he did seem different, but not a monster. Lumber didn't cower at the sound of his voice anymore; Lumber didn't pant. The dog just looked at him. Why was that stupid old dog looking at him?

The man reached over and lifted the dog's bangs.

"Oh my god!" He pulled his hand back like he thought Lumber would bite it off. Beneath the white bangs he saw luminous silver eyes. Now he knew that somehow this wasn't Lumber at all.

The spectral phantasm guided Lumber's instinct. Lumber didn't hate the old man; Lumber could see he was weak and full of blood. It was the blood that Lumber craved. Once, the man's rages had filled Lumber with terror. Once, the man's violence had driven Lumber's boy away. He thought of all the days the man starved Lumber, all the days with an empty bowl in the garage.

There would be no more empty bowl days for Lumber.

A ghostly spectral tentacle from the phantasm reached out across the bedroom and caressed the man's frightened brain. Lumber wanted the man to be calm, and then he was calm. Lumber felt this new power within himself. The man's eyes grew wide, blank, and placid.

Lumber reached up and pulled back the covers. The paw was different again. Lumber marveled at it. Fingers from beneath the white matted hair; fingers with long black claws.

Lumber climbed up on the bed. He didn't know what to do next, but the instinct from the phantasm guided him, the phantasm having fused itself with Lumber's mind and nervous system, and it fueled the shapeshifting with alien spectral energy. Lumber and the phantasm were now one being, and Lumber had only begun to discover what the phantasm could do.

Lumber was so hungry.

At first, Lumber thought he wanted to bite the man, but he discovered that he wanted to do something else. He gazed upon the man's bare chest and neck until he saw what he wanted: the blue vein in the crook of the man's arm. Lumber licked, and the man did not move, still under the spell of the spectral tentacle from Lumber's brain. As natural as drinking water or taking a bite, Lumber's snout shapeshifted into something else: a special mouth perfect for sucking. Lumber fastened it to the crook of the man's elbow. Lumber discovered the special tooth to make the incision. The blood flowed.

Lumber's new mouth fit the crook of the elbow like a baby's at the nipple. Yes, this was what Lumber needed; this was what the phantasm needed. Lumber sucked and sucked; the eradication of the hunger felt too good to stop, and Lumber didn't stop.

Lumber didn't know he had drank too much until the spectral tentacle found nothing more to fasten to. The man's mind was gone, just an empty organ. The man was dead. Lumber's mouth dribbled blood and saliva on the man's chest as the dog stared into the blank eyes of his former master. As quick as a dog shakes off a wet coat, Lumber shook his head and his snout returned to normal. Lumber didn't hate the old man, but he wasn't sorry. Lumber was full, and it felt good to be full.

Lumber didn't want to stay too close to the house. He should have stopped sooner, but the man owed Lumber his blood; a master owes his dog food. This was the man who had driven away the woman and Lumber's boy Toby, so maybe the man owed Lumber his blood. Perhaps the man did deserve to die.

At dawn, Lumber sought refuge in the strip of forest that followed the creek throughout the city. Lumber walked on the trail next to the creek that led to the large forested park by the graveyard and the sea.

For several days, whenever Lumber heard people approaching, he ducked beneath a fallen log or hid in the ferns next to the embankment. When people did see Lumber, they would marvel at the massive shaggy dog. Sometimes, people would tentatively pat Lumber's head and say "good dog." When this happened, Lumber remembered Toby and all the times they played catch in the park by the sea. Lumber wanted to belong to a boy again. Lumber wanted to be a good dog.

Lumber walked past the old house with the man that Lumber killed. For many days nothing happened as the mail piled up and the newspapers formed a small mountain on the porch. One day, as Lumber passed the house, he could see that many strange people milled about inside.

Lumber knew that he had done something wrong. He shouldn't have taken so much blood, even if the man owed him.

Afraid that he would take too much again, Lumber chose not to feed, and the hunger inside him grew. He passed runners on the trail by the creek, or he watched the mothers with their baby carriages in the park, but he was afraid he would drink too much.

Lumber waited too long.

Lumber walked down the alley in a stupor of desperate hunger. He found himself standing next to the old filthy pickup truck shell where he used to live. He looked up at the dark house where his boy used to live, and Lumber thought about all the delicious life blood that the man gave him after so many years of kicking Lumber and forgetting to fill the bowls in the garage. Just at this moment of remembering the fulfilling taste of the man's blood, a little girl in a rain jacket walked up to Lumber. The starving dog didn't even hear her approach, so lost in the memory of feeding.

The little girl named Georgiana lived in the neighborhood. She always patted Lumber's head when she passed his shell on her way home from school. The little girl didn't think twice about walking up to the gigantic shaggy creature that was covered with matted lumps of filthy hair from sleeping in muddy holes in the park and along the creek.

"That's a good boy, Lumber," Georgiana said.

The hunger overwhelmed Lumber. His front legs became strong arms as he grabbed the girl and pulled her into the shell of the pickup truck. The girl screamed only once.

When Lumber finished, he knew he had really done something wrong this time. The dog crawled out of the old pickup shell where he used to sleep, and he looked back to see the yellow rain jacket of the girl peeking out from the shadow of the shell. Lumber's gigantic tongue licked at the remaining blood on his snout and in the matted hair. Lumber ran for the strip of forest by the creek, passing by the gigantic tree where Lumber had found the portal to the Black Orb. Now it was just a rat-infested hole. Lumber had waited too long, and he had fed too much.

Gordon Watt, the famous paranormal investigator, waited in the hallway outside Georgiana's hospital room.

Gordon frequently consulted psychics in his research. Through his numerous psychic contacts, it became clear that some kind of significant paranormal event had occurred. He heard from several different sources about visions of shaggy white hair. He didn't know what this meant.

Gordon's own hair had turned completely white over the past few years, even though he was only in his late forties. Sometimes he joked that the white hair was due to so many encounters with the world of the paranormal—just like the old wives' tale of a man's hair turning white from fright. Gordon was skinny enough, with his peculiar horn-rimmed glasses and his white hair slicked back to reveal a V-shaped widow's peak. This man hardly looked like a crusader against the forces of darkness.

When Gordon was finally admitted into the girl's hospital room, he introduced himself to Georgiana's mother. The little girl was doing very well, her mother told Gordon. The blood transfusions had been successful and there appeared to be no infection from the animal wound. In fact, little Georgiana was awake and drawing. She was drawing pictures of a gigantic white dog.

Kevin walked home through the late afternoon drizzle. He had stayed late after school for play practice, and now the forested trail grew dark as Kevin followed the creek on his way home, his heavy backpack filled with textbooks and the flute he played in the Junior High orchestra. Next year when he started high school, he hoped to play for their orchestra, and he knew that his father expected that he would.

Kevin had lived near the creek for his whole life, and he didn't think of any possible danger as walked along through the deepening shadows. He hadn't heard that the police and the humane society were searching for a dangerous animal that had wounded a small girl and roamed loose in the neighborhood surrounding the creek.

Kevin followed the trail around the bend in the creek where Lumber slept beneath the fallen log.

For the past few days, the people had come looking for Lumber. He knew he had done something wrong with the little girl, and the people came as a consequence. Twice people walked right up to the fallen long where Lumber slept, but somehow Lumber's will reached over and overwhelmed them before they could speak into their walkie-talkies. It seemed so simple and natural now, as simple as drinking water from the creek. Lumber reached out and a spectral tentacle from Lumber's brain connected with their brain, and they would get that look in their eyes, and they would lie down next to Lumber in the muddy nest beneath the fallen log. Now Lumber didn't wait too long before feeding, and Lumber was so careful.

During these feedings beneath the fallen log, Lumber discovered that he could lick the bloody spot after he finished feeding, and it would heal over like he had never hurt the person. The spectral energy that coursed through Lumber's nervous system could heal the bloody wound just like it gave Lumber's snout the power to shapeshift into a sucking mouth. And Lumber could create a black shadow in their mind so they wouldn't remember. These new powers seemed so obvious and easy, just like reaching out and opening a doorknob where before there had been an impenetrable boundary.

Lumber could smell the boy coming down the trail, and in the twilight beneath the towering trees by the creek, Lumber spied on the boy's shadow, remembering when he belonged to a boy, when he followed the boy's every movement and played catch down by the cemetery next to the sea. Lumber knew it was better to live with a boy than to live under a log in the mud, always watching for danger.

Kevin stopped on the trail when he saw the enormous white creature emerge from the dark nest beneath the fallen log. For a moment, Kevin didn't know what he was looking at, the matted fur entangled with branches and stained with mud and blood, Lumber's eyes entirely concealed beneath the deep shaggy veil. Kevin didn't know how to read it. Was it threatening? Was it friendly? Then the white creature started panting, and the ominous threat dissipated. Kevin knew it was just a big shaggy dog.

"Are you a good dog?" Kevin asked and patted the head of the dog.

This was a question that Lumber recognized, and Lumber yearned to be a good dog again and to belong to a boy who cared for him like Toby did.

Kevin started down the trail again.

Lumber followed.

"I usually like to meet who I'm working for," said the new janitor to the pair of church elders who offered him the job.

"We can assure you, Mr. Landing," one of the elders said, "the new pastor has reviewed your application thoroughly and believes that you are perfect for the job. Since his arrival, he has been very very busy."

"When am I going to meet him?"

"In a sense, you're working for the entire church community," the other elder said.

"Yeah, I know that too," Landing said, "but if the new pastor is my supervisor..."

"The new pastor is convinced that you are perfect for the job. We would like to take you on a tour."

During his sixty years, the janitor had worked many different jobs, but nothing that gave him the creeps like this new church janitor job, and he had always considered himself a good churchgoer. But the elders seemed nice enough as they took him on a tour of the church. The job might actually be a lot of work, Landing thought. First there was the old sanctuary with the towering stained glass windows and the meeting room downstairs. But in the new addition there were two floors of classrooms, offices, and bathrooms. Landing didn't think a church would need so many classrooms, but nobody asked him.

The church elders gave Landing a big ring of keys.

"This is very important, Mr. Landing," one of the elders said. "We are entrusting you with keys to all of the rooms in our church. You will see most of the keys are labeled for the various offices and classrooms and the closets that store the vacuum cleaner and the mop and bucket with all of the supplies for the bathrooms."

They stood on the ground floor in the new addition when the elders told him this. Landing noticed the door right behind the elders. "You have free reign of the entire place—access to the all of the sensitive materials in the offices and all of the rooms in both buildings. We are placing a great deal of trust in you, Landing. You can go absolutely anywhere except through this door. This is the key here. We are leaving it on the ring in case of an emergency, but I want to stress that under no circumstances are you to use this key."

Landing had a puzzled look on his face.

"I know it may seem strange," Landing, "but I can assure you this is only due to the insurance company. Downstairs in the storage area we keep some very sensitive records."

"Yes, personal records," the other elder said. "And the insurance company makes us restrict the access. Of course we want the key on the ring in case of emergencies. But we want to make it clear that you are not to go into this storage room for any reason."

Landing had cleaned the church at night for an entire week before he finally unlocked the door to the forbidden storage room. It had filled his thoughts perpetually since he began working for the church. Every toilet he cleaned, every patch of carpet he vacuumed—his thoughts were filled with the forbidden door. It was silly, really. Obviously, he was an employee of the church, so the insurance company couldn't really have a problem with him going down into the basement. After all, like the elders said, what if there really was an emergency? A fire or something. They had given him the key. Who else would do something about it but him? Of course he needs to go down and see the storage room if he is to be entrusted with it. Didn't they entrust the entire building to him?

As soon as Landing opened the forbidden door, he smelled something strange emanating from the basement below—not foul or rotten, not even stale, but strange. Something sweet. And something fishy beneath the sweetness, a smell like the sea. Landing expected to find a light switch inside the stairwell going down to the storage room, but he felt only smooth drywall, beneath him the unfinished wooden stairs descending below with many muddy footprints on the stairs. See, he thought—they clearly need him to tidy up down here.

This would be a good time to lock the door and walk away. There were no lights down there. It was night, and he would probably lose his job if they knew he trespassed against their wishes. But now the door was open. He had already crossed the line. Why not find out what was really down there. They would never know. The church didn't have a security system. How would they ever know that he had been down there.

Landing went to the storage closet and got the flashlight.

He started down the stairs into the storage room, knowing all along this was a stupid plan—he really needed this job, but the threshold had been crossed. As soon as his feet touched the earthen floor at the bottom of the stairs, he was surprised by the massive size of the basement room.

This was the thought that flashed through his mind before he noticed the line of people standing along the wall of the room. He quickly looked behind him and saw the stairwell already filled with men of the church to block his retreat. In the black basement room, the congregation launched into a hymn at the top of their voices. The sound of all those voices suddenly singing in unison knocked Landing to the floor in surprise and terror.

What were they all doing down there in the darkness—waiting for him?

He shone the flashlight around the room at all the faces of the people—young, old, even children singing in the darkness, all of them singing merrily.

Landing saw the pit.

The gigantic shaggy dog followed Kevin all the way home.

Kevin lived in one of the large two story houses that backed up to the forested trail running along the creek. A short chain link fence marked the boundary of Kevin's backyard. Kevin opened the latch on the gate and entered the yard, Lumber being just one step behind him, stopped by the gate, watching as Kevin crossed the yard and climbed the steps to the deck. The boy opened the back door with a key around his neck on a shoestring.

Lumber marveled at the beautiful back yard. This was the perfect yard for him. In his mind, Lumber could see himself playing catch with the young boy here in the yard. They could walk together on the trail. They could walk to the park by the sea. Lumber could see it, wondering if the boy would place a collar around his neck. The boy would throw the ball, and Lumber could hear the jangling dog tags as he chased the ball and brought it back. Over and over again. Lumber continued the sweet daydream, knowing the boy would love him and make Lumber his very own dog like Toby did once before. At night, Lumber could sleep at the foot of the boy's bed and protect him. Lumber knew he could be a good dog again.

Kevin passed by his bedroom window, which faced the back yard and the creek, as he tossed his backpack on the floor and changed his shirt. About to close the blinds, he saw the white shaggy fur of the filthy stray dog at the back gate. Kevin wondered if the dog was hungry. It wasn't the first time Kevin had heard of stray dogs living by the creek. Kevin closed the blinds.

Kevin's parents, Dr. Mortensen and his wife Harriet, who went by the nickname Harrie, were putting dinner on the table when Kevin came downstairs and noticed an orange flyer with the newspaper on the kitchen counter. The flyer advertised the new community congregation that occupied the historic church building overlooking the sea. Kevin set it aside and noticed another flyer: a flyer about the white dog.

Dr. Mortensen, Kevin's father, wanted Kevin to tell him everything he remembered about the white dog.

"It was hiding under the fallen log in the bend of the trail," Kevin explained. They had lived in the house for years and Dr. Mortensen was familiar with the trail.

"Did the dog growl at you or seem rabid in any way?" Dr. Mortensen asked.

Kevin didn't know what rabid meant.

"You know—foaming at the mouth," Harrie said.

"It seemed like a nice dog. It was just really dirty, and it was gigantic—a big smelly dog."

"It seems ridiculous that they can't find such a large dog," Harrie said.

"You should see it, dad. It's probably the largest dog I've ever seen, and it's completely covered with mud."

"Well thank God it didn't attack you like it attacked that little girl in the neighborhood."

"Until they catch that thing, I want you walking home through the neighborhood. It's obviously hiding in the woods by the creek," Harrie said.

Dr. Mortensen didn't waste any more time. He called the number on the flyer and reported everything that Kevin said.

Kevin's bedroom floor was covered with tangled jeans, socks, underwear, and sheet music for the orchestra. Underneath a sweatshirt, he found his geometry textbook that he searched for everywhere because he needed to finish his homework. It was already 9:30 and he knew his dad would check on him soon. Kevin turned off the computer, which sat on the desk by the window. He opened the geometry book, took one look at the problems, and closed the book again, instead grabbing one of the comic books from a pile on the desk. After turning off the desk lamp, Kevin climbed to the top bunk and crawled under the covers to read his comic book with a flashlight.

Dr. Mortensen entered the bedroom a few minutes later, finding Kevin asleep with the flashlight sitting on the opened comic book next to him. His son was fifteen-years-old and still reading comic books. Dr. Mortensen didn't exactly approve. Quietly, he removed the comic book and flashlight and placed them on the desk, stepping on the boy's dirty clothes and books. He shook his head at the deplorable state of the room. As he set down the comic book and the flashlight, for some reason he decided to check the latch on the boy's window, even though the bedroom was on the second floor with no way for anyone to climb up.

Gordon Watt settled his Recreational Vehicle in a park at the edge of town, also renting a car so he could pursue leads in the vicinity. At the table in the RV he spread out all of the information he had on the case and studied the information. Night had closed in and it started to rain. The private investigator, Nettington, supplied Gordon with police files concerning the man who had been mysteriously exsanguinated, the owner of the dog named Lumber. Gordon had some photographs of the pickup truck shell where they had found the wounded girl. The team was working closely with the humane society and the local police. In a case like this, the agencies were willing to accept all of the help they could get. Clearly, the dog needed to be captured—if it was a dog at all.

Gordon knew that something big happened in the seaside town. The psychics working with Gordon's organization kept receiving conflicting visions about white shaggy fur and teeth. But also something else, something from the sea. Gordon knew about the spectral phantasms, and the psychics claimed that some of them fed on the blood of the living in order to survive, but Gordon had never heard of a psychic phantasm in a dog.

Kevin awoke a few hours after his father visited the bedroom. In the nightmare, the boy walked along by the creek, something following him beneath the surface of the murky water—like the opposite of a shadow—a gigantic white shadow, growing and growing. Kevin tried to open the latch on the gate when he heard a tremendous splashing behind him, something emerging; he woke up. He heard the scratching at the window. Kevin knew none of the tree branches came near the window, and the window was too high up for anyone to reach. Instead of scared, Kevin felt a strange curiosity to know the origin of the scratching.

Kevin jumped out of the top bunk and turned on the desk lamp. Opening the blinds, first he saw his own reflection in the window, but beyond that—a pair of luminous silver eyes.

The next morning Kevin felt sick to his stomach, his head hurting and his limbs weak, and that terrible wet dog smell filling his room. He didn't remember getting up in the middle of the night; he didn't notice the screen to his window had been stashed behind the desk, and he didn't notice the muddy smudge on his geometry notebook resembled the print of a dog.

Kevin opened the blinds and pulled up the window slightly to let in a little fresh air, flashing back to the silver eyes disembodied in the darkness, except it seemed to be just a dream. He had dreamt about that gigantic shaggy dog too—it licked peanut butter off of his neck, and Kevin remembered the dog's wet clammy chin on his chest and a strong hand holding him down. For a moment, it occurred to Kevin to tell his father about the dream, but he felt embarrassed somehow, as if too personal to share.

There was a respite in the rainy weather, so Kevin and his father decided to take advantage of the nice Saturday afternoon to play catch in the backyard. Kevin always joined the baseball team in the spring, and Dr. Mortensen played catch with his son as often as possible so Kevin's skills didn't diminish over the long rainy winters. Dr. Mortensen still had his baseball glove from when he played baseball in college, and Kevin's baseball glove had been a new gift from his father during the most recent baseball season.

Kevin stood by the back fence while Dr. Mortensen stood next to the deck. Dr. Mortensen threw the ball hard, aiming right for Kevin's chest. The boy didn't mind the brief stinging sensation when he caught a fast throw. He tried to match the force of his father's throw, but he tended to go too high, and

Dr. Mortensen would raise his long arm into the sky to keep the baseball from crashing into the porch.

Dr. Mortensen gave his son some pointers on how to adjust his follow-through when Harrie peeked her head outside the screen door.

"There's a call for you from the office," she said.

Dr. Mortensen threw the ball once more, and this time it bounced off the end of Kevin's glove and hit a tree trunk on the other side of the fence, landing somewhere in the bushes on the embankment.

"I'll be right back, son," Dr. Mortensen said.

"Okay. I'll go find the ball."

Dr. Mortensen ran up the steps to the deck and stepped inside to take the call from his psychiatry practice.

Kevin unlatched the gate to go search for the ball in the bushes.

Lumber waited there with the baseball in his mouth, waited to play catch with his new boy.

The white dog was even larger than Kevin remembered, the boy cringing at the sour smell of wet dog; Lumber had been wet for weeks, the dog's thick shaggy coat completely matted, the underside of the dog dark with wet mud. Brown blood stains covered the snout and the chest of the dog, twigs and fern leaves sticking out of his coat, his eyes hidden behind a thick wall of hair. Kevin backed up and latched the gate behind him, running up the deck and calling to his dad.

Kevin looked over the depiction of the dog on the flyer while Dr. Mortensen called the telephone number. The dog had run off again. It must have been the most difficult dog to draw, the face just a big blurry mass of white hair with a black nose, Kevin thought to himself, impossible to see the eyes or the ears; the whole head was unreadable.

This time, Dr. Mortensen's call was forwarded to Nettington, Gordon Watt's private detective. While Dr. Mortensen waited for the call to go through, he stepped out on the deck and remembered that he had set his baseball glove on the grass when he went inside to take the call. Dr. Mortensen had reached down and almost touched the baseball glove before he saw it: a large pile of dog shit deposited directly on top of the baseball glove. But the gate had been latched.

This time Gordon Watt was ready. With the help of Nettington, Gordon mobilized his team of volunteers. They congregated in the park in fifteen minutes. Nettington had hired a man named Keegan who kept and trained bloodhounds. Keegan was there with four of his best bloodhounds; Keegan hated nothing more than a dog who hurt children, eager to capture this menace to their community.

Gordon supplied the volunteers with guns that fired tranquilizer darts, but Nettington and Keegan carried shotguns—just in case. Gordon decided not to carry a shotgun himself, but he kept close to Nettington who knew to aim for the brain, the location of the spectral phantasm. The volunteers assumed they hunted a feral, potentially rabid dog, only Gordon and Nettington suspecting it might be more than a dog.

They found Kevin's baseball on the trail. Keegan was thrilled. The bloodhounds got the scent of Lumber from the saliva and they tore down the trail in pursuit. Keegan kept the hounds on a lead until they passed through the residential area where Kevin lived. Once they entered the large forested arboretum, Keegan let the bloodhounds loose. Gordon and Nettington, eager to stay on top of the pursuit, attempted to keep up with them. Keegan, who had more trust in following the baying of the hounds, stayed farther back. He knew the bloodhounds would corner the dog.

The dogs left the trail, following the scent of Lumber deep into the forested park. Watt and Nettington had trouble making their way over the steep hills and the dense undergrowth.

Keegan knew that sound; the hunt was almost over.

Then they heard the horrible squeals of terror and pain.

Gordon and Nettington caught up with what remained of the dogs at the edge of a large stagnant pool fed by runoff from the hill. The dogs bodies, torn to pieces, lay all around the edge of the pool.

"Oh my god," Gordon whispered. "What is this thing?"

Nettington subtly gestured back toward the pool, readying the shotgun.

The top of a slick white head poked up out of the pool.

Nettington and Gordon cried out in surprise as Lumber erupted from beneath the surface. In one leap Lumber landed on the muddy bank, Nettington falling back into the bushes and Gordon jumping for cover behind a fallen log. The creature had shapeshifted into something that barely resembled a dog. Covered with green slime from the stagnant pool and muddy water streaming off his white coat, Lumber reared up on his hind legs like a grizzly bear, his paws transformed into a set of six-inch black claws that had torn the bloodhounds to pieces. Lumber's mouth shifted from the snout of a dog into the mouth of a monstrous ape with elongated fangs as it emitted an unnatural roar. Lumber's luminous silver eyes met Gordon's before the creature turned and ran deeper into the forest.

Gordon paid Keegan in cash for the lost animals as the man wept bitterly, putting in more than a little extra to keep Keegan quiet about what really happened in the forest. It could have been much worse; those dogs slashed to pieces could have been members of the search party.

Kevin was at school when Dr. Mortensen noticed the missing screen from Kevin's window. He had been raking leaves in the yard when he happened to look up. Dr. Mortensen always took Mondays off from his practice to do work around the house.

Upstairs, he found it right away behind Kevin's desk. Dr. Mortensen couldn't figure out what this meant. Did Kevin sneak out of the house at night? No, the window was too high off the ground with no footholds to climb. Dr. Mortensen saw the streaks of mud on the windowsill, which matched the mud on the desk and on the carpeting beneath Kevin's dirty clothes. The room was a pigsty.

Dr. Mortensen got the extension ladder from the garage and climbed up to replace the screen from the outside. The frame had been twisted out of shape; Dr. Mortensen would have a few words for his son about the cost of window screens. While climbing, Dr. Mortensen noticed more of the muddy streaks on the side of the house. Dr. Mortensen saw the deep gashes in the wood—at least three or four of them, almost like someone had struck the side of the house with an ax. When did this happen?

Dr. Mortensen decided to go on his run to process what happened to the side of the house, perhaps Kevin could tell him something when the boy returned from school. His striped socks pulled up to his knees, Dr. Mortensen ran along by the creek and entered the network of trails that crisscrossed through the arboretum.

He saw the massive shaggy dog approaching him from the other direction. So they were wrong after all. The dog didn't really escape into the mountains. Dr. Mortensen stopped, considered turning around, but it wouldn't make any sense to run away from the animal if it pursued him. Besides, the dog didn't appear to be in a threatening posture or approach—he knew the body language of dogs. In fact, the dog appeared to be prancing down the trail.

Dr. Mortensen was relieved when the dog simply trotted past him without pausing. He wished he had his cell phone on him so he could call that number again. Dr. Mortensen resumed his normal pace and rounded a corner as the trail zigzagged through the dense forest of the park.

Dr. Mortensen heard a crash in the bushes to his left, almost as if a tree had fallen. He turned toward the source of the noise when he saw a flash of white hair, and Lumber emerged from the dense bushes, the powerful clawed hands grabbing Dr. Mortensen and pulling him down into the depth of the undergrowth.

Lumber ran through the forest, ran as fast as he could to escape what he had done to the man, ran as fast as he could with a full stomach.

Lumber's jealousy, a dark shadow of the dog that once lived beneath the pickup shell, rose up and consumed Lumber. The man stood in the way of Lumber becoming Kevin's dog—just like the man in the other house had driven Toby away. Lumber hated the man; Dr. Mortensen got to play catch with Kevin, and when Lumber tried to play catch with Kevin, the boy ran inside with fear and revulsion. But now the man would never play catch with Kevin again; he would never get in the way again.

Lumber was desperate now. He had been visiting Kevin's bedroom in the night, but Lumber didn't want to sneak into the house. Lumber wanted his own doggy door; he wanted to belong to the boy and—most importantly—to be a good dog, a loyal dog. Lumber wanted it all: he wanted a collar; he wanted to play catch, to go on long walks with his boy, to snuggle all night next to him in the bed.

Lumber smelled something strange and familiar, the smell of the alien clay flesh of the Black Orb. Lumber turned a corner and there stood the open portal in the middle of the trail. Lumber felt the overwhelming pull of home emanating from the portal, as if Lumber knew his mother waited on the other side.

Lumber was drawn into the portal.

He awoke in the weightlessness of the Black Orb's labyrinthine tunnels, no sense of how long he had floated there. The great consciousness of the Black Orb interfaced with the spectral phantasm wired into Lumber's brain, and Lumber felt great joy and comfort to be back inside.

In the center of the Orb, floating before the luminous ball of water, Lumber felt ashamed, ashamed he had drank too much from the old man and the little girl, ashamed he had torn out Dr. Mortensen's throat in anger and jealousy; Lumber was a bad dog.

The Black Orb soothed Lumber's rising anxiety as the dog drank from the water. The Black Orb didn't judge Lumber; the Black Orb had a purpose for Lumber.

As the matted veil of fur rose up in the weightlessness, allowing Lumber to clearly see the pictures in the water, the Black Orb showed Lumber images of Kevin walking him to the park by the sea. Lumber noticed the leash and the collar. Lumber wanted that again. The Orb showed the boy brushing out all the tangles from Lumber's thick white coat. The Orb showed Lumber sleeping next to the Kevin in the bed, the dog content after drinking just enough of the boy's blood.

Lumber felt overwhelming love for the boy.

In the Black Orb's images, Lumber's coat was fluffy and glowing white, not the tangled muddy ropes with crusted blood.

How would Lumber ever make the boy love him?

Just as the question formed in Lumber's mind, an image of a beautiful woman appeared in the luminous ball of water. Lumber memorized her face, and the woman spoke a name: Abby.

Julie smoked a cigarette at the back door to the basement where she ran a dog grooming business with all of the best stainless steel bathtubs and top-rated professional equipment. Over the past five years, she had gained a wonderful reputation in the town, so she was always booked with clients. She only had time for a quick cigarette before getting back to work.

Lumber emerged from the bushes across the yard.

"Oh my goodness!" Julie blurted out, and she tossed her cigarette in the coffee can by the door.

From across the yard, Lumber recognized the woman from the vision in the Black Orb.

Julie couldn't believe the horrible state of the gigantic white dog. Immediately she knew he must be a stray. The long shaggy fur hung in filthy matted clumps all over the dog's body, accompanied by a terrible odor because Lumber had been wet for weeks. With the scum of the pond and the huge amount of blood from Dr. Mortensen (Lumber couldn't drink it all—it came out so fast), Lumber hardly looked like a white dog at all. Julie noticed the blood and wondered if Lumber had wounds beneath the coat.

Despite all of the dogs waiting for their baths, Julie brought Lumber immediately inside. At first, Julie placed Lumber in a pen off to the side of the room, but the smell of Lumber became too much to bear; she decided to groom Lumber right away.

She raised Lumber up on the grooming table and looked for wounds beneath the coat, but fortunately found nothing.

"Have you been fighting?" she asked Lumber. "Are you a good dog?"

Lumber perked up at this question.

"You sure are a big boy," she said, pulling back the veil over Lumber's eyes. When she saw the luminous silver eyes, she whispered, "Oh you are a special dog. You're very special indeed. We'll just make sure to leave enough of your bangs so not everyone can see."

No point trying to clean all of the deep mats and tangles in Lumber's coat, so first she used the shears. All of the smelly matted hair came away from Lumber's skin. To Lumber it felt wonderful, like finally getting out of wet clothes.

Once Julie sheared away all of the matted hair, the dog looked like a different animal altogether. Julie expected Lumber to be skin and bones underneath the coat, but surprised to find an incredibly muscular frame.

"You must be a fast runner," she said.

Julie pulled back the bangs again for a second look at Lumber's silver eyes. Lumber reached out to her mind and hypnotized her, able to quickly drink some of her blood right there on the grooming table. She didn't even need to sit down; Lumber was getting better at this. The spectral energy sealed the little wound, and Julie woke up again with a puzzled smile.

Next, she brought Lumber into the large silver bathtub. As she scrubbed the close-cropped white coat, she discovered that she felt better and more energetic than she had in weeks. She teased Lumber while she scrubbed his back. "Are you a good dog?" she repeated.

And Lumber barked in reply.

As Lumber gained more skill in feeding without leaving a trace, he also discovered that he could give something back. He didn't have to just take the life force of the blood; he could give some of his spectral energy to the person while he fed. Lumber wanted to be good, and Lumber was in ecstasy as Julie scrubbed all over his body in the warm soapy water after being so cold and uncomfortable for so many weeks.

When Julie finished, Lumber truly looked like a different dog. Instead of an undefined mass of muddy, shaggy fur, all bouncing like foaming waves of the surf, Lumber was neatly trimmed, brilliantly clean with white fur cut close enough to reveal the lean, muscular shape of the dog beneath.

"Now you're all nice and clean," she said to Lumber. "You're as white as the Abominable Snowman—that's what I'll name you: Abby, short for the Abominable Snowman."

Over the next few weeks, Lumber felt very much at home in Julie's house, slipping easily into Julie's bedroom at night, even managing to eat enough of the horrible dried meat nuggets that Julie fed to Lumber in a bowl. Lumber hated dog food, but he ate enough for show. Julie kept Lumber warm and clean and fed, but she never had time to play, always tending to the normal dogs that came in day after day. Lumber used to be one of those strange, stupid creatures.

One day Julie had a special surprised for Lumber. She brought home a dog collar. Lumber knew this meant that he belonged to someone again, and now he hoped he could come and go in the world without being hunted by those men and their hounds. Julie brought Lumber to a vet, and the vet gave Lumber some shots, although Lumber was immune to all diseases, and now everyone called Lumber by the name Abby. The vet declared that Abby was a healthy dog, and with the clean, short white coat, Abby looked nothing like the dangerous beast called Lumber.

Lumber officially became Abby; that's what the dog tags said.

It was almost time for summer vacation. Kevin decided not to go out for baseball this year, and he told everyone, including his mother and his new psychologist Dr. Karen, that it had nothing to do with his dad's death, although clearly Kevin was depressed, and Dr. Karen recommended that Kevin start taking some antidepressant medication.

Four months passed before they found any trace of Dr. Mortensen. Harrie and Kevin were in financial trouble after the disappearance, the insurance company unwilling to pay out the life insurance policy without Dr. Mortensen's body, but Kevin knew his father was dead.

Of course, the police asked lots of questions about extramarital affairs, but all of Dr. Mortensen's belongings remained in the house, including his wallet. He didn't run away with some mistress; he just vanished.

In early June, a jogger discovered a jaw bone in the forested park, and the dentist was able to positively confirm the identity of Dr. Mortensen with dental X-rays, so Harrie and Kevin got to bury a jaw bone in the cemetery. It was all the closure they had.

Gordon Watt visited the jaw bone in the cemetery.

Once they buried the jaw bone, Harrie and Kevin were finally able to collect the life insurance money and save the house from foreclosure.

Kevin would be turning sixteen very soon, and he pleaded with his mother to buy him a car with the insurance money, but Harrie wasn't ready for her son to be driving; she declared that Kevin could not get a driver's license until he turned eighteen. It was the subject of many fights, but Harrie stood her ground. She knew she had to put up a strong front or else Kevin would walk all over her. No driver's license, and no car.

Kevin went to visit his dad's grave at the cemetery, which overlooked the sea, the cemetery only a few blocks from the church that Harrie started attending. She wanted Kevin to go too, but he refused—his way of getting back at her for not letting him get his driver's license.

Kevin stood at the grave, vacantly staring at the name and the dates printed on the headstone. He put his hands in his windbreaker jacket, thinking about that jawbone. What happened to him in the arboretum that day? Why would someone murder his dad? A deranged patient, perhaps? Or did he fall and break his neck on the trail? Maybe scavengers pulled his body apart. He wished they had found the rest of his body.

Kevin thought about the jaw bone and his mother going to that new church on the hill, and he thought about Dr. Karen and the antidepressant pills, and he thought about not going out for baseball, and he thought about the stupid insurance money and how he wanted his mom to let him get a car. Tears of anger spilled down his face, so furious about the driver's license. He dropped to his knees and allowed himself to gush big painful sobs until he heard a funny jingling noise and felt a big wet tongue on his cheek. Kevin fell to the side and saw a big white face staring into his face.

"Abby! Stop it!" called a woman's voice.

Kevin got back up to his feet; the white dog jumped up on him, trying to lick the tears off the boy's cheeks.

"I'm really sorry about that," Julie said, grabbing Abby's collar. It was one of the rare days when Julie wasn't grooming dogs, so she took Abby for a walk through the cemetery. "We were playing catch and he just got away from me... I'm really sorry." Julie snapped the leash on the collar.

"It's okay, really," Kevin said, and it was completely obvious that he had been crying.

Julie, who had never been able to resist helping stray dogs or crying kids, asked Kevin, "Hey, are you okay? Is that your dad?"

"Yeah," Kevin said, embarrassed, wiping his eyes. "It's just his jawbone."

"What?"

"They only found his jawbone. I know it's completely..." and Kevin stopped.

"Horrible," Julie finished the sentence.

They stood there for a moment in awkward silence. Julie thought of something. "Do you want to play catch with Abby... it's a stupid thing to say, I know, but it's a beautiful day." She tossed the saliva-drenched tennis ball to Kevin, who caught it and laughed, despite his tears.

"That's disgusting," he said. And he threw the ball. And Abby brought it back to him, running with joy over the graves.

Julie convinced Kevin—and eventually Kevin's mother—that Abby was the perfect dog for them, totally thrilled for Kevin to adopt Abby. None of them thought for a moment that this might be the stray dog that terrorized the neighborhood for weeks. Kevin purchased a new dog tag with the Mortensen's address and phone, and he found a new collar, since the old collar belonged to Julie, and she helped Kevin find the right brushes he would need to care for the dog's thick white coat.

Lumber could have wept with joy on the day that Kevin placed the new dog collar around his neck; his dream of belonging to a boy again had finally come true.

Since Kevin decided not to go out for baseball that summer, he had lots of time to play with Abby and take him for long walks. Kevin took Abby down to the park by the sea where the freezing cold waves crashed against the rocks; they played catch with a tennis ball. Abby would lie still while Kevin brushed out the dog's coat, which slowly grew longer and longer. At night, Abby fell asleep at the foot of the bed while Kevin read comic books, and in the morning Kevin had no recollection of the dog coming into the bed or the weird clawed hand that gripped Kevin's shoulder while Lumber fed.

Lumber's skills increased; he almost never left a drop of blood on the sheets. The few times he did, Kevin assumed he had a bloody nose in the night. Lumber's spectral phantasm willed the boy asleep the entire time. Everyone could see that the boy was much happier than before Lumber came to live with him—even the mother could see—so Lumber knew he wasn't doing anything wrong. Lumber knew that the boy needed him.

Gordon Watt decided to bring Marilyn Redding, Gordon's primary contact with the psychic world, for a visit to the seaside town. Most of the residents had forgotten about the strange stray dog that attacked a young girl under a pickup shell, but Gordon would never forget. He wanted to know if Marilyn might perceive some kind of psychic trail that could lead him back to Lumber.

Gordon drove a few hours to pick up Marilyn from the airport. On the drive back to Gordon's RV, they talked about recent research into psychic phenomenon and the secret organization that funded Gordon's investigations. He noticed Marilyn growing tense and distracted as they approached the town. Gordon thought he could see her becoming visibly paler as the car reached the seaside town.

Back at the RV, Gordon put on some hot water for tea. He sat down at the kitchen table with his notes, maps, and research scattered all around in piles, and Marilyn sat across from him in a swiveling chair. Marilyn had lost all psychic traces of Lumber from her home on the East coast, so Gordon hoped that being closer to the geographical area would produce new leads about the creature.

However, as Marilyn attempted to hypnotize herself in the chair, something she normally had no difficulty with, she became even more pale; she began to pant with intense anxiety.

"What's wrong, Marilyn?" Gordon asked. "What do you see?"

"Gordon, I'm so sorry—I wish I could help, but you're going to have to take me back to the airport. I'm not going to be able to see anything here."

"What do you mean? I was hoping to take you on a walk where the creature was hiding."

"No, Gordon... it's not the creature. It's something else. It's like the entire town is covered in a black fog. I can't see anything. Something is terribly wrong here, Gordon. I try to reach out and it feels like I'm drowning. There is something very powerful here. And it sees us. You're in terrible danger here, Gordon."

Slowly the blob built its church.

One by one, the faithful undertook their baptism. The blob pastor opened an orifice for them to climb inside, not to be digested like the offerings, the lambs, but to discover their rank in the order of the blob church. Only one or two of the parishioners could climb inside at one time. Inside the dark innards of the massive organism, the pastor learned the strengths and weaknesses of the parishioners' minds, and decided how they could best serve the pastor.

The blob contained many spectral phantasms inside, a phantasm for each of the numerous brain masses spread throughout its enormous body mass. It kept the pockets and veins of digestive acid separate from the brain masses and separate from the parishioners in its belly. The blob could multiply spectral phantasms; they divided like cells.

Each phantasm was born for a specific purpose within the blob's hive. In some of the parishioners, the blob implanted a breeding phantasm. Some of the phantasms gave their hosts the ability to shapeshift into an attack blob, their purpose to protect their master from outside dangers—and to gather protein. Once the master blob selected a phantasm for a parishioner, they were reborn again from a birth orifice with a new body.

Lumber lingered outside the door to Kevin's bedroom, listening to the boy weep into his pillow. This hadn't happened for a long time.

Lumber had grown to love Abby, the new happy dog that Lumber pretended to be, the dog that belonged to Kevin, the dog that played catch in the park and went on walks, not the shaggy beast that hid in ponds and attacked children. That dog was long gone.

Kevin hadn't closed the door all the way, so Lumber pushed it open with his snout. Inside he found Kevin sitting on the bed with his father's baseball glove in his lap. Lumber hated to see him crying, so he jumped up on the bed and licked Kevin's face until the boy laughed. "Cut it out, Abby."

That night Lumber buried the baseball glove deep in the forest.

It was time for Kevin to start high school. On the first day, he put on his new blue jeans and flannel shirt, collecting his new notebooks and pens inside the backpack his mom gave him. Lumber watched him getting ready, growing more morose and wishing that the summer would never end.

As Kevin walked down the forested trail toward the the high school, he felt another pang of frustration and anger about his mom not letting him get a driver's license until he turned eighteen, which was still over two years away. Most of his classmates would be driving to school, while he still had to walk along by the creek.

After Kevin's choir class, he lingered in the hallway where many of the upperclassmen in the choir had their lockers. Kevin didn't know if he expected anyone to initiate a conversation, or if he wanted to start one himself, but his shyness got the better of him and he turned away. It was silly to think he could make friends with upperclassmen, Kevin thought as he turned around too quickly and ran right into Roland, a large boy with thick hands and long curly hair.

"Oh, I'm really sorry," Kevin said and he helped Roland pick up the books that he dropped on the floor.

"Hey—you literally ran into me," Roland said.

They walked down the hallway together and Kevin heard that someone was playing the piano on the stage of the auditorium.

"Kevin, I wanted to ask you if you wanted to come to the club I belong to after school. We just talk about stuff and play games, you know. It's a totally new club this year, and so you would be like a charter member, so to speak."

It was true that Kevin wanted to find some new friends; he lost a bunch of baseball friends after quitting the team. "Where does it meet?" Kevin asked.

"I have a flyer," Roland said, pulling an orange flyer from one of his books. "It's called Students with Spiritual Aspirations, or the SSA. It meets just down the hall from here."

"Is it like a Jesus group?" Kevin asked.

"No, not really. Do you hear that piano playing?"

Careful not to barge in, Roland and Kevin entered through the backstage door. It was dark behind the stage, but when they parted the black curtain, they could see a boy at the piano, completely alone in the large auditorium.

At first Kevin thought the boy played some kind of jazz, but Kevin didn't recognize a jazz rhythm, and the music seemed too violent to be classical music. In fact, it didn't seem to be very musical at all, just a dynamic series of discordant notes building and crashing like waves on a beach. The boy at the piano wore an army fatigue jacket, and his hair was dark black.

Roland recognized the player and he rushed over to him, not caring if he interrupted the piano playing. "Holy shit, Andrew. I didn't know you could play piano like that."

Andrew stopped playing, a bit annoyed at being interrupted by Roland.

"Who wrote that?" Roland asked.

"I did," Andrew said.

Roland appeared to be almost embarrassed at this piece of information, as if the music were so strange it made the composer freakish. "Andrew, are you coming to the SSA today?" Roland asked.

Andrew didn't answer at first, instead he looked over his shoulder and saw Kevin standing back by the curtain. "Yeah, I think so."

Kevin knew that he would go to the group too. "Sorry to mess up your playing," Kevin said, not wanting to be associated with Roland's rude interruption.

Andrew smiled.

Kevin walked closer to the piano bench. "You don't have any sheet music."

"No. I don't have any sheet music."

"Are you a senior?" Kevin asked.

"No. I'm a sophomore—just like you."

"How did you know I'm a sophomore."

"I'm psychic."

Roland said, "You see Kevin, Andrew's coming to the group after school, and you should come too."

Kevin could see that Andrew's black hair was really hair dye, the bright blonde roots showing beneath. Kevin had never heard of a blonde person dying their hair black before.

"Do you guys want to come with me?" Andrew said. "I have a secret to show you."

Both of them were eager to go along.

On the opposite side of the stage, an emergency exit door opened to the outside where a screen of trees overlooked the soccer fields.

"This spot is totally secluded," Andrew explained. "It's the best place to smoke on campus."

Both Kevin and Roland were shocked.

Andrew pulled out a package of cigarettes and a lighter.

After Andrew lit his cigarette, he offered the package to Kevin and Roland. Both of them thought about it, but declined the offer.

In the locker room, Kevin took off his shirt and jeans for gym class; Andrew appeared from around the corner just as Kevin stood there in his underwear. Kevin felt embarrassed at his scrawny body, and he could smell cigarettes on Andrew as he walked up to Kevin.

"Can we share a locker?" Andrew asked. "I didn't bring a lock from home yet."

Kevin looked carefully at Andrew, thinking that Andrew might be trouble, mainly because of the smoking, but Kevin was astonished at the piano playing he heard, and for some reason he liked the thought of being associated with Andrew, if that was even possible. Kevin thought for a second that Andrew was looking at his body, and Kevin quickly put on his gym shorts and said, "Yeah, of course—you can share the locker."

The locker room filled up with students as time got closer to the bell.

Kevin could feel his cheeks flush as Andrew took off his clothes, and Kevin noticed that Andrew had a little tuft of hair on his sternum, which Kevin couldn't stop thinking about all through the gym class as the students played rounds of volleyball.

It was the end of the school day. Quietly Kevin and Andrew changed back into their normal clothes, and Kevin thought to ask Andrew if he wanted to go to the group that Roland told them about. Andrew said first, "Do you want to come over to my house after school?"

"What about Roland's group?"

"You can go to that, if you want to."

"Oh, I'll go with you then. I mean, yes, I do want to come over."

Andrew lived in a large apartment complex with his father. Before Andrew brought Kevin upstairs to the apartment, he showed Kevin the laundry room with several rows of washers and dryers, some storage cabinets for the residents, and a little recreation room, including a Ping-Pong table. Tucked in the corner, stood a small piano. They played Ping-Pong for a few minutes, although Kevin didn't have strong Ping-Pong skills, and Andrew kept taking advantage of this to slam the ball after Kevin's serve.

"Would you play some more piano?" Kevin asked. Andrew smiled.

The little piano in the laundry room was nothing like the grand piano in the high school auditorium, but it served as an adequate vessel for the bizarre rolls and crashes of Andrew's strange music.

Up in Andrew's bedroom, the two boys sat cross-legged on the floor, and Andrew put an ashtray on the floor between them. Kevin had movie stars on his bedroom walls at home, but Andrew had posters of people Kevin had never heard of—avant-garde piano players. Andrew threw his army jacket on the bed, but not before taking the cigarettes out of the pocket. He wore a white T-shirt, and Kevin couldn't help looking at Andrew's body, thinking about what he saw in the gym. Kevin looked at Andrew's bare feet and noticed he had a little bit of hair on his toes.

Andrew lit a cigarette and handed the pack to Kevin, as if this time it was expected that Kevin would partake. And Kevin did. Andrew didn't even ask if this was the first time Kevin smoked a cigarette, telling Kevin to breathe in deeply and laughing at Kevin's intense coughing. Andrew leaned over and rubbed Kevin's back.

Lumber had learned the secret of invisibility. He extended a spectral tentacle from his mind and he could will someone to not see him. Sometimes, Lumber could make three or four people not see him at once, but that required much more concentration.

Since Kevin started going to the high school every day, Lumber could hardly bear the long days alone, and Lumber waited for Kevin in the bushes outside of the school, following Kevin on the way home, but making himself invisible until they arrived back, Lumber not wanting Kevin to know that he snuck out of the house.

Lumber followed Kevin and Andrew from the school to Andrew's apartment. They went there almost every afternoon. Lumber had left his dog collar under the couch at the house so they wouldn't hear the jingling of the tags. Lumber climbed the tree with four clawed hands, and he could see inside Andrew's bedroom from his perch outside the window.

Lumber felt a rage of jealousy as Andrew leaned over the burning cigarettes in the ashtray and placed his hand on Kevin's neck, drawing him closer. Lumber let out a painful sob as he watched Andrew kiss Kevin on the lips. When the kiss was finished, Lumber saw the look in Kevin's eyes, the look of complete trust and wonder.

Here the two boys had only known each other for a couple of weeks, and already Kevin felt like he knew Andrew. After one kiss, Kevin knew he was in love, like only a teenager can.

Kevin got a headache from the cigarettes as they talked in Andrew's room until twilight arrived. Kevin wanted to know why Andrew dyed his hair and why he wore and army jacket and where he learned to play the piano.

Andrew told him that he hated having super blond hair, and he wore the jacket that his own dad had worn in the army, and Andrew had taught himself how to play the piano, and he didn't even know how to read sheet music. Andrew was almost 18; he had been held back at his previous school, which Kevin found to be wild and fascinating, to actually flunk two grades in school. It seemed unimaginable. They left before Andrew's father returned home from work.

Andrew walked Kevin to the head of the trail by the creek, and Andrew told Kevin that he was beautiful. He kissed Kevin again in the shadow of the trees.

Lumber watched from beneath the ferns, knowing he could kill this boy, throw his body in the creek, and still get home in time to put his collar back on before Kevin returned, but it would be close. Lumber had his killing claws out, but then Lumber saw that look in Kevin's eyes again, a look of complete surrender. Lumber wanted to rip out Andrew's throat for trying to steal Kevin from him, but Lumber also knew that he couldn't bear to see Kevin sad again after Lumber had already made Kevin so sad.

Kevin turned back twice to see Andrew walking away.

Kevin saw Abby running toward him on the trail. The white dog was very excited to see Kevin, and he jumped up on Kevin and licked his face.

"How did you get out, Abby? I'm glad to see you too, boy. I wasn't gone that long, was I? Where's your collar, Abby?" Kevin let Abby lick his face, and Kevin was so happy about what had happened with Andrew that his joy spilled over into seeing Abby.

Back at the house, Harrie was upset with Kevin for being so late for dinner. Of course, she was glad to hear that Kevin had made a new friend at school, but she wanted Kevin to try and remember to call home in the future. Harrie had no idea how Lumber got out.

"Mom, did you put Abby's collar back on?"

"No, Kevin. By the way, someone else called for you. Someone named Roland. Actually, he called twice."

Kevin's mind was full of Andrew and the way Andrew looked at him. And Andrew wasn't even exactly beautiful. He had crooked teeth and a funny shape to his nose, but Andrew exuded something Kevin had never encountered before.

When Roland called again after dinner, the boy sounded annoyed. "Hey Kevin. This is Roland. What happened? I thought you were coming to the SSA meeting."

"Oh. Something came up."

"Well, I guess that's cool. Can we count on you to come to next week's meeting? We really want to get all of our new members on board for the new year."

"I don't know, Roland. I'll think about it. I've gotta go. See you in choir tomorrow."

Roland hung up the phone. He was in the meeting room on the second floor above the pit of the pastor. Ten students from Kevin's school, all members of the SSA, eagerly waited to hear what Kevin said, all of them disappointed with Kevin.

"What am I going to do?" Roland asked, sounding a little hysterical. "The pastor wants new members for the SSA. Everyone managed to bring a new person today except for me."

A girl named Jackie tried to calm Roland down. "The pastor understands, Roland. Not everyone who comes to an SSA meeting even ends up becoming a member anyway. The pastor understands."

"But the pastor's patience only holds out for so long."

"You'll get somebody, Roland," Jackie assured him.

"And watch what you say about the pastor," said an adult voice from the back of the room. It was Dr. Karen, one of the elders of the church and Kevin's psychologist.

Harrie met Nathan at the gym, but she had also seen him at recent church services. She noticed him first on the exercise bikes when he appeared to be talking to himself, which Harrie found to be cute. The first time they actually talked was by the free weights, when he asked her if she needed one of the dumbbells.

After church service, everyone walked from the historic sanctuary to a meeting room in the new addition. The congregation added the new walkway to connect the buildings; otherwise, everyone would have to walk out in the rain. Harrie noticed that Nathan stood off to the side, greeting some elderly ladies and drinking a cup of coffee. Harrie approached him and mentioned the gym. His face lit up and he remembered her.

On their first date they met for dinner, followed by a drink at a subdued local nightspot, and they ended up having another drink over at Harrie's house, although she had hoped to see the inside of his house. It was her first date after losing her husband, and Harrie wondered if she should tell Nathan about the weird circumstances of her husband's death. Once it came up, he would probably start asking questions, and she would have to bring up the jawbone, which was ghastly. She didn't want to scare him away, and he might figure out they had a lot of money from the insurance policy. She didn't want him to know that yet.

The following morning, Kevin was lost in his own world at the breakfast table. Harrie had seen less and less of Kevin since he made his new friends at the high school, especially the new friend Andrew that Kevin mentioned frequently. Harrie suspected that Kevin had started smoking, but Dr. Karen assured her that a little rebellion was to be expected, especially considering Kevin's age and their recent loss. Perhaps Andrew was a bad influence on her son. She was sure Kevin never would've started smoking if he had stayed with the baseball team.

Harrie mentioned that she was going out for dinner with her new friend again.

Kevin raised an eyebrow. "Is it OK if Andrew comes over?"

"Yes, as long as you two boys stay in your bedroom, so I can meet with my friend downstairs."

"Okay—I suppose we can stay in the bedroom." Kevin turned away to conceal a smile.

Harrie knew it was only a matter of time before Kevin started dating. She felt glad in her decision to wait for Kevin to get a driver's license until he was eighteen. She didn't want him feeling the pressure of taking girls out on dates quite yet; she wanted him to enjoy being a kid and having sleepovers for a while longer. She also felt glad that Kevin had found Abby. The dog had been a delightful addition to their home since the tragedy, Abby always brightening the room with his loyal exuberance.

Harrie took her time getting ready for the date. It felt good to be going out and not playing the grieving housewife. She did miss her husband, especially the partnership of raising Kevin, and the events of his death lingered like a fog bank on the periphery of her mind. If she thought about it too much, the fog bank rolled in and consumed her, so she continued to focus on this new little romance, and tried not to think about the jawbone.

When Nathan came to the door, she noticed he wore something very similar to what he wore at church, and for a moment Harrie felt overdressed.

"Good evening, Harriet," he said with a large awkward smile.

"Hi Nathan—please call me Harrie. Harriet is for little old ladies."

Nathan laughed a little too loud. "Sorry, I can't seem to get used to that."

Harrie wished she had remembered to put Abby into the back yard because the dog kept trying to smell Nathan, and clearly Nathan wasn't on friendly terms with dogs. Harrie thought about calling up to Kevin's room to say she was leaving. She usually said goodbye whenever she left the house, but Kevin was with his friend, and she didn't want to pull them away from their video game. Besides, she didn't feel quite ready to introduce a date to her son.

As soon as Harrie and Nathan left the house, Kevin led Andrew to Dr. Mortensen's stash of whiskey bottles in his father's old den. They took one of the bottles and a couple of glasses back to Kevin's bedroom. Kevin turned on the radio, but they didn't pay too much attention to it as they sat on the lower bunk with a bunch of Kevin's old stuffed animals piled behind them. Both of them choked down a small glass of whiskey.

"Your bedroom is like a little apartment," Andrew said, stroking Kevin's hand. Andrew leaned over and kissed Kevin, and Kevin pushed the stuffed animals to the floor so they could stretch out on the lower bunk, both of them still wearing their shoes. Kevin loved the feeling of Andrew's weight on top of him. Andrew gently kissed Kevin's neck and nibbled on his ear, carefully sliding his hand under Kevin's shirt. He stroked Kevin's hair and gazed into his eyes; Kevin tried to gaze back at him, but he became embarrassed and looked away. Kevin kept thinking to himself that high school was the most wonderful thing that ever happened.

They poured another drink and decided to go out on the deck for a cigarette before things progressed further. When Andrew opened the bedroom door, he almost tripped over Abby who slept right up against the door in the hallway. "Watch out, Abby," Andrew said and patted the dog's head. Abby followed them to the deck. Rain had fallen earlier in the afternoon, but now they could see a clear fall night full of stars.

"When did you know that you liked boys?" Andrew asked after lighting a cigarette and handing it to Kevin before lighting his own.

"I guess I always thought about it a little, but then I really knew it when I saw you."

"Do you think you'll tell your mom?"

"I'm not sure. I wouldn't want to tell my dad, but I might tell my mom. Did you tell your dad?"

"Not exactly. He accidentally saw one of my dirty magazines once, so he probably suspects it."

"Is it a gay magazine?" Kevin asked.

"Yeah—I'll show it to you sometime. Hold this for a second."

Andrew ran inside where he had hidden something inside Kevin's open garage earlier before ringing the doorbell.

"It's for you, for your birthday," Andrew said when he came back.

"But my birthday's not until next week."

"I know, but I thought tonight was the night to give it to you."

It was heavy package. Inside, Kevin found a birthday card that said "Sweet Sixteen" on the front. Inside the card, it read, "Happy Birthday. I love you. Andrew."

Kevin liked how bold it was, and he blushed when he read it; he didn't know whether or not to say "I love you too." He opened the package, which contained a heavy ashtray that Andrew had made in his pottery class.

Back in Kevin's bedroom, a horror movie played on the television with a lot of screaming and vampires being executed with stakes. After drinking another glass of whiskey, Kevin's head whirled. Andrew had more experience drinking, but he also felt drunk from the liquor.

Kevin closed the bedroom door after pushing Abby into the hallway. Standing in the center of the bedroom, they both undressed while watching each other. At first they smirked, then laughed at the awkwardness. They had watched each other undress in the locker room everyday since they met, but this time they both could really look and they both had bulges in their underwear. They touched each other, laughing. They crawled under the covers of Kevin's upper bunk. While the horror movie played on, they kissed each other in new places. When Andrew looked up, he saw Abby staring at him from the crack in the door.

"Oh shit, Kevin, your dog is watching us," Andrew said and burst into laughter. Kevin thought he had closed the door. Andrew climbed down from the bunk bed. "Sorry, Abby, but you can't join in," Andrew said, closing the door and laughing again. Kevin laughed too while watching Andrew's naked body in the light of the television.

They held each other while the horror movie finished, the moon shining into the bedroom through the trees by the creek. Kevin felt like he had never been happier in his life.

They held hands and went into the bathroom where they cleaned up with a washcloth while looking at each in the bright light.

Abby waited in the hall as they went back into the bedroom, both of them stepping over the dog and closing the door behind them again.

Kevin and Andrew got dressed in some shorts and T-shirts for pajamas, so everything would look like a normal sleepover when Harrie and her date came back, although Kevin knew he better try to avoid seeing her or she could tell he was drunk.

Harrie had a nice time at dinner, although she felt like she did most of the talking. She felt angry with herself for telling too many details about the death of her husband. She promised herself she wouldn't talk about the jawbone, but she did anyway. As the story came out of her mouth, it sounded so ghoulish and morbid.

Nathan was very warm and supportive, however, even reaching for her hand when she talked about the jawbone, and Harrie fought the instinct to keep apologizing for darkening the mood.

Back at the house, Harrie offered Nathan a drink. Nathan wanted a glass of wine. Harrie brought out the wine with a tray of fancy cheese and crackers. She turned on the gas fireplace, and they talked for about an hour, mainly about the new church and the parishioners they knew there. Kevin and Andrew kept to themselves up in Kevin's room.

At the door, Nathan gave Harrie a big hug and said he would call her tomorrow. Overall, it seemed like everything was going very well. Nathan seemed like someone Harrie could enjoy doing things with. He didn't try to kiss her, and Harrie worried that it seemed like she wasn't over the grief of her husband's loss.

Nathan had already passed through the innards of the master blob that referred to itself as the pastor. Inside the depth of the blob, the master had placed a very special spectral phantasm inside Nathan's brain, the spectral phantasm of reproduction, the only phantasm that could create new offspring outside the body of the blob. Nathan was key to making sure the blob's seed continued to spread throughout the community; after all, not everyone could be as lucky as Nathan to pass through the blob's body mass firsthand. Nathan's wife had also passed through the blob, and she waited for him at home, eager to hear how his work for the pastor went that night. Their four children hadn't passed through the blob yet.

Harrie knocked on Kevin's door after a while, happy to see the two boys playing a video game together on the floor of the bedroom. She didn't get close enough to smell the whiskey, but she did smell cigarettes from Andrew's clothes. She would have to talk to Kevin about that. She said goodnight.

After Harrie closed the door, Kevin leaned over and whispered in Andrew's ear, "I love you too," in response to the birthday card from earlier. They kissed, and Andrew's player on the screen died a horrible death.

Kevin put on another horror movie and they curled up together in the upper bunk, Kevin saying they didn't need to worry about his mother walking in because he could lock the door.

Lumber was hungry.

Lumber's hand tried to open the bedroom door and found it locked. Lumber's furious jealousy rose up from beneath the happy exterior of Abby the dog.

Outside, Lumber's front legs became strong arms with sharp claws for climbing the side of the house. Lumber perched outside the window, clinging to the top of the frame, a spectral tentacle traveling through the pane of glass. Andrew stirred. He looked up from the bed and he saw Lumber's luminous silver eyes outside the window. The influence of the spectral tentacle overwhelmed him. Andrew got up from the bed, careful not to disturb Kevin. Andrew climbed down from the bunk and pulled up the window.

Lumber fought the urge to grab Andrew and carry him off to the forest where Lumber could consume his blood and tear his body to pieces. Kevin would never know what happened to Andrew. Instead, Lumber commanded Andrew to sit in the chair at the desk. Perching above him on the desk, Lumber's canine snout shifted into a blood-sucking mouth, and Lumber cut Andrew's neck, feeding off the blood spilling from the wound.

Lumber was thirsty and Lumber hated Andrew. He knew he shouldn't drink too much or else Kevin would be sad all over again, but Lumber's thirst blinded his judgment. Lumber knew he was taking too much.

Kevin cried out from the upper bunk: "Stop it, Abby!"

There, in the middle of night, awoken from dreams, Kevin seemed to know what Lumber was, as if the truth about Lumber rose up from the secret place in Kevin's mind where Lumber kept it buried. The horror-stricken cry from Kevin made Lumber stop feeding immediately, and the dog creature looked up at the desperate boy he loved while blood and drool ran from his mouth. Lumber couldn't bear to see Kevin heartbroken again, and Lumber couldn't bear to hear Kevin's wretched crying, even if Lumber did hate Andrew for trying to take Kevin away."

"Don't, Abby. I love him."

Lumber calmed Kevin with a spectral tentacle inserted into his brain, and Lumber created a shadow there, so Kevin wouldn't remember seeing this. Andrew, still in the trance, was alive, and Lumber licked the wound on his throat, offering to Andrew the healing power of the spectral energy that coursed through Lumber's nervous system.

Lumber helped Andrew back up the ladder into the upper bunk, and Lumber shapeshifted into the white dog named Abby, falling asleep with a full stomach beneath them.

Gordon Watt and a young psychic named Jessica drove past the front of the Mortensen house, parking the rental car in a spot down the street. Since Marilyn refused to set foot in the town, Gordon had to bring in Jessica, a powerful but unstable psychic.

Jessica could also sense the horrible cloud that made the town unbearable for Marilyn, but Jessica was more resilient, and she told Gordon that she could sidestep the dread of the psychic cloud and help figure out what was going on.

"Do you think Lumber is in there?" Gordon asked.

"I think so, but I need to see the dog to be sure it's the host for a spectral phantas," she said, tossing her cigarette out the window.

Roland wasn't stupid. He knew that the pastor didn't like him. Roland had tried to bring some more high school kids into the SSA club, but he didn't have any luck, and he knew that Kevin and Andrew were avoiding him.

Roland's parents had become devout disciples of the pastor, so he couldn't turn to them for help. Roland wasn't going to end up a sacrificial lamb for the pastor. He put some clothes and supplies in a backpack and rode out to the bus station, abandoning his bicycle in the rack outside.

As he waited for a bus to Seattle, a feeling of nervous dread began to grow; he felt like someone was watching him. At this point, Roland had no idea how many members the church had under its control. The bus station waiting room was full of people—any of them could be a spy for the pastor.

In a moment of panic, Roland abandoned the bus station idea and decided to try hitchhiking, heading out for a quiet, serpentine road that ran along by the coast. Two hours later, feeling safer with the hood on his rain jacket up, Roland walked along on the shoulder of road. Now that he was a good distance out of time, he decided to start flashing his thumb. He got a ride much faster than he expected.

The college-aged girl driving the car seemed nice, and she seemed to be much more comfortable than Roland, as if she had picked up hitchhikers many times before, so this put Roland at his ease.

"Put your bag in the back seat," she told him. "My name's Cindy."

"Thanks a lot. I'm Roland."

As she navigated the sharp turns of the road, Cindy hummed along with the radio, and Roland started to feel a little nervous again. He tended to start jabbering when he felt nervous, but something held him back this time. But this girl had to be safe, he told himself. It appeared to be a normal car for a college kid, messy with old CD covers, cigarette packs, and fast food bags, but then Roland wondered what the car of a religious zealot would look like anyway.

"So do you go to college?" Roland finally asked. She didn't answer, but just smiled at Roland. "Are you going to answer?" Roland asked. He always let his big mouth get the better of him.

Instead of answering, Cindy hummed a different tune, one of the hymns that the congregation regularly sang in the pastor's church.

"Do you mind if I get out to take a piss?" Roland asked. He spotted a place where she could park on the shoulder, shouting, "right here would be perfect. Unless you want me to piss in your car."

Roland planned to abandon his bag and go right over the guardrail, slide down the embankment, and escape into the trees.

Cindy slowed the car, Roland's hand on the handle.

"Before you get out to pee, I want to show you what comes out of my belly," Cindy said as she brought the car to a complete stop and lifted up her shirt. A tentacle of red-black blob flesh erupted from a split in her stomach and grabbed Roland's ankle as he attempted to escape the car. A smile of delight on her face, she said, "I've waited for this day. Now I can become the pastor's flesh."

Roland pulled free and fell to the ground, rolling away from the car and colliding with the guardrail. Looking back, Roland saw Cindy's face melting, viscous streams of blob flesh spilling from her mouth and eye sockets. The tentacle from her abdomen caught up with Roland and wrapped around his throat. The girl melted into an attack blob in just a matter of moments, faster than it took for the tentacle to strangle Roland to death.

The small blob settled in upon Roland, engulfing his head and torso to begin the digestion process. The blob burned human flesh on contact; digesting an entire human body could be accomplished rapidly, the parked car shielding the blob from the passing cars on the road. Once the blob liquefied Ronald's torso, it pulled the rest of the boy's limbs inside its body, went up over the guardrail and rolled down the embankment, heading for the sea.

A few moments later, another car parked on the shoulder, a servant of the pastor running from the passenger seat to the driver's seat of Cindy's car. He didn't mind sitting in the sticky residue of Cindy's transformation as he drove the car away from the scene of the murder.

The small blob, covered with leaves and twigs from its short journey from the road to the shore, was happy to reach the cold water where it could swim rapidly. It waited offshore until after midnight when the blob rolled up on the beach and made its way up the hill to the church, guided by the telepathic connection to its master, hiding in the bushes for a car to pass before crossing the street.

In the shadows outside the building, a member of the church waited at a side entrance, opening the door for the small blob to roll down the stairs to the basement where it was warmly received by the master blob in the pit, and the blob that once was Cindy felt grateful to deliver this small gift of Roland's protein.

While Kevin played a video game in his bedroom, Nathan and Harrie shared some wine and cheese by the fireplace.

"It's wonderful how much the church has helped the real estate market. People are moving here from all over just to be part of our new congregation," Nathan explained.

"People are moving here just to go to the church?" she asked.

"Of course."

Nathan leaned in for a kiss. Harrie knew she didn't want to go too fast, but a kiss in front of the fireplace sounded nice.

The spectral phantasm reached out to Harrie's mind to calm her, to prepare her for the implantation as Nathan stripped off her clothing, his bloodstream teeming with embryonic phantasms, all of them waiting to be deposited into a new host, all of them seeds for the blob.

Nathan looked up and saw the white dog staring at him from the staircase. For just a flash, he thought he saw the eyespot of a spectral phantasm looking back at him from behind the fluffy white veil of hair, but he had never heard of a phantasm inside an animal.

Lumber could see all of the phantasms coursing through Nathan's body.

"That's a good boy," Nathan said to the dog, unafraid. He could hear the low rumbling growl from the dog, knowing that with only a thought, the agents of the pastor waiting outside would enter the house and kill the dog.

The dog ran back up the stairs to guard Kevin's door.

Nathan unbuckled his pants and inserted himself into Harrie, depositing a spectral phantasm inside her with a large spurt of fluid.

Eventually Kevin agreed to attend the church with his mother.

His birthday was coming up in only a few days and Kevin wanted Harrie to relent and allow him to get his driver's license. They could even afford to buy him a new car, Kevin kept saying. Harrie explained that it wasn't about the money; she didn't think that Kevin was ready for the responsibility. Kevin said that it was Harrie who wasn't ready. Kevin said he would agree to try the church if she let him get his driver's license. However, she tried a different strategy. She told him that Andrew was attending the church, which Kevin didn't believe, so now he wanted to go along to prove her wrong.

Kevin dressed up in shirt and a tie, and he patted Abby on the head, calling the dog to come downstairs.

Once Kevin and Harrie left the house for church, Lumber went back upstairs to Kevin's bedroom. Lumber's paw shifted into a crude hand and opened the bedroom door. Lumber searched through the piles of dirty clothes on the floor. Lumber found what he was looking for: Kevin's backpack. As Lumber inspected the bag, his entire body changed. Lumber sat back, and his hips shifted; his legs stuck out like the legs of a sitting ape as his hands became dexterous enough to open the zipper on the backpack. Lumber's snout flattened and his forehead raised, pulling back the bangs from his silver eyes. Lumber pulled out the contents of the backpack: a geometry textbook, a novel, folders, and a spiral bound notebook. Lumber flipped through the pages, until he discovered what he wanted to see.

The day before yesterday, Lumber noticed that Kevin kept looking at Lumber and scribbling in the notebook; Lumber wanted to see what Kevin had been drawing. At first, Lumber only found pages with scribbled words and numbers, but finally Lumber happened upon the picture that Kevin drew. It was a portrait of Abby: the shaggy ball of fur with a black button nose and gigantic lolling tongue. Lumber saw more doodles in the notebook, images of Kevin and Lumber walking along together, connected by a leash.

Tears streamed down Lumber's face, the first tears Lumber had ever cried. The boy did still love him. The portrait was proof, even if that other boy wanted to steal Kevin away from Lumber.

Lumber found another drawing in the notebook: a creature with red ink for blood dripping from its horrible fangs. Kevin's subconscious mind knew what Abby really was, even if Lumber had created the shadow in his mind.

Dr. Mortensen had never taken his family to church, and Kevin didn't know what would happen in the service exactly, but he expected more about the Bible and Jesus in the sermon. In fact, he didn't see any Bibles in the pews in front of him, and he didn't hear anyone say the name of Jesus. The minister kept referring to the pastor, as if the minister at the pulpit was just a substitute teacher, and the nameless unseen pastor was the real minister.

Kevin enjoyed singing the songs, the words projected on a big screen that covered the cross. When the children's choir sang their songs, Kevin noticed that several children appeared to be the same child, although dressed differently.

Halfway through the sermon on the topic of forming community and spreading the love of the pastor, Kevin noticed Andrew sitting all the way at the back of the sanctuary. His mother was right. Andrew smirked when Kevin saw him.

Harrie was relieved to see Andrew attending the church, Kevin's new best friend commanding a lot more attention from Kevin than Harrie did. Hopefully both of them could persuade Kevin to willingly join the pastor, she thought.

At the conclusion of the service, Kevin rushed over to Andrew, who, unlike Kevin, didn't appear to be dressed up at all. Andrew was with his father, a severe looking man with deep wrinkles on his face and bags under his eyes. He looked like he could be Andrew's grandfather.

While the rest of the congregation gathered in the meeting room for punch and cookies, Andrew led Kevin out back where they could hide behind some trees near the church playground.

When they were sure no one could see them, Andrew kissed Kevin, but Kevin pulled back.

"Why didn't you tell me that you were going to the church?"

"My dad makes me go. He's the janitor here. If I come to church he looks the other way when I steal his cigarettes."

Andrew started to kiss him again. This time, Andrew interrupted: "Kevin, is that your dog?"

"Where?" Kevin asked, and when he turned around, he didn't see Abby anywhere.

"Now I don't see him."

Kevin and Andrew walked down to the sidewalk in front of the playground, but no sign of Abby anywhere.

"Don't worry," Andrew said. "It was probably another dog. If it was Abby, I'm sure he would have come over here."

"That's true," Kevin said.

Andrew pulled out a cigarette.

"We shouldn't do that here," Kevin said. "We're too close to the playground."

"Okay. Come with me," and Andrew put his arm around Kevin.

"Maybe I should say goodbye to my mom."

"She knows you're with me, and we're only a couple of blocks from your house."

"Okay."

"I want to show you a secret place," Andrew said.

As Andrew and Kevin walked down the sidewalk, smoking their cigarettes, Lumber noticed that several of the children on the playground watched him carefully. Two of the girls were the same girl; Lumber could see that. Lumber tried to make himself invisible to them like he had made himself invisible to Kevin and Andrew, but found he could not put a shadow into their minds. Lumber looked at the children with his other sight, with the sight of the spectral phantasm's eyespot, which revealed all the children had luminous phantasms in their brains, and they were all interconnected with subtle spectral threads that spiraled back toward the church and the pit beneath.

Behind the apartment complex at the back of a small dirt lot, the management allowed Andrew and his father to park their old RV.

"My dad and I lived in this RV for a couple of years. We traveled around a lot. It's why I'm really behind in school."

"I thought you were behind because you got in trouble a lot," Kevin said.

"Well, that too," Andrew said.

Outside, the RV was covered with spots of green moss. Inside, the furnishings were old with some cigarette holes in the cushions.

"My dad hates this RV. It reminds him of the past. But now he's got a good job with the church, and he never comes out here anymore. Sometimes I sleep out here when I want to be alone. My dad doesn't notice."

It started to rain; the sound of the raindrops on the roof of the RV was comforting, and it felt cozy inside the RV. There was a large ashtray full of cigarette butts. Andrew emptied it in the little kitchen trash can and lit new cigarettes for Kevin and himself.

"I hide my magazines out here," Andrew said. "I got them a couple of years ago from this guy I met when we lived in Denver. I'm almost old enough to buy magazines myself now."

"Was he your boyfriend?"

"Not really," Andrew said. "He was a lot older."

Andrew showed Kevin a couple of the magazines from the secret box stored underneath the couch cushions. Kevin was curious, looking at the pictures while he smoked his cigarette. Kevin had never seen pictures like this before.

Sitting on the couch together, Andrew undid Kevin's tie and started to unbutton his shirt.

"Do you want to try anything you saw in the magazines?" Andrew asked.

Lumber peered inside the windows, but they had closed the curtains.

Lumber sensed the children behind him. He looked back. Four little girls from the church playground had followed Lumber, all of them with different bright dresses and different styles of hair, but they were all the same eight-year-old girl, and Lumber could see the phantasms in their brains.

One of the phantasms emitted a spectral cord that connected with the phantasm in Lumber's brain. At first it fed Lumber some images and messages. People, lots of people, men and women, all of them telling Lumber what a good dog he was, and Lumber saw the master blob rising from the sea. And Lumber could see the pit. All kinds of children played with Lumber, brushing his coat and weaving flowers in his hair. And they showed images of a special dog house next to the playground by the church and a special room where the neighborhood boys would lie down on the couch while Lumber drank their blood. The message was clear: the blob would provide for Lumber. The blob would bring Lumber all the blood he would ever need. The cord did more than just pass images; it exerted influence over Lumber. The phantasm in Lumber's mind did not like this and shut out the cord.

Lumber had to get these weird children of the blob away from Kevin.

Lumber ran until he reached the trail by the creek. When he looked back, the four girls ran after him. Lumber didn't want to lead them back to his house, so Lumber kept running toward the depth of the forested park where Lumber had killed the hounds. As Lumber ran, spectral energy radiated throughout his body; his muscles grew larger and his claws grew sharper as his speed increased. The little children of the blob kept up with him, running faster than any normal human child could run.

At the stagnant pool where Gordon saw Lumber's monstrous form, the four girls caught up with Lumber.

Lumber turned to face them, ready to fight. Lumber raised up on his hind legs. His front legs shifted into arms, the right arm forming a long black claw like a reaper's scythe, which terminated in a sharp point. As the girls entered the clearing next to the stagnant pool, Lumber swept his claw-scythe and decapitated the first girl, her body disintegrating into viscous blob flesh as the spectral phantasm inside her head pulsated and ruptured; it was dead.

The three remaining girls melted into attack blobs, the special drones that protected the master blob from outside threats. If Lumber could not be seduced into joining the pastor, the dog monster must be destroyed. The little girls, now red-black blobs, left behind their church dresses, saturated with foul-smelling liquid, and rolled toward Lumber with one purpose: to kill him.

Lumber's chest heaved in great breaths of rage and terror as the three blobs rolled toward him.

A long slimy tentacle like a frog's tongue jumped out and wrapped around Lumber's throat. With one quick motion, Lumber severed the tentacle with his claw-scythe. Lumber attacked the nearest blob. Impaling the mass repeatedly with the sharp point of his claws. The blob revealed a nipple on its underbelly; the nipple emitted a focused acid spray. Lumber felt the acid eat through his coat, and the pain electrified the right side of his body. He let out a howl of agony. He could see the other two blobs closing in.

Lumber pulled himself back; he felt certain that he would be killed.

Lumber remembered to see with the vision of the spectral phantasm in his brain, which enabled Lumber to see more than just the undulating masses moving in to destroy him—he could also see the spectral light of the phantasms housed in the brain masses, which resembled hard fleshy nodules inside the amorphous flesh. With canine eyes, he couldn't see where the brain mass was located inside the blob, but the spectral phantasm could see.

With one quick leap, Lumber landed on top of a blob and speared the brain mass with his claw. The blob trembled violently and disintegrated into a puddle, but not before Lumber's back paw landed in a pocket of acid, which ate it away completely. Lumber squealed and fell back into the stagnant pool. A blob jumped in after him. Inside the black murky darkness of the pond, Lumber could still see the spectral energy pulsating through the blob as it approached him like a jellyfish. Ignoring the horrific pain from his back leg, Lumber pushed off from the bottom of the pond with his good foot. The blob tried to dodge the spear of Lumber's claw, but with the help of the phantasm's vision, he nailed the fleshy organ, and the blob dissipated into the water of the pond.

The last blob hesitated on the edge of bank, rolling back and forth indecisively, not sure whether to return to the master or jump in after the dog creature. Lumber rose up out of the pond, roaring. The last blob was ready, spraying acid from a nipple that burned Lumber belly. The tentacles of the blob wrapped around Lumber's arms as Lumber landed on top it. They became completely entangled. Lumber let out a howl of pain. The blob disintegrated as Lumber hobbled away with the small blob's brain mass crushed inside his bloody jaws.

Large patches of Lumber's white coat had been burned off during the entanglement with blob, and he had severe burns over most of his body; he was missing an entire foot and an ear. Lumber limped a few feet away from the pond and collapsed.

Lumber awoke from a horrible nightmare about the burning spray of the blobs, floating through one of the countless labyrinthine passages in the cold dreamy darkness of the Black Orb. Lumber could barely move, paralyzed by the pain crashing through his body in waves; the light of his spectral phantasm was fading.

As Lumber approached the globe of water in the Black Orb's cavernous center, Lumber yearned to refresh himself; Lumber drank and drank.

In addition to serving as a conduit for spectral phantasms to enter this world, the water was charged with the spectral life-force of the phantasms. As Lumber drank, the phantasm in Lumber's mind renewed its light. Lumber's damaged body was flooded with the powerful spectral energy, his burned skin healing and his white coat returning thicker than before. Lumber's paw and ear regenerated. The white shaggy veil over Lumber's eyes grew dense, but he learned more and more how to see with his other vision, the vision of the phantasm's eyespot.

Harrie set out the tray of cheese and crackers on the coffee table by the fireplace. Edgar, the man she met at the gym, nibbled on the cheese while Harrie went back to the kitchen to pour a couple glasses of wine.

"Do you need any help?" Edgar asked. He dressed in a nice shirt that he kept open enough to show off a dark tuft of chest hair. Harrie looked fantastic in her bright new dress and new hairdo from the stylist she met at church. Edgar had seen Harrie at the gym before, but tonight she looked amazing, almost as if she had lost ten years.

"No, I've got it. You just stay right there."

Edgar had gone on quite a few dates since his wife Ginnie had passed away, but this definitely appeared to be the most promising. Edgar considered himself adept at reading body language.

Harrie turned on the stereo that played romantic easy listening, switched on the gas fireplace, and toasted Edgar as he hungrily checked out her figure in that new dress.

It wasn't long before the small talk about Edgar's window washing business and the virtues of his long dead wife Ginnie turned into making out and heavy petting on the couch. Harrie grabbed Edgar's hand and led him up the stairs to the bedroom.

Harrie pushed Edgar onto the bed, and he started to unbutton his shirt as she removed her dress.

"The master needs protein," Harrie said as she violently trembled all over her body. She started to melt, the red-black flesh of the blob running from her nose. Edgar emitted a horrible scream of surprise as her stomach exploded.

Jessica and Nettington sat in a parked car outside of Harrie's house. Both of them had smoked an ashtray full of cigarettes while watching the house for signs of Lumber. They heard the scream.

Jessica and Nettington stepped out of the car and approached the house. They only got as far as the front gate when a large object flew out the upstairs bedroom window, which had been left open. The object, Harrie in her blob form, hit the ground with a wet splat, leapt over the fence, and rolled down the street unharmed.

Jessica and Nettington began to run after the blob when they saw three men approaching them from across the street.

"Good evening, gentleman," Nettington said with his hand on the revolver.

"Nettington," Jessica whispered. "They're blobs. Shoot the brain."

"I can't just start shooting them."

"Run, Nettington. Run."

The first man's face split open, the flesh of the blob spilling out like a stream of red-black vomit.

The other two men watched their companion melt into an attack blob as Jessica grabbed Nettington's arm, pulling him back to the car, seconds before the blob could form tentacles and spray acid.

They scrambled into the car. Nettington turned the ignition as the full weight of the blob hit the driver's side door, its mass stretched over the window. A tentacle shattered the window and wrapped around Nettington's throat. Jessica grabbed Nettington's revolver as Nettington hit the accelerator and crashed the car into a van across the street. With a horrific screech of metal on metal, Nettington dragged the car across the length of the van, pulling the blob off the side like scraping a smashed slug off of a shoe. Nettington was free of the blob, but his neck burned with the touch of its flesh. They had escaped.

"They're a lot easier to kill when they're in human form," Jessica said.

"Next time I'll shoot."

The blob that was once Harrie made its way back to the church, full of the protein from Edgar to offer the master. At the back door, a servant waited to let the blob inside. It was a thrilling prospect for the new blob to rejoin its master, full of its gift of protein. It rolled down the stairs to the pit where it dived in and joined the massive organism.

Twelve hours later, the master blob raised a large orifice to the top of the pit and gave birth to a naked woman with no hair and covered with warm slime. The woman looked somewhat like Harrie, although many years younger, her features seeming less formed somehow. The clone opened its eyes. Several of the parishioners helped her to her feet.

Kevin and Andrew spent the night in the RV again. They both awoke in the late morning after school had already begun.

When they stepped outside the RV, Lumber waited for them.

"HI Abby," Kevin said. "How did you find me, boy?"

Andrew kissed Kevin goodbye, and Kevin walked back home with Abby, passing Lumber's old pickup shell and the fallen log by the creek where the boy first encountered Lumber.

When they entered the back door, they encountered a group of three elderly women from the church; they sat at the kitchen table, drinking tea and waiting for Kevin.

"What's going on?" Kevin asked.

"Oh, Kevin dear," one of the women said. "Your mother has taken ill."

Kevin entered his mother's bedroom. The women from the church, who still lingered downstairs, already informed Kevin that his mother's hair had fallen out. Kevin didn't open the curtains or turn on the light. He saw his mother's head, a bald pale ball, resting on the pillow. In fact, Kevin could barely recognize her at all. It seemed her features had been scrubbed away, and now she resembled a department store mannequin. The eyes opened momentarily and closed again, but showed no recognition of Kevin who stood over her.

"We've got a serious problem in this town, Gordon." Nettington said. The private investigator, Jessica, and Gordon sat around the tiny table in Gordon's RV, drinking coffee.

"Now that they've identified us as a threat, do you think we're safe here at the RV park?" Gordon asked.

Jessica looked troubled. "The blob has invaded this entire town. That was why Marilyn couldn't stomach being here. She could feel the shadow it cast. It completely drowned her psychic ability."

"But not you," Gordon said.

"She isn't me," Jessica said.

"How can we save this town?" Gordon asked. "It's not like we can start letting entire communities fall under the control of blobs."

"It's worse than that, Gordon," Jessica said. "The blob is assimilating this town."

"We've got to drive it out from under the church and back to where it came from," Nettington said.

"It came from the sea," Gordon said.

"We've got to drive it back into the sea, then, unless it can be killed."

"You would have to kill every one of the brain masses in order to kill it," Jessica explained. "You saw how hard it was to kill the blob that attacked the car. The master blob will be a hundred times bigger, so it probably has hundreds of brain masses."

"Back into the sea it is then," Gordon said.

"I don't think it's going to be satisfied with fish for long."

"Could we bomb the church?" Nettington asked.

"We would need a serious bomb to reach the depth of the pit," Gordon said. "There must be another way. I'm going to get on the phone with the leaders of the organization, perhaps they can gather together some emergency funding before it's too late."

Kevin sat on the bed with Abby's shaggy head resting on his lap as he thought about the condition of his mother. Kevin had never heard of a condition where someone loses all their hair overnight and starts to look younger. But not just younger, his mother looked fetal somehow. The trio of church women had camped out downstairs. When he looked out his window, he saw men in the yard. Something was very wrong. Kevin wished he had a phone in his room, because he couldn't go downstairs and call Andrew. The old women could hear. And he knew they were guarding his mother—and keeping him prisoner.

Kevin tried to distract himself by playing a video game. Lumber sat by the bedroom door. If Lumber could get past all of the blobs downstairs, he would take Kevin out of the house before it was too late, before they took Kevin away from Lumber, before they invaded him and corrupted his mind.

Someone was at the door. Lumber growled. The person on the other side looked through the door with a spectral phantasm. Lumber looked back and saw four men in the hallway.

The door opened. A strong man grabbed Lumber's collar while a second man put a muzzle over Lumber's snout. They pulled Lumber into the hall as someone familiar to Kevin walked into the room. It was Dr. Karen, Kevin's psychologist.

Kevin turned off the video game. "Don't hurt my dog," he said, his voice dripping with anger and confusion. More than anything, the appearance of his psychologist in his bedroom surprised Kevin, and he didn't imagine the danger.

The balding man, with his wrinkled face and glasses, spoke to the boy with the same calm and authority as if they sat together in Dr. Karen's office, nothing aggressive or threatening about his manner.

"I know you're very worried about your mother, Kevin, but I can assure you that everything is going to be fine. I've overseen this kind of transition for the pastor many times now."

"What kind of transition?"

"This is an exciting time, Kevin."

Outside the bedroom door, Nathan stood in readiness.

Two strong men dragged Lumber downstairs to the door of the basement. Lumber growled and struggled against the combined power of the men, but he could not bite them through the muzzle.

Halfway down the basement staircase, Lumber stood on his hind legs and pushed the first man with great force. The man flew backward and landed on his back on the cold cement floor. Lumber turned to the other man and grabbed his throat with a clawed hand, tossing him down the stairs while tearing out his throat. The first cried for help, his voice deepening as he trembled in the first stage of becoming an attack blob. Lumber removed the muzzle as his snout elongated into a monstrous set of jaws. His right hand shifted and formed the claw-scythe. The man began to melt as Lumber landed on him and impaled his brain with the long claw-scythe three times, the man screaming and disintegrating into a puddle. The second man tried to escape, his throat pouring blood. Lumber's left claw ripped open the man's back as he started up the stairs and Lumber took off his head with one swipe of the claw-scythe.

The spectral phantasm in the mind of Dr. Karen radiated powerful tentacles that calmed Kevin's mind. Nathan entered the room, the same agent of the blob that implanted the spectral phantasm into Harrie by the fireplace. Kevin was now pliant with the spectral influence of both men. They placed Kevin's body face down on the side of the bed and removed his jeans. Nathan prepared himself to implant the spectral phantasm into Kevin.

A horrible knock sounded on the door as if being struck with an axe. Dr. Karen had remembered to lock the door. The two men looked at each other in confusion.

Lumber crashed through the door, breaking the lock and knocking the door loose from its hinges. The men cried out in shock at the sight of the massive shaggy beast, Lumber's hideous maw of sharp teeth roaring at them. With one quick swing of Lumber's arm, Nathan's severed head landed on Kevin's desk. Lumber could see the numerous embryonic spectral phantasms of the blob in the torrent of blood that spilled from the stump of Nathan's neck.

Dr. Karen turned and jumped headfirst through Kevin's bedroom window. Lumber looked out the window and saw Dr. Karen running through the back yard to escape, uninjured.

Lumber saw at least four attack blobs waiting in the back yard to block Lumber's retreat.

The rest of the women from the church, now all in their blob form, rolled up the stairs—three more blobs coming up the stairs to kill Lumber.

Kevin, lying face down on the bed, was still unconscious from the influence of Dr. Karen. Multiple attack blobs gathered in the hallway outside the door that Lumber had smashed. With his hands, Lumber pulled up Kevin's pants and picked up the helpless boy in his arms.

The first attack blob leapt into the room and rolled into the corner behind the bunk beds while another blob slid into position behind the television. The blobs knew they had the advantage because now they knew Lumber's weakness: his love for Kevin. Two blobs in the bedroom, another in the hallway, and numerous blobs waiting outside to attack, if Lumber should escape.

The instinct for survival raged inside Lumber's mind, his body electrified with spectral energy like powerful adrenaline. In this most desperate moment, Lumber turned inward, remembering something he had glimpsed inside the globe of water in the center of the Black Orb. And Lumber knew he had not yet discovered the true extent of his powers.

The blobs, uncertain, readied for attack as Lumber dropped into a ball on the floor, and for a moment it seemed the creature had become a gigantic ball of pulsating shaggy hair that covered the boy.

Lumber, with massive powerful arms, grabbed Kevin off the floor and leapt through the open window. The blobs tried to catch them, springing tentacles to grasp them and spraying acid, but Lumber had moved too fast.

A dozen blobs now waited in the back yard to attack Lumber as he landed, but two gigantic bat wings of pink skin and shaggy fur unfurled as Lumber and Kevin left the bedroom window. Lumber emitted a roar of exertion as the spectral energy pulsated through his body and powered the massive wings. Lumber flapped the wings that carried him and Kevin over the tops of the trees and away from the blobs.

And people saw the horrible white creature with the boy in its claws.

At the church, Andrew's father worked on a faucet in the restroom while Andrew watched, handing his father tools as requested. A puddle of water had collected on the linoleum, and Landing told his son to get the mop and bucket from the janitor's closet.

Andrew walked down the hallway toward the closet, past the secret locked door to the black basement. The door was ajar. He passed by the open door without noticing it until he caught a whiff of something strange—a sickly sweet fishy smell. The smell was strange and powerful enough for Andrew to pull open the door all the way. Andrew didn't even know that the new church building had a cellar.

He saw the unfinished wooden stairs going down. Something wasn't right. The darkness of the basement consumed the bottom of the staircase like a fogbank. The light from the hallway stopped halfway down. Andrew felt a horrible sensation of dread, about to close the door, when a powerful spectral tentacle from the depth of the pit entered his brain. The tentacle aroused portions of his brain that created an undeniable sensation of curiosity. Then, a strange confusion overwhelmed him and he didn't know where he was. From within the dark shadow downstairs, he heard crying. Andrew saw Kevin, dressed in his gym clothes, emerge from the black shadow, his nose having bled all over his face and down the front of his shirt.

"What's wrong, Kevin? Did someone hurt you?"

Andrew ran down the steps to Kevin who held his nose and wept.

"Who hit you, Kevin? Tell me who."

Andrew's father closed the door at the top of the stairs.

Andrew felt a momentary sensation of strangulation and dread as the darkness surrounded him. The hallucination of Kevin vanished and Andrew saw bright fluorescent light against white tile.

Andrew walked into the darkness of the muddy basement where the deep pit concealed the master blob. In Andrew's mind, he walked into a brilliantly lit room with white tiles. In the same spot as the blob's pit, Andrew saw a swimming pool.

The power of the master blob's influence completely disoriented Andrew. It seemed perfectly normal for him to go swimming in the pool. He had arrived for the purpose of going swimming. He loved to go swimming. He looked all around him. Since no one else was around, he could swim naked and no one would see. He unbuckled his jeans as the pastor arose to the very edge of the pit.

Andrew pulled off his shirt and placed his clothing on top of the shoes with his socks balled inside. The servants of the blob, invisible to Andrew, gathered up the clothing as Andrew walked closer to the edge of the pit.

There was a little diving board. It would feel so good to dive naked into the water. Andrew could even smell the familiar chlorine smell of the swimming pool, not the sickly-sweet stench of the blob. Andrew stood at the edge of the diving board, his toes curling over the side.

In the church sanctuary, the congregation trembled with great excitement and sang joyous hymns as the blob opened a warm orifice to catch Andrew once he jumped from the diving board.

The pastor had chosen Andrew to be the host of a very special spectral phantasm, the seed of a new master blob to start a new church. Andrew would spread the glorious word of the pastor to a new town and a new community.

Standing naked on the diving board, Andrew felt a shudder. He looked all around him; he looked into the depth of the crystal clear swimming pool, which for a moment appeared as black as tar, but became shining and clear again. It looked inviting. Andrew dived in.

Lumber began to tire.

Keeping aloft with Kevin's extra weight exhausted all of Lumber's spectral energy. He had flown with Kevin to the east over the mountains, which were heavily forested and desolate.

Just as Lumber looked for a clearing to attempt a dangerous landing, afraid he might hurt Kevin, Lumber noticed a disturbance in the mist above the treetops a few hundred feet away. A portal, directly in Lumber's path, began to open in the mist. A moment later, the Black Orb drew Lumber and Kevin inside its tunnel.

With great relief, Lumber released Kevin's unconscious body, which now drifted weightless under the direction of the Orb, and Lumber drew his wings to his sides and floated with Kevin to the central chamber.

The Black Orb maintained Kevin's sleep, and the boy levitated near the silvery ball of water. Lumber lapped up the water and drew upon the spectral energy to restore himself, unconsciously shifting back into his canine form.

Once Lumber was back to normal again, the Black Orb lifted Kevin's veil of sleep and the boy's eyes fluttered awake.

"Where am I?" he called out, fighting back the sense of panic in the zero gravity.

"You are with friends," Jessica said as she emerged from the shadows at the back of the chamber. She removed her jacket and put it around the freezing boy.

Lumber growled at Jessica, but the Black Orb calmed the dog.

Kevin looked upon the shimmering globe of water with awe. "Is this a dream?"

"You must drink from the water," Jessica said, holding him in her arms.

"What?"

"The Black Orb will give you a wise and ancient being to guide you and protect you. Think of it like a guardian angel. The Black Orb will deliver it through the water."

"I don't think I like the sound of that—is it the blob?"

"I will show you." Jessica grabbed Kevin's shoulders and faced him. She revealed the spectral phantasm in her brain. Kevin could see the consciousness in the alien eye spot and the numerous silver tentacles that radiated from the phantasm and swayed peacefully like ropes of seaweed beneath the waves. Kevin saw the spectral phantasm, and he was not afraid of its alien form.

"The phantasm will protect you from the blob and the creature named Lumber," Jessica said and gestured toward the dog who floated a few feet away across the chamber.

"That's not a creature," Kevin said. "That's Abby, my dog."

"It once was a dog," Jessica said. "Its real name is Lumber. It murdered your father and it drinks your blood like a vampire."

"What?"

"Lumber also has a spectral phantasm, but the phantasms need the life force that can only be found in human blood, so Lumber is forced to become a vampire."

"Abby drinks my blood?" Kevin said, but somewhere deep inside, he already knew the truth.

A horrible look of guilt and confusion crossed Lumber's face. He knew that he had been a very bad dog. Lumber broke free of the Orb's hold and floated over to the wall of the chamber. His paws transformed into hands and he propelled himself down a tunnel to hide himself from the accusatory look on Kevin's face.

"But once you have a spectral phantasm, Lumber won't be able to drink your blood anymore," Jessica explained. "The life in your blood will be bound up with the spectral phantasm. And it brings gifts."

"What kind of gifts?"

"Gifts of sight—and other powers. The blob will never be able to control you."

Kevin paused. "My mom is dead, isn't she?" he asked, but before Jessica could respond, Kevin said, "I know that she is."

"We will avenge her."

"How?"

"We will destroy the pastor's church."

Kevin nodded, and the Black Orb brought him into the water like a baptism.

A long van pulled up to the front of the church, the door sliding open as Gordon, Jessica, Nettington, and Kevin walked up to the front step. Instantly, servants of the blob appeared around the sides of the building, and some stepped outside the front door. The blob could use anyone as a host.

"We have come with a message for your master," Gordon called out to the people. "We know what you are and we know what you are trying to do."

"The pastor has done nothing wrong," an overweight man said. "The pastor takes good care of his children."

"We are here to say that your master is not welcome here. We are offering you one last chance. We will not abide your presence here. Tonight, in the darkness, your master has one chance to return to the sea."

"The pastor is the foundation of our church," an elderly woman shouted.

"If your master does not return to the sea tonight, it will be destroyed. Your church will be destroyed. This is the message we are here to deliver: leave the church tonight with all of your followers, and we will not destroy you."

"This is the pastor's home."

"The blob must return to eating fish, or choose death."

They got back in the van and quickly drove away.

The following morning at dawn, three black vans pulled up to the side of the church. As the van doors slid open, black-clad mercenaries with automatic weapons and Molotov cocktails ran out, tossing the incendiary devices through the stained glass windows into the church sanctuary.

The followers of the blob, in their human form, emerged from side entrances and ran toward the men. This time, Nettington didn't wait until they transformed, giving the order to fire, and the machine guns rang out, striking followers of the blob in the brain. The quiet residential street was now filled with gunfire and screaming.

Gordon Watt and Jessica watched from down the street.

Outside the church, the mercenaries encountered heavy resistance, the followers having melted into their attack-blob forms as the fire in the sanctuary continued to grow. The mercenaries fired their machine guns at the attack blobs, but they could only guess the location of the brain mass, so they riddled the blobs with bullets until they struck upon it. A blob leapt up and engulfed a fighter's helmet, penetrating inside and digesting his head with a pocket of acid. Another mercenary screamed out in agony as a blob sprayed his face with acid from an underbelly nipple.

As the fire consumed the historic church building and the new addition, the master blob flowed out of the ground floor doors and windows, a red-black wave of viscous flesh like a lava flow. When the blob began its slow descent down the hill, another wave of a dozen mercenaries, all armed with flamethrowers, moved in, attempting to contain the massive organism and corral it toward the sea.

The master blob revealed a long row of nipples and liquified a pair of mercenaries with a gush of acid. The blob targeted a tentacle strike like a frog's tongue, latching onto a soldier's throat and whipping him back into the blob where a pocket of acid consumed him. Grenades struck the massive flow of the blob, spattering burning chunks of the blob flesh, but despite the destructive power of the grenades, the blob only seemed to reconstitute and continue forward.

The remaining attack blobs and servants of the pastor escaped directly into the flowing mass of fiery blob flesh, to be carried out into the sea with their fleeing master, Dr. Karen among them.

At the rear of the blob, the mercenaries continued to spray flamethrowers to force the blob down the hill, large swaths of the organism burning as it swept over parked cars in its path.

Gordon and Jessica watched as the massive organism disappeared into the surf and the vast ocean beyond.

Once the blob disappeared under the waves, and the mercenaries cleared away their dead and left the scene in their black vans, the local authorities arrived with sirens blaring to put out the church fires and restore order, all carefully orchestrated by the powerful organization that employed Gordon Watt.

They entered the empty lot behind the apartment complex: Andrew, bald and frail after being reconstituted by the master blob, and three members of the church, a heavy man with thick lumberjack hands, a tiny old woman with strong knees again after passing through the master, and the clone of Kevin's mother with a fresh layer of downy hair on her head. They had slipped out before the battle had begun. Andrew was planning to escape the town with the only means at his disposal: the old RV. Andrew had the seed of a new master blob in his mind. If he escaped, he would be able to establish a new blob hive in another church.

The intuition from Kevin's new spectral phantasm showed him this terrible outcome. Kevin had to keep this from happening, but he never expected that the clone of his mother would be there. The boy Kevin had loved was gone forever; his mother was gone forever.

"You have the seed of the blob in your mind," Kevin said from the front step of the RV.

"I am the new pastor," Andrew said. "I'm very sorry to see that your mind has been spoiled."

"My mind isn't spoiled," Kevin said.

"Now you can never join us," Andrew said.

"Why would I want to do that?"

"Because you were mine once," Andrew said.

Andrew had a strange smirk on his face as he walked toward the RV. The large man stepped in front of Andrew, grabbing Kevin's arm, pulling him from the front step, and shoving him down to the dirt and gravel. Kevin knew he didn't have a chance against three servants of the blob, but if he could slow them down, he would.

Andrew slipped inside the RV and put the key into the ignition, but the engine didn't want to turn over.

The heavy man and the old woman both pulled long hunting knives from their belts as they stood over Kevin, but they stepped aside for the clone of Harrie, who trembled slightly as tears of blob fluid ran from her eyes. The pastor wanted Kevin to see his own mother melt into the blob before consuming him.

Just as the streams of blob flesh began to pour from her mouth and eye sockets, a horrific scream sounded above as the white bat-creature flew overhead. Lumber was upon them, his wings outstretched as he descended upon the large man who tried to stab at Lumber, but Lumber fixed the long claws of his right hand in the man's skull and twisted off his head in a torrent of blood and blob flesh. Lumber's wings retracted and the shaggy form of the bat-creature transformed into a white fighting beast.

Kevin watched in horror, paralyzed on the ground as Harrie's clone split open, the shell of her body falling away and the attack blob fully emerging. Lumber leapt upon the blob as it sprayed acid, and a large swath of fur and skin was burned away. Lumber roared in agony, clawing out the brain mass of the blob, tearing it apart with his teeth and tossing it aside.

The old woman, now in her blob form, leapt upon Kevin and smothered his body. The blob moved the pocket of acid within its mass to immerse Kevin's head. Lumber clawed at the blob that covered Kevin, spilling the pocket of acid before it reached Kevin's face. Lumber's claw eaten away by the acid, his arm shifted into the claw-scythe, spearing the brain mass like a pickaxe. Kevin gasped for breath as he scrambled to get the disintegrating flesh of the blob off of him.

Andrew, unable to start the engine, emerged from the RV in his blob form. Now he had to fight for his life.

Lumber, wounded and burned by the acid, roared and charged toward the blob, aiming his pickaxe claw at the brain mass. Treacherous tentacles leapt from the blob like frog tongues, wrapping around Lumber's limbs and throat. The blob pulled Lumber towards its center. Lumber's claw-scythe lashed out, severing multiple tentacles at once. The blob's nipples sprayed the acid, burning away more of Lumber's coat and skin. The blob engulfed Lumber's hind leg and ate it away. Lumber howled in pain, piercing the blob's brain mass, finishing off the new master blob, which dissolved into a large puddle of red-black fluid.

Kevin retreated into the RV, the key still in the ignition. The engine started on the first try. Kevin put the RV into drive, pulling away from the scene of the horrific battle. The RV went too fast over the uneven ground as pans crashed in the cupboards and dishes broke in the sink. He reached the street, turning the RV toward the highway and stepping on the gas.

Lumber dragged his wounded body into the bushes to die.

Gordon and Jessica inspected the ground where the battle occurred, taking photographs of the black puddles and scorched gravel where the blobs disintegrated. Gordon followed a trail of blood across the ground and into the trees.

Behind a screen of bushes, Gordon came upon a naked boy.

The boy was unconscious on the muddy ground. He looked so pale, at first Gordon thought he might be dead, but the boy was only sleeping. He had no hair anywhere on his body, but Gordon noticed tufts of white hair on the ground all around him.

"Jessica, you better come see this," Gordon said.

Jessica came up behind him. It took her only a moment before she recognized what had happened. "Oh my god, Gordon—it's Lumber."

"He's transformed into a human boy."

Jessica grabbed a blanket from the trunk of the car, wrapping it around the boy who slowly regained consciousness. They helped him into the back seat of the car where he curled into a ball with the blanket around him.

"Don't worry," Gordon said. "You're with friends now. You're safe."

Lumber didn't speak, but Gordon thought he saw some recognition in the boy's silver eyes before he closed them and went back to sleep.

AFTERWORD

IN 1996, I GOT A bartending job at the only gay bar in
town. It was a cursed bar, haunted by ghosts, a tragic past,
and *The Twilight Zone* pinball machine. I was twenty-three
that summer, in the closet, a recent college graduate with
an English degree, working full-time at the local bookstore
and living upstairs at my mom's house. It was the summer I
decided to become a horror writer.

I had a tragically brief romance with the manager of the
local dinner theater, an older man named Matthew who played
the lead in the production of *Anything Goes*; when he sang
"You're the Top," I imagined that he sang it directly to me in
the audience. He had a beautiful tenor voice with just a hint
of raspiness. He had dark hair and freckles on his shoulders,
which I loved. Introduced by a mutual friend, I met Matthew at
a popular pizza joint after my shift at the bookstore. We were
holding hands under the table by the end of the night. It was
sheer luck—destiny, I thought; I didn't have many gay friends
and I felt buried alive in the closet.

As I fell in love with Matthew, I started to feel like I had
really conquered the closet at last. But I was desperate and
needy for reassurance, which was typical for a young man
emerging from the closet, and I smothered him.

With some of Matthew's friends, we took a trip to a nightclub in Denver where they pumped waves of slippery foam into the dance floor. The patrons shed their clothes and danced in the foam pit, but I couldn't join them because I was so reserved and shy, and I was the designated driver, having borrowed my mom's car for the night. Matthew got drunk and left me at the edge of the foam pit until closing time.

I drove everyone home, but Matthew was drunk and distant. He wouldn't return my calls for days after that.

My need for constant reassurance was a pit.

It was over. I was devastated; I had to do something or else get sucked back into the closet, which felt like crawling back into a grave.

So I applied to work at the only gay bar in town: The Phoenix. I told Matthew that I applied, and he put in a good word for me with the owner. But Matthew warned me. He thought I was too green, too fresh out of the closet.

Next to the miniature golf course on the highway, across from the only strip club in town, The Phoenix was a scary bar, especially when empty in the afternoon as I prepared for Happy Hour alone. The dance floor itself was cavernous, lined with tables on the perimeter. It didn't have any windows, and there were many empty back rooms, sections closed off and filled with spare equipment and furniture, and the back hallways had red-carpeted walls. It had a terrible mice infestation; sometimes I found their little bodies in the cupboard.

It was a cursed bar.

The original bar burned down one Christmas season in the '80s when the bar was full on a busy Saturday night. At least two people died from asphyxiation in the bathroom. The flames made it impossible to escape. Closeted married men, the rumor went. The fire started when an angry lesbian threw matches at the dried-out Christmas tree in the bar. She had to serve a brief prison sentence. The regulars during Happy Hour told me all about it.

In 1996, the gay community was just emerging from the worst of the AIDS epidemic. I know I felt the fear of it every day, and it cast a dark shadow on my coming out.

I didn't know how to enter gay culture without a mentor. With Matthew out of the picture, the only thing I could think to do was dive in. Working at a busy gay nightclub was definitely diving in. However, the bar—the literal bar where I set down the drinks—became like a barrier for me, my own personal ramparts to separate myself from the customers and from my purpose. I didn't know how to be on the other side of the bar where the people danced and socialized and hooked up.

One of the regulars for Happy Hour, a man who ordered many pitchers of Bud Light and played the trivia video game all afternoon, told me that the bar was haunted, and suddenly everything made sense. I had felt such an overwhelming sensation of dread on so many afternoons. I always assumed that this anxiety stemmed from my own struggle with the closet, but could it be a ghost?

Once, when the bar was crowded and busy, I heard a strange cascade of voices call my name like an echo throughout the bar.

The DJ for the bar seemed to be the most sensitive to the presence of the ghost. She called it "Mr. Thing," and she said when she saw it on the dance floor, the ghost looked like a moving shadow. And I did see a running shadow one afternoon next to *The Twilight Zone* pinball machine.

The Twilight Zone pinball machine, released in 1993 by Midway, is highly regarded among pinball aficionados. An incredible game to play, it is extremely complex and difficult, layered with references to a wide variety of *Twilight Zone* episodes, prominently featuring the central and iconic image of Rod Serling himself. Serling's voice, portrayed by an actor, can be heard at times along with creepy motifs based on the unforgettable theme music.

One afternoon, as I was plugging in *The Twilight Zone* pinball machine, I was surrounded by flashing spectral light like a strobe light. I stepped out of the corner, and it vanished. I stepped back into the corner, and I was surrounded by the light again.

When I finished my Happy Hour shift around 9:00 or 9:30, I loved to stick around, have a few beers, and use my tips to play the pinball machine. I always got lots of quarters in my tip jar. After playing a game, I could turn around and watch the young men on the dance floor.

I was setting out ashtrays in the empty bar before opening, and about halfway through the dance floor, I had to stop and turn back—I sensed something in the corner where there stood several large stacks of extra chairs. The rest of the afternoon I stayed put behind the bar, eyeing that corner of the dance floor. When the D.J. showed up for her shift a few hours later, she said to me: "Mr. Thing is back there in the corner," and I felt a chill because I knew it too.

I felt a presence walk up behind me as I prepared the till. I turned around and there was no one there.

I saw a white figure wave at me in my peripheral vision as I handed a customer a "greyhound" across the bar. It vanished when I turned my head.

On a dead weeknight in March, I lost the battle with my fear of the bar. A drunk, belligerent customer threatened to cut my throat. He had come from the strip club across the street, and I refused to serve him because he was already sloppy drunk. The second he walked out the door, I locked it behind him, afraid he might come back, even though it wasn't midnight yet.

Instead of calling the police, I just decided to close the bar. The only customer was my friend who had witnessed the whole thing. When the owner stopped in unexpectedly, I was still cleaning up. The owner immediately fired me for closing early.

Last August, when I visited my hometown after being away for many years, it was a strange shock to discover that The Phoenix had been completely demolished. In its place stood a bank.

Does Mr. Thing haunt the bank after hours?

I discovered that Matthew died from AIDS a few years ago. I searched online to see if he had a Facebook page and found his obituary instead.

It felt like The Phoenix had become a ghost bar, vanishing into the mist, along with all of its stories: the horrible fire long ago, my lost love Matthew, and the mysterious ghosts that haunted the dance floor where I came out of the closet and played *The Twilight Zone* pinball machine.

Was the ghost in my imagination? Was everyone feeding me stories because they could see I was afraid? The bar itself was dark and gothic enough to push anyone's imagination. Over the years, I speculated the ghost in the bar was just a projection of my own anxieties about being gay, a shadow figure of myself, but then I remembered how the D.J. and I both sensed something in the corner by the chairs. With its flashing, disorienting lights—like the dance floor—and its pitfalls, twists, and turns, *The Twilight Zone* pinball machine embodied my experience at The Phoenix. More than that, I felt like I was in *The Twilight Zone*, venturing into the strange and dangerous world of being gay.